Copyright

Chapter 1

A star is born

The year was 1964 and the landscape of Britain was set to rock n roll music, London fashion, beautiful women all declaring peace and love as they marched hand in hand with the flower power movement. The decade of love and joy painted a romantic notion, however the harsh realities of life for many of those in Scotland was quite different.

High unemployment due to the decline in farming in the highland areas drove countryside families into the bustling industrial cities of Glasgow and Edinburgh looking for work. Mass migration from Ireland continued to add to the already simmering religious issues and conflict in the underbelly of the city. Catholics and Protestants alike, both forced to live side by side in the newly erected tenement buildings. The beauty of Glasgow, steeped in such violent history, was rapidly becoming the most dangerous city in Britain.

About thirty miles away was the town of Stirling. This historic area, once the scene of battles between the armies of England and Scotland had its own share of issues. The Gypsy travelling communities, some forced out of Ireland due to family battles and the pressure of surviving, paired with the desire to be on the move as is engrained into the DNA of travellers, often found the natural beauty of the Stirling area to be an ideal choice to settle. An area surrounded by sweeping hills and plentiful rivers would offer these families the chance to create a future.

One of those families were the McAfee's. Head of the family was Billy, a small man in stature, with what some would say a Napoleon complex, Billy had the heart of a lion. A very much old school hard man you rarely come across in modern times. It would be a stretch to call him five foot seven, however few would argue in his presence. His hairline receding since his late teenage years, he now sported a brown thin crown of hair around the side and back of his head, covering small shapely ears. His glasses sitting perched in centre place, milk bottle thick to try and aid his lack of vision. What Billy lacked in height, he made up in strength, his arms thickened from years of manual labour. Both arms scattered with tattoos to remind Billy of memories past. A man is truly gauged on masculinity by the size of his shoulders and biceps in worlds like these.

The travelling mentality which generations past had lived by had long gone by the time Billy's generation came around. Billy was years settled in a home built with bricks and mortar, not a caravan in sight. However, that travelling gypsy heritage is something Billy liked to point out whenever a situation arose, as a vocal weapon to ensure any potential threat understood the heritage of the man in front of them, as if to somehow add to the level of violence one could inflict should it be necessary. Respect for this generation was always the most important thing.

Billy's heart belonged to his new wife, Jackie. For all the chest pumping and bravado of Billy, the real warrior in the household was Jackie. A woman that was born during the Second World War, it was a difficult start to life. Almost as tall as her man, Jackie stood with a slender build and sharp features, complimentary of the diet at the time in lower class households. Thick brown hair decorated as best she could with the tools available. Her skin soft, with scattered groups of freckles creating a map like expression. The touch of her skin wrinkle free, despite the pressures of life. Truth be told, life with Billy was not an easy one. Billy often finished conversations with his fists.

In a generation where a wife dares not speak out, Jackie suffered in silence. Billy, a brick layer by trade, was not a bad man; he had just been raised through generations of violence. It was a story repeated behind many doors in the village they called home, the Raploch.

The Raploch was a small village on the outskirts of Stirling town centre. It was an honest place with family being the single most important thing. However, with the lack of funding in the area for development and growth, it could also be a breeding ground for villains and crooks. One thing the people of the Raploch could never be called was scared. Each family filled with fiercely protective individuals, proud of the heritage they followed. The people of the Raploch did not consider themselves bad, they just found solving issues with your fists took a whole lot less effort and made a whole lot more sense. It was a world that had violence and day to day living blended as one. And in November 1964, this small village was about to be introduced to its newest member, Kevin McAfee. The first born to Jackie and Billy, Kevin was the apple of his mother's eye. Kevin was like a little cut out version of his father. With the mirrored features of Billy, and the temper to match.

4

With Billy often away working long hours around central Scotland, the newly erected homes of the future carefully constructed with his strong hands, the task of raising Kevin sat with Jackie. Now every mother wants to believe her boy is a salt of the earth good child, but Jackie knew incredibly early on that Kevin was not your average young boy. With a temper to match that of his father, young Kevin was certainly unique.

By five years old, Kevin's reputation in the village proceeded him. It would be no surprise to have parents of other kids coming to the family home to tell tales of how the bold Kevin had just handed out a beating to one of their sons. When Jackie would point out that the child involved was a lot older than Kevin, the protesting mother would find herself leaving the property as instructed by a forceful Jackie, who was equally as fierce as her young son. Clearly hinting that the same fate might fall upon them. The turning point for Jackie came during a train journey when Kevin was six years old.

The thick paisley pattern dressed over each passenger chair, carefully picked to offer the premium ambience in this game changing style of transport. The thought of travelling in a beaten up old double decker bus held no appeal to this generation, but the luxuries and esteem which matched the train journey was a gain in status for each passenger in the nether regions of their mind. Above each passenger stretched rows of wooden storage plates, allowing those travelling the journey with significant baggage the opportunity to be freed from the clutter, tucked high away above them, waiting for the mutual destination.

The train marched along nicely on the recently laid fresh track between Stirling and Glasgow. Since the war, regeneration of the centre of Scotland had really been picking up pace. And young Kevin's generation would pick the fruits of this through the work no doubt available in the manufacturing and heavy industry sectors over the coming years.

Sitting together looking at the outside world from the carriage window, Jackie could tell Kevin's anxiety levels had started to grow. The cause of this was a child not much older than young Kevin on the seat behind them. A young boy, with thick chunky legs holding place on the soft chair, velvet shorts hugging the tops of his knees. He had an equally tight short sleeved white shirt, with each button fighting for its place to remain intact, with his full oval belly offering as much resistance to this stand off as possible. The small boy had thick NHS prescribed glasses

5

on. Fashionable they were not, but when you are not required to offer any payment towards the product, you smile and nod your head with the best they offer! The young man had thick black hair which offered complete sun coverage around his portly face. A face which his mother would systematically clean with the small cotton hanky produced from her handbag. Each intervention fought off by the young boy, insistent on the fact that "he was fine!"

While the boy played innocently with his toy train, a thin blue double carriage tinplate Great Western that looked more expensive than any toy within young Kevin's collection, it was clear Kevin was on a different level of maturity...

"Choo choo" the young boy would declare as he actioned the toy train flying. "Choo choo" repeatedly. Kevin could feel the blood in his veins begin to boil as his rage increased. The levels of anxiety mirroring that of a tight rope walker. "Choo choo, choo choo, choo choo."

Kevin's agitation grew each moment until he could hold it no longer, he burst into action like a jack in the box long since played with. Bouncing over the chair and snatching the train from the young boys' hands, Kevin focused on his rival with an expression cold as ice. He darted his focus at his prey and declared

"Choo Choo now ya bastard!" The carriage of the train fell silent. The embarrassment from Jackie was clear. But the victory from Kevin in his mind was enough to justify his actions.

Jackie removed the train from the grip of Kevin's small rounded hands, however he refused to drop his deathly stare. The young tubby boy exploded with emotion, uncontrollable tears and pre-pubescent cries filled the section of the carriage they inhabited.

"I am so sorry" Jackie pleaded with the young boy's mother, hoping to salvage any form of dignity that might remain in the situation. The defending mother refused to offer a response, as her sights locked on young Kevin in sheer disbelief at what she had just witnessed. "Say sorry Kevin!" Jackie declared, hoping to distance herself from her son's actions by offering similar shock to those viewing the episode. Kevin refused; still sure his reaction had been justified. "You will be sorry when your dad sees you" Jackie warned Kevin as she moved in to ensure nobody else picked up on the thinly veiled threat, knowing the viewpoint from those around would be of a mother unable to control her young son.

Returning to the family home, a small mid terraced property with two small bedrooms, the rage within Jackie had failed to subside. As she made her way through the poorly decorated hallway, coated with cheap purple paint Jackie had used in an attempt to offer some sort of character within the home, they could see Billy sitting at the kitchen table, cigarette in hand as he looked over an old copy of the Angling Times. Jackie explained the incident to Billy, who beamed with pride as he took in the details.

"That's my fucking boy!" he declared, to which Kevin took immense pride. With any form of aggression Kevin displayed, Billy would celebrate this as if his boy were coming of age. In a world like this, a man had to be tough. For Billy, this display of behaviour merely reassured him that his boy would be able to handle himself with the many things' life would throw at him.

Jackie thought a decision had to be made. At this point Kevin was not alone. Younger brother Davie now had to be part of any decision Jackie would make. She could see the direction her eldest was following and despite only being six years old, Kevin was trouble. With that, she decided the family needed a fresh start.

Chapter 2

New beginnings

The family decided to start again in the town of Falkirk. Around twenty miles from Stirling, Falkirk was at this point a heavily industrialized area. Most employment came in the form of factory work within the various foundries. They moved into the small village of Camelon. At six years old this was now a new warzone in Kevin's mind. He felt he had conquered the Raploch in his brief time on earth, and that the respect he had from children around him would be enough to see him through childhood into adulthood. But Falkirk, this was a strange place to him. Joining the new primary school as a young outsider, it was up to him to make his mark early on to avoid any future issues. And make his mark he did....

While Kevin made his way to the playground for first playtime of his new school day, he took in his new surroundings. Various pieces of athletic equipment lay scattered around the hard-concrete floor, and faded markings showed different activities from earlier financial investment in the school, which had now cried out for reinvestment. Snakes and ladders, most of which had faded to a distant memory after years of harsh Scottish weather, twinned with the traffic which had passed over it through the years. Beyond that he could see the remnants of hopscotch print, again, long abandoned by this generation of kids due to the difficultly to see the markings. The school exterior was harsh, almost soviet like, as the building architecture cut into the surrounding fields.

Kevin was met with obvious glares of interest from the other kids. He could hear the giggles from each cluster of groups, and he prayed that someone would come and offer a helping hand. The dynamics of the playground already clearly visible to him. The athletic boys playing football with the small battered tennis ball, the group of girls, despite their early age, discussing which of the ghastly boys would eventually take their hand in marriage. Then there was the bullied group of intellects. Kids making every effort to go unnoticed and avoid any form of physical punishment that day from their tormentors. Tales of space and science between these young men allowing them to imagine their day in faraway lands filled with heroes who would defeat the bad guys.

Kevin looked round wondering which of these factions would adopt him and offer him sanctuary. But that welcome hello did not come, instead he was met with the words of hostility that would end up defining his life in this new world. "Check this wee cunt out", roared a large boy towering over Kevin.

Taking after his father, Kevin was small in height for his age. Even at six years old most of his fellow primary three classmates towered over him. The problem was, just like his dad, Kevin had the heart of a lion. He stood with his rusty blonde hair; his body covered with the new colours of his school uniform. His small feet shielded from the world by a pair of brogues which felt slightly too big. His mum had assured him he would grow into them.

Turning to look at the three boys who stood in front of him, testing his resolve to see what he was made of, the required course of action was clear for Kevin. Without a single word of reply, he lifted the ringleader off his feet with a clean right hook. No sooner had the first blow landed, that Kevin's focus now turned to the other two boys. In an instant the playground burst into life. All the kids ran over to create a human ring for these young gladiators to battle inside.

Kevin took a good beating that day as the three boys proved too much for the young lad, but it also sent out a clear message to everyone. Kevin McAfee takes shit from no man! Like most environments for both children and adults, a pecking order needed to be established. The intellects knew their place in the order, the athletes understood who amongst them was at the top of the pile and on that first day, Kevin had just firmly established himself towards the top. The gasps of shock at the fact this small boy, not much to look at in all honesty, had defiantly taken on three combatants at the same time, meant that instant respect filled the playground for this young man.

Primary school in a social sense went by smoothly for Kevin after this. The dynamics of most childhood environments usually hold those who can fight towards the top of the pile. The other factor which sat well for Kevin was his ability to play football. Kevin was a natural player who would stalk the wings of any football park he graced. His small frame and bursts of pace made him a standout in most teams. Kevin could always be found with a ball when not at school, although the ball often found its way inside Kevin's school bag going to school, much to the dismay of Jackie.

School was not all plain sailing for Kevin though, and the work in class proved the biggest fight for a young McAfee who clearly showed signs of dyslexia. Unfortunately, in the sixties and seventies, there was less understanding and awareness of this, and it was seen more as a lack of application from the pupil. At seven years old Kevin was struggling. Now in primary four, the desire to want to learn and progress was clear, however any failings from Kevin that had been highlighted by the teacher were quickly met with aggression from a young Kevin. Unfortunately for Kevin, the aggression was reciprocated by the teachers in the form of the usual discipline and punishment, the leather strap or 'belt' as it was referred to. An almost lethal and torturous instrument designed to put the fear of god (and the fear of whoever was holding it) into the minds of the young children. The 'belt' was at least a quarter of an inch thick, more than two inches wide and both rigid and long enough to deliver with great accuracy a resounding, painful slap with its two leather tongues across the hands of a hugely fearful yet expectant child.

"Eight times six McAfee", Mr Harris roared, as if the nine feet between them was a far greater distance.

Kevin looked at his nemesis with a clear desperation in his eyes as if begging Mr Harris to move on to someone else with the question. Could he not see Kevin was sinking here? Was he doing this on purpose? Some of the girls behind Kevin began to giggle. This only added to the anxiety which by this point was bursting out of his young head.

"Get up here now McAfee!" Mr Harris demanded. If a pupil in his class was not willing to learn, then by god he was going to make sure they remembered the consequences.

Kevin knew what was coming. As if the humiliation of not knowing the answer was not enough, he was now going to get six lashes of the belt which would no doubt draw him to tears. This sort of humiliation was common for Kevin. Even by the tender age of seven, he had inadvertently made himself a target within the school.

Harris was about fifty years old, with a military look about him. Tall and slim, giving the appearance of a man that always stood to attention. Grey was the colour of choice. Everything about him, just grey. It was as if any form of life or imagination had long left this cruel shell, replaced by a robotic, bullish persona of a wolf amongst the sheep. His long fingers stood out from his thin arms, as if they had been especially sculptured to hold the notorious belt and offer the young children such intense assaults. His cold dark eyes shielded by thick bushy eyebrows, which always pointed directly at his long-crooked nose as he scowled at the kids. Just like the old saying, if the wind changes, you will be stuck with that look. Clearly Harris didn't listen. He really had no place around children. The violence he handed out, along with the mental abuse, was no help to any young child growing up looking for guidance.

The small classroom was desperately out of date and in need of renovation. The row of tables made from brown hardened oak wood, each scattered with the graffiti from pupils who had previously sat at them. Generations of children creating timelines of attendance with the help of a pencil, or the sharp point of a compass. The floor under them forged from hard maple wood, the environment offered an unwelcoming, harsh atmosphere.

By the fifth lash Kevin could feel the tears running down his soft cheek. He could feel the eyes of every pupil in that class on him, and he could feel the built-up rage of the animal holding the belt. As Kevin made his way back to his seat, Harris walked to his desk and placed the belt back down, his face lit up by some perverted notion that he had just bolstered his own masculinity by abusing a young boy, who would have no doubt put him in his place once upon a time when Harris was that age.

As Kevin sat back down, a voice softly spoke out to him. The voice from a boy who would grow into a man alongside Kevin. A voice that Kevin would go on to hear more than a thousand times in his life asking the same thing.

"You ok Fe?"

Fe. You see the only people who called Kevin by his Sunday name was his mum and dad, everyone else knew him as Fe. Now Fe was obviously a play on McAfee, but Kevin chose to spell it with only one 'e' instead of the natural two 'ee's you would expect, ('Fee'). Clearly the dyslexia even played a part in the spelling of his nick name. And the voice offering genuine concern came from Fe's best and closest friend in the world, "big" Sanny.

Now in an ideal world, one would like to say that Kevin and big Sanny got on like a house on fire from the first moment they met, but the reality was that young boy who tested Fe's resolve on the first day of school, was in fact big Sanny. That first punch Fe had thrown on the first playtime, the punch that would forge a young Fe's standing within the school, had landed right on big Sanny's chin. The problem for a young Fe on that day was that big Sanny could fight for Scotland! However, something from the steely resolve of a young Fe really warmed to big Sanny, who immediately took Fe under his wing.

Sanny was a big boy and even at seven years old, was one of the most feared young men in the full school. Sanny had strong features, often allocated to the alpha male of environments, the kind of look which immediately put him on a higher level and way ahead of his peers. Respect from other kids was expected in Sanny's presence. His short black hair expertly cut by his mother, now refined by experience of being a barber to six sons. His strong jaw line cut a look of athletic prowess. For Sanny, fighting came easy. He had five brothers, which meant there was no shortage of sparring partners each evening when he got home from school. But despite his reputation and sheer physical size, Sanny absolutely detested bullies. Make no mistake, that episode on Fe's first day was clearly just to test if he was worthy of Sanny's time and attention. A young Fe clearly passed the test.

"You need to tell your old man", Sanny declared, as he tried to keep his voice at a level so as to not allow Harris to hear and dish out to him the same fate that Fe had just met.

"Fuck that, my dad would kick my arse for not knowing the answer" Fe replied.

"Would he fuck, someone needs to sort that bastard, it's not fair." A statement both young boys knew to be true, but what could they do? Harris was indeed a bully.

While the two boys walked home together, Sanny's comment played over and over in Fe's head. Harris was a bully bastard. He prayed on young boys, not just Fe but the full school and with any boy Harris viewed as a threat to his power. Fe knew that if this was someone Harris's own age, that behaviour would not stand. Fe also knew his dad was home for the week doing work around the house. Should I mention it? The young boy fought over the decision in his head. As he stood at the gate leading into the small front garden, he could see his dad through the window staring out to him.

Fe stopped in his tracks. He knew the beatings his mum often took had not only been reserved for her in the house, Fe himself had often been on the end of his dads' drunken fists. Since the move from Stirling, Billy's hometown, his father had become disillusioned with his new life in Camelon. This strange unfamiliar environment was full of new threats who had known not of his physical accomplishments in the Raploch.

Billy was a hard man, and they did not appreciate this. It was a tough pill to swallow for Mr McAfee. He tried in vain to reignite that once stellar reputation he held. Working away throughout Scotland on various building sites, he would often not come home for days at a time, the distance of travel making the ability to arrive home for dinner each evening impossible. However, you could be sure McAfee would always be home by Friday evening, his intentions to head straight for the local pub. He would offer the usual conversation to the small group of friends he had now gained, but once the whiskey kicked in his mind-set shifted to testing himself against the natives.

The battles were many. On the occasions in which Billy was victorious, he would return home a champion and celebrate as such, handing money out to his two kids while explaining to the now disillusioned Jackie how he'd conquered the unbeatable! However, when the fight did not fall in Billy's favour, he would return home looking for retribution, which usually landed at the feet of his family.

Fe knew he could end up being on the receiving end of another beating at the hands of the man he once adored if this ended badly. Deciding this was not worth the hassle, he took a deep breath and resigned himself to the fact that this was his fight and his alone. As he closed the gate behind him he turned again, but this time his glare was caught directly by that of his father, and like a breath of fresh air, his old man gave a subtle wink of the eye to his young puppy as if signalling "I got you". With that small but uplifting and protective gesture, the decision was made in a young Fe's mind. He was going to tell his dad.

As Fe made his way towards the entrance of the end terrace house, significantly larger than the property they had waved goodbye to in the Raploch, he pulled on the small steel handle of the front door and made his way inside. The lobby was covered with an old Persian rug, wounded and worn by years of people marching over it. The look told a story that this rug had been spread over many floors before this one. The walls remained bare and in need of attention as the family had not yet managed to decorate the entire property in the twelve-month period they had lived there. As Fe made his way into the living room, the mix match array of furniture offered little in the way of home comfort, at least not yet anyway. Most of the furniture had joined in the travel from Stirling, some of it looking a lot worse than before it went into the removal's lorry, clearly a casualty of the journey.

"Well son what did you learn today? Have you been showing every cunt in this wee shite hole of a town just how smart us McAfee's are?" Billy questioned Fe as if the family had drastically downgraded their lifestyle in order to move into the area.

Billy stood with faded denim jeans on, marked and scuffled from the labours of DIY. His top half covered with an old Glasgow Rangers shirt. The glasses perched on his healed broken nose, a trophy from battles past.

Fe laughed nervously and replied with a soft "aye dad." His father looked at him puzzled. Even with the distance that had been driven between them by Billy's actions over the previous twelve months, he could tell something was wrong with his boy. A father's intuition tells him when one of his own is hurting and for Billy, this was unacceptable.

"Look at the fucking face on you, what's wrong?" At only seven years old, stood in front of his fearsome father, a young Fe struggled with the words.

In his father's eyes he had always been a soldier, a young fighter scared of no man. He recollected the pride in his father's eyes when overhearing of tales about his young son. Even at his young age, he could feel the pride in his father's voice as he described the antics of his young son to friends and acquaintances. "That's my fuckin boy."

With a deep sigh, Fe looked at his dad, then breaking the glance only to regain it with a sudden surge of adrenaline declared, "Dad I am getting it from my teacher at school"

"Getting it? The fuck does that mean, you are getting it, getting wit?" Billy replied, already knowing what his son meant, but needing a few seconds to process the information in his anger and disbelief. "Did some cunt rattle you?" Billy roared, his own adrenaline rushing now he was fully grounded with the reality of the situation and the potential events about to unfold.

"Aye, my teacher gave me six in front of everyone" a now nervous and frightened Fe whimpered, not knowing if his visibly angry dad was now going to dish out to him a similar punishment for weakness he displayed as they stood on the old tattered rug in the front room.

Silence fell on both. Only a few seconds passed with no interaction, but it might well have been a lifetime in the mind of a young McAfee. He dug deep into his busted old boots knowing he could be moments away from his dad lifting him out of them.

"What for?" his dad asked, now significantly lowering the volume to a level of dark rage.

"What do you mean what for" Fe replied, knowing exactly what his dad had meant, but now struggling to connect the dots in his young mind as the fear took over.

"What did he rattle you for ya daft cunt" his father roared, now taking the volume back up to maximum level.

At this point Fe's mum walked in. Jackie had been in the back garden hanging out some washing when she heard the commotion inside. Fearing for her young son and readily willing to jump in the line of fire for him should Billy decide to get violent, she stood at the arch of the door, looking ten feet tall in the eyes of her son who knew she would protect him should the situation turn violent.

"What's going on?" Jackie enquired, as if looking to share the burden of information now sitting on Billy's shoulders.

"His fucking teacher gave him six of the belt" Billy roared, looking for an ally in this now heated episode.

"Who was it Kevin?" Jackie asked softly, with genuine concern echoed in her voice.

"Harris mam" the young Fe replied, knowing he now had his mum backing him.

"And what for son?" she questioned, already aware that her son could be a handful at the best of times. His dad stood behind, taking in the information as if to reserve judgement based on the facts unfolding in front of him...

"Fucking didn't know what eight times six was" a young Fe declared, now clearly becoming angry as the episode became known again in his mind.

"You mind your fuckin language boy" his mum roared, as if putting all other issues to one side and reminding her son just who his audience was.

"Eight times six?" ... his dad exclaimed! "What cunt knows what eight times fucking six is for fuck sake, and who needs to know fuckin arithmetic anyway when you're working in a fuckin foundry." Billy clearly holding what he considered were reasonable expectations for the future of his son.

"So, you're telling me that bastard put hands on my boy over fuckin eight times six", the anger now clearly displayed on his dad's face. At that point, the young Fe knew he had both his mum and dad on side. This was a good thing, wasn't it? Billy and Jackie looked at each other. No words were exchanged, but the understanding was evident in the unspoken language between the two parents whose offspring was in trouble. Despite the issues and the clear rift in their relationship that sat firmly between them both now, a moment like this united them as their focus was the concern for their son.

"You away out and play son" Billy offered kindly to Fe in a rare moment of parenting and fatherly support, "and leave this to your old man."

Chapter 3

Game changer

The following morning Fe woke up, the prospect of dealing with Mr Harris had been weighing heavily on his mind for quite some time of late. For kids, most troubles become amplified as they play it over, unable to implement the reasoning an adult would, and this was the same for Fe despite his display of bravado at times. However, today felt like a new day and a weight had been lifted from his small shoulders. The reaction from his mum and dad the previous night had really caught him off guard. The display and experience of unity and support between the three of them, and the warmth this brought with it, was something he had not felt in a long time. The once sacred sanctum of the family home in the Raploch was a now long distant memory.

The bedroom offered little in terms of styling for Fe and his brother Davie and was still decorated in the feminine style of the earlier tenant, a point Fe highlighted to his mum on a regular basis in order to push the point of urgency. The new house again had only two bedrooms, this time with the boys at the front of the house and the master bedroom at the rear of the property overlooking the back garden. The boys had two single beds and an old set of oak drawers which provided sanctuary to their small collection of clothes. They had a cupboard at the side of Davie's bed which housed the unopened boxes still waiting to be unpacked and introduced to their new surroundings.

Fe swung his legs out of bed and his younger brother Davie looked over at him. Davie was now four years old and idolised his big brother. If Fe's dad had once been a superhero in the eyes of Fe, then for Davie, the only hero in his life was his big brother. Fe was fiercely protective of his younger brother during the time they spent on the streets with other kids. It had been a year since the move and Fe had found a group of friends who would stand by him through most of his life. One thing he made sure of was the fact that his younger brother would grow up to have that same level of security and affinity from the group of boys.

"Heard dad and mam last night downstairs", Davie whispered to his older brother so that his parents could not hear. "You reckon dad will sort him" Davie questioned, digging to find out what was on his big brother's mind. Even at an early age, Fe was a thinker. He would analyse every situation in his head to try and determine the best course of action. Often the final decision was not the most productive course of action whatever the analysis of each situation.

"I don't fucking know" Fe snapped back, as if the thought had not even crossed his mind when in truth, he could think of nothing else.

The two boys dressed for school. Davie had just started primary one a few months earlier. His long black hair covering his ears like a helmet perched on the head of a soldier going into battle. Davie had big brown eyes and dark features he had inherited from his mother. If Fe was a cut out of his dad, then Davie took his looks from his mum. One obvious physical attribute that was always going to see Davie as a target had been the shape and size of his ears. Fe often said as they grew up that Davie could "pick up satellite signals on those bastards." Davie did not have to defend this point with kids at school because by the time he joined primary one his big brother was now a well-established primary four pupil with a fearsome reputation. It was not unknown that his brother Fe would easily go head to head with primary five and six pupils and was feared by the older boys in equal measure. With big Sanny as additional back up, Davie had no reason to be concerned about his own position in school. Only a few "do you know who my big brother is?" on his first few days at school removed any potential threats or issues.

Harris stood in front of the blackboard deep in thought. They would be here shortly, the filthy ignorant little ruffians. The boys with their pathetically expectant faces, waiting to learn something new and then failing to do so because of their own stupidity. And he would need to teach them a lesson, again. The girls, with their short vulgar skirts exposing too much flesh, pretending to be innocent, encouraging him to look at half naked little bodies. How on earth did he end up in this godforsaken lower-class cesspit they had the insolence of calling a school?

No, this is not the direction his life should have taken. He had bigger plans following his expensive education at the elusive boarding school paid for by his wealthy parents. Until his father left them penniless and in debt of course, and he had to look after mother on his own. Years of caring for mother and her fragile emotional state, yet not too fragile that she didn't rule him with a rod of iron. Yes mother, no mother, three bloody well bags full mother.

Harris was tired of being told what to do and when to do it. "Don't dress like that" mother would say. "You will only attract attention to yourself and you know you're not exactly pleasing on the eye. It's one of the reasons your father left."

Well he would show those little vermin and teach them a lesson alright, he wasn't going to take any nonsense from any of them. He was in charge and its time they all knew it, he decided as the bell rang!

At the sound of the school bell, the boys split into opposite directions in the playground. By this point Fe could almost hear his heart beating through his chest. Had his mum or dad phoned the school? Would Harris be waiting on him to offer even more punishment to teach him a lesson for speaking out? The questions played over and over in his head as he walked down the corridor.

Turning the corner, he could see Harris standing at the entrance of the class. His emotionless expression as the kids walked past was impossible to read. As he got closer Harris would offer the occasional outburst to other kids as they walked past.

"Move faster boy, you should be sitting down by now," or "will you straighten your back laddie, this isn't the playground now." It was the same bullshit he spouted daily, and Fe realised his hatred of this man was only going to grow. Within feet of the door, a young Fe caught the attention of Harris. "Ah McAfee, late as usual, but do not worry we will all wait for you." With this comment Fe could tell Harris did not know he had updated his parents about the incident from the previous day.

That smug look on his face only added to the resentment Fe harboured for him. "I hate that cunt" McAfee said as he took his seat beside Sanny.

"And me Fe, horrible cunt he is", Sanny replied.

Fe had now resigned himself to the fact that Harris had gotten away with it. With not only humiliating him in front of his peers, but also taking personal pleasure in physically hurting a young boy. An act Harris played out daily with plenty of the boys in the school. An act he had no doubt enjoyed over the years.

"Books out, page six, and I want one of you to stand and start reading, who is offering?" The usual hands went up. The girls with the pig tails that Harris would stare at for just a moment too long, in an uncomfortable sort of way. No doubt the image of these young girls in short skirts and the punishments he doled out with the leather belt would stay lodged in the mind of this abusive monster when he went home. "Ah McAfee, thank you for offering, now stand up and read."

Fe looked up confused and replied, "Sir I didn't have my hand up."

With an explosion of rage, Harris shouted "I didn't ask you if you had your hand up, I asked you to read, do you not understand boy, do we need to have a repeat of yesterday boy? Answer me boy," giving Fe no time to respond to his repeated questions which shot out of his mouth like machine gun bullets. The fear which Fe had allowed to subside after the previous evenings' reassurance from his parents had now returned with a vengeance.

As Fe slowly got to his feet from his chair, the class fell silent. "The Mary Rose was ship," Fe struggled but continued "the Mary Rose ship was..." Fe, clearly out of his depth as he looked at the written text from the book.

"The Mary rose ship was!" Harris roared, as if to cement the fact that the young boy in front of him was incapable of reading a sentence.

In that moment, as the satisfaction of Harris's abusive behaviour reinforced his power over his young charges, and spewed from every part of his body, the abuse of young boys mentally and physically that this man craved, the door swung open! The collective gasps from the children sat in the air as Harris swung his head to the door to see who dare interrupt him during a lesson. Standing there, no more than five foot seven inches tall, broad shoulders from years of lifting bricks, was Billy McAfee.

"Can I help you?" Harris smirked, not realising who the man in front of him was. As if some lost nomadic wanderer had stumbled upon his class by accident.

But this was no accident, the man standing in front of Harris knew exactly what he was doing, where he was going and why. Every hair on Fe's body stood to attention, as he waited with bated breath for what was about to happen.

"You ya cunt" Billy shouted as he verbally attacked Harris. "You're the cunt who thinks he is a hard man for picking on wee boys?" Billy continued before Harris could respond. "Well you picked on the wrong fucking laddie this time."

By now Billy was standing directly in front of Harris, as he trembled with shock, disbelief and terror – just like a terrified child. For Fe and the rest of the children, this was a complete transformation of the monster Harris, their nemesis, who had only ever sought to terrorise and control them. The man who sought only pleasure when he belted them. But now, that power and arrogance had vanished, replaced by a weak, bumbling excuse for a man. The tables had finally turned!

Before Harris could speak or offer an explanation regarding the situation, without warning Billy drove his head directly into Harris's face. As with most bullies, Harris had no response. He dropped to his knees and held his face in his hands, his nose having exploded in red claret. A loud cheering erupted from the class, particularly loud from all the boys who had been on the end of Harris's abuse. Mrs Walton, a teacher from the class next door burst into the room and bravely placed herself between McAfee and Harris. But the battle was over, and Billy had no intentions of dishing out any further justice or a sustained attack. He knew what Harris was. And this was a message, not only to Harris, but to his boy.

"Nobody fucks with us son," he declared as his eyes met with those of his son.

After his dad walked out young Fe sat in the classroom, no nerves evident as one might expect in a normal child reaction to this event. There was only satisfaction in the mind of this small boy. His tormentor was beat. His dad, despite the issues they often faced, had come through for him, had backed up all the drunken promises of protection he would make after a return from the pub on a Friday night. Victory was his. Following the incident, the teachers would think twice about subjecting Kevin to any form of capital punishment.

Chapter 4

Father and son

By 1974 Fe had found comfort in his new surroundings. Falkirk was now home. Any warm memories he held of the old life in Stirling had long passed and were replaced with new ones from his new life in Falkirk. Now ten years old, the world was starting to become a more recognisable place for him. His friendship with Sanny was stronger than ever, but the group they had was now considerably bigger. All the boys from that age group wanted to be part of the gang. They did what all kids of that generation would do. If not spending time on scrambler motorbikes taking chase from the police, they would be out fishing or hunting.

From an early age Fe was crazy about fishing. A big trout fisher himself, Billy would often take young Fe around Scotland visiting the lochs as they looked for that elusive catch. For Fe though, only one type of fish offered any real form of excitement, and that was the pike! The Forth and Clyde canal, running right through the village, with the Union canal also situated in close proximity provided Fe with the opportunity to catch pike from an early age! Fe now found the bond between him and his dad stronger than ever and was still happy to tag along when his dad went in search of trout.

Things at home continued to be tough for the family, and the relationship between his mum and dad was now at an all-time low, but Fe knew that a lot of kids had it worse off than him.

One of those kids was Tam, who came from a large family of siblings, with neither of his parents working, and both being fond of the bottle. It was a tough life for Tam, who found his only solace was in spending time at Fe's house. Tam, like all his siblings, was blessed with a head full of fire red hair, with cheeks to match. Tam's poker face was a tough gig as his cheeks would always give away the game whenever a situation requiring a cool head would arise. A bright red glaze beaming from each cheek whenever he was put on the spot. Tam was thin in stature, no doubt brought on by fighting for the scraps of food available at home throughout his short life. He was a bit taller than Fe, but nowhere near as well rounded. Big blue eyes shone from a face which had laid sight to many hardships over a brief period. The gateway for the damage that would follow him into adulthood.

With Billy often being out on the road, Jackie was to run the show at home with the two boys on her own. The introduction of Tam to the fold was no issue for Jackie, as she was aware of his situation at home. Despite the difficulties in her own world, Jackie was the type to always look out for others. That mentality would pass down to her sons. Although not official, Tam would spend days and weeks at a time living at Fe's house, nurtured by Jackie as best she could.

One thing that Fe and his dad did not agree on, was the colour of Glasgow. For Billy, Glasgow was red white and blue. A huge fan of Glasgow Rangers, Billy was also a protestant, and a member of the local orange lodge.

He did not mix his words when discussing his feeling for Catholics, or Fenians as he would call them. It was a sore point for Billy that his son, a young talented footballer himself at this point, was a massive Celtic fan! Mesmerised by the achievement of the Lisbon lions just seven years earlier, a young Fe dreamed of one day being as good as his idol, Jimmy Johnston.

Fe based his full game on "Jinky," playing in the same position on outside right, and having the same skill set. Billy managed to put his hatred for the club to one side and would often take his young son to Celtic games. The belief that one day his son would grace this football pitch was enough to have the biased views put to the back of his head. A point that did not sit well with other members of the lodge, but he was Billy McAfee, and he answered to no man!

This acceptance to take his son to the Celtic games paying off one day when the young Fe finally managed to grab Jinky's attention after the game, and the legendary outside right agreed to sign the ball Fe had brought with him. The grip of the ball intensified on the journey home as the new prized possession in this young man's life made the journey back to Falkirk.

With Fe sitting on the end of his bed doing keep ups with his now signed and sacred football, Tam looked over in envy. The memories created that day for father and son was something a young Thomas could only dream of. Billy was good with the young lad, but Tam knew he was not one of the family, at least not in his eyes. He would often pass his mum and dad in the street, both heavily intoxicated, without any recognition

23

from either of them. Considering troubled adults, is it the reality that this is how life for them usually begins? A toxic circle of substance abuse and violence passed from generation to generation. Tam was a good lad, but he would grow into a broken man.

Sitting in class, the teacher began to read the requirements for the upcoming school trip. She highlighted that the only child still to pay for the trip was Tam.

Before Tam had the chance to respond, a young girl behind him declared, "Miss, Tam's mum and dad are poor, so Tam won't be going on any school trip." The full class began to laugh, all except Sanny and Fe...

"Aye miss, my mam will sort the money for tomorrow." Tam knew this was a lie. As Fe turned to Tam, he told him all he had to do was ask Jackie and she would pay it for him. But despite the situation Tam had grown up in, he was a proud boy. He hated asking for anything. Even having a meal offered at night to him by Jackie was met repeatedly with gratitude, with a constant "thank you" and "you did not have to". Jackie however knew that she did.

During the walk home, the boys passed the row of private houses on the left-hand side. Tam would often imagine his mum and dad waiting inside one of those houses for him, with a grand meal awaiting the young lad after a long day at school. Tam turned to Fe and told him he needed his help.

"I told you, it's nae hassle, my mam will pay for it." Fe casually said, but Tam shouted back "that's not what I mean." By this point Tam was visibly angry.

"I am going to get the money myself" Tam declared, with clear passion in his eyes. Fe burst into laughter.

"And just how you going to manage that then, your ten years old, nae cunts giving you a job." He laughed at his own comment, but Tam did not laugh.

"I'm going to break into the chip van at the top of Wall Street." This stopped Fe in his tracks.

The boys had been in trouble in the past, but nothing too serious as far as they were concerned. Fe recently shot the school janitor in the arse with his point 177 air rifle because he would not give him his ball back.

24

But never anything serious. This was different though. This was big league stuff.

"You going to help me?" Tam enquired. Fe knew Tam would do anything for him, so there was only one answer he could respond with. As both young men made the rest of the journey back to Fe's house, silence fell over them. Both deep in thought as the details of the upcoming heist played over in their minds.

Tam's plan was easy enough, pop the van's sunlight hatch and in he goes. He knew big money would be out of the till, but he also knew the kitty tin of change sat under the driver seat. That loose change would be enough to pay his fair for the school trip, and some sweeties for the bus ride. It was almost nine pm, and the streets sat settled in the knowledge another day had almost come to an end. Families taking refuge in the warmth of their home, blind to the amateur criminality unfolding around them. The chip van had been parked off a side street, with little in the way of street lighting offering adequate security. The owner obviously confident that no one would attempt to rob a chip van knowing the money is cleared out the till each evening.

Approaching the van, Fe felt a sudden rush of adrenaline. What was this? He assumed the fear would kick in and he would turn and run, but this was different. He enjoyed the rush. At ten years old, he stood as much of a man as any in this wee town at this moment. "Un fucking touchable" he told himself under his breath. Could a life of crime he had been warned against by his mum really be so bad?

Tam made his way to the side of the van, looking to find grip on the off side of the wheel arch. With the protruding durable plastic, he was able to lift his small frame up high enough, then used his body weight to force himself over the breach. As Tam stood on top of the van, ready to pop the hatch, Fe wondered why more people never thought of this.

Fe's moral compass appeared to be missing at this point... No sooner had he pondered this question when he heard a crash from the van.

"What the fuck?" Fe looked around, but Tam could not be found. "Tam, Tam, where the fuck did you go?" A few seconds passed with no response, then suddenly Tam appeared behind the driver's seat of the van. "You mad bastard, what the fuck have you done?" Fe roared...The battle to hold in his laughter proving to be one of the biggest fights in this young man's life. While seeing the best way to pop the hatch, Tam thought it a promising idea to stand on top of it. No sooner had he placed his full body weight on the hatch, was he sitting next to chip fryer number two! Both boys looked at each other and struggled to hold the laughter.

"Get out ya mad bastard" Fe shouted, hoping this was the end of Tams comedy show. Tam ruffled around with the till, eventually popping it to reveal nothing more than a few old hardened chips that had managed to make their way into the till drawer during the days work. Moving towards the front of the van, the smell of stale cooking oil sat in Tam's throat, momentarily giving him the urge to vomit. However, once he identified the small coin tin placed carefully under the passenger seat, wrapped in an old Falkirk football club scarf, any thoughts of sharing the contents of his stomach quickly passed. Victory was his!

Making his way back out the hatch, Tam looked down to Fe and shouted "catch." The old tin coin box landed sweetly in Fe's hands. "Job done!" Fe said to himself as he turned to walk away from the van and await Tam to join him.

"Catch" Tam declared again, much to the surprise of Fe.

"What the fuck Tam, what have you got now?" Fe questioned, as he struggled to hold the laughter. No sooner had the words left his mouth than a box full of mars bars came hurtling towards him. As Tam dropped himself to the ground from the side of the van, Fe asked him what the idea was behind the mar's bars.

"Just wait" Tam winked, as if the masterplan were almost complete.

The following day the class sat as the register was called. Tam, normally still half asleep at this point, was as bright as a button. Fe, still intrigued as to what his friend was up to, sat and observed. Mrs Walton stood to hold the class to attention, her soft long blonde hair and petite figure embraced the fashion of the era with such grace. Her silk oriental dress falling just below the knee, with the remainder of her legs wrapped in soft skin like tights, offering a darker tone to her natural colouring. Her lips tinted with the faintest of colours offered from the lipstick of choice, big blue eyes sat engaged with the young minds in front of her. It would be difficult to sell the fact that this small beauty had been the heroic force that stood between Mr Harris and young Fe's father only a few years earlier. Mrs Walton had no love for the methods of Harris and teachers such as him. The barbaric methods of punishment individuals such as him would dish out had no place in education in the eyes of Mrs Walton.

She held a soft spot for Fe, no doubt after overhearing endless conversations from her fellow teachers regarding how much of a bad boy he was. In her eyes it was all nonsense. The boy was struggling with the content of the work and she understood this better than anyone.

"As mentioned yesterday, we have our trip to Bannockburn coming up, and we need to take the final payments." As the attention of the class turned to Tam, the crowd of girls who took immense pleasure in mocking him yesterday waited to attack. Each of them sitting with matching outfits, the standard school colours blending with the soft cotton stockings chasing the tops of the knee with the vigorous task of staying in place. Each girl with pig tails dangling at the side of the head in unison, the only difference being the shades of hair colour each girl had. This gang of young vixen ladies had been as brutal as any boy gang within the school. Not in the physical obvious sense, but with the words they would dish out to anyone who did not meet the grade they expected. That verbal assault often causing more, long lasting damage than any flurry of punches. Tam clearly falling well short of the benchmark with his often-tattered clothes and hand me down look.

"Yes Mrs Walton, I have the money here" Tam declared, pride shining out of him like a warm summers day just exploded from inside.

As the whispers died down, Tam then stood up, took his bag from under the desk, and said he also has a wee present for everyone on the bus. Mrs Walton, caught off guard by this declaration, stood watching. Tam proceeded handing out a mars bar to every pupil in the class. As he made his way to the group of girls who had spent the best part of the term tormenting him, he smiled, dug deep in the box, and handed each of them a mars bar. None of them said a word, clearly shocked by what they had just witnessed.

The pieces of the puzzle had just fallen into place for Fe. This was not just about the money for the trip, this was Tam having a moment in life where he did not feel less of a human being than the others. A moment where he could sit side by side with anyone, with everyone. He was just as good. Better even for that split moment. As Tam sat back down, he did not say a word. The expression on his face said it all.

Many years later in the grip of a serious heroin addiction, Tam would tell Fe that the day with the mars bars at school was the best day of his life...

27

Chapter 5

Daisy Daisy

It was 1977, the year Red Rum would win the Grand National for the third time, The Clash would release their debut album and Celtic would lift the league title for the thirtieth time in the club's history. But all of that was insignificant in comparison to the event which took place in thirteen-year-old Kevin McAfee's life. He found love for the first time with Daisy, only a couple of months younger than Fe, and the youngest of two children. She was built like a racing snake, with thick blonde locks of hair curling around her snow-white cheeks and blue eyes open to the world around her. Features which some would declare as unremarkable, however in the eyes of young Fe, this was perfection in its absolute purist form.

Life was not easy for Daisy. Money was scarce in the family home and Daisy had been raised on hand downs from her older sister. This made Daisy a target during primary school, which could be found on the opposite side of the village from that of Fe's school. But as the various primary school pupils merged as they joined the same high school, Daisy was soon to have that knight in shining armour, the one she had only dreamed of coming and fighting the monsters in her world.

Both youngsters were now in their second year, and neither had come across each other before. Fe, still struggling with the content of work given, found himself in remedial classes for most subjects. Daisy, despite everything going on in the playground, tried hard to better herself, in the hope one day she could give herself the better life her parents had failed to. By this point Fe was now coming into the awkward teenage period all boys go through. His face ravaged with acne; it was a tough time for Fe to hold much self confidence in his appearance. His only saving quality would come with the fact that nobody in the school was brave enough to highlight his imperfections. None except his friends of course. Sanny and Tam took immense pleasure in pointing out how he was starting to resemble a "fucking dartboard."

With his thin moustache and bleached blonde/ginger hair, it was certainly a unique look for Fe. It seemed like a promising idea at the time, "dye my hair blonde, get a few tattoos and a wee moustache on the go, the girls will love it" Fe told himself as his mum stood over him with the peroxide, declaring he is going to look like a "fucking idiot." Fe had now grown well into his young body, clearly displaying the same features as his father, with the broad shoulders giving him an appearance of being several years older than his thirteen years.

He had also started getting tattoos from the local artist, known locally as Beast. Beast was an old school tattooist, rarely sober when working. Fe had come across Beast through his love of motorbikes, a culture beast had been part of for a long time. It was said he was once a member of the feared "K4 Rottweiler biker gang" from the borders, a group of outlaws consisting of Scottish bikers and counterparts from the north of England. Something unique to this group of bandits had been the fact that when on the road, you could often find the hardened biker with a companion between his arms holding firm above the gas tank. Not the standard blonde beauty you would expect, instead you would find a muscle-bound Rottweiler holding court, as if a dog standing pride of place at the front of a Harley Davidson was the most natural thing in the world. The patch emblazoned on the back of the vest each biker wore would have the head of a Rottweiler, teeth exposed as to show intentions. The dog would have an old-world war two German helmet on. It posed a menacing sight, and one which affirmed the point this gang were to be taken seriously. The Rottweiler was a massive part of their culture, club houses around the country with each chapter having the breed littered around, walking in line with the bikers like a common community. Often the dogs were held in higher esteem than the new prospects vying for a place within the gang.

None of the boys ever had the bottle to ask if he was part of the gang. But the signs had all been there. The two big Rottweilers that would greet you upon each visit, both giving clue to the man's past. Once you have loved a rottweiler, that love never dies. Truly a breed like no other. The first time Fe had gone to Beast for ink, he was charged at the door by the two giants protecting the home from unwanted visitors. Lola and Loki were spectacular, and once beast had assured the dogs that Fe and his group of friends had been no threat, the relationship between Fe and the dogs was something to behold. His friends often said that Fe got on better with animals than he did with people, as if the canine counterparts could understand Fe like humans had failed to.

Beast was a giant of a man, standing well over six foot and coated in ink from head to toe. His hair extreme with a high mow hawk, a style Fe had seen increasingly with the arrival of the new punk scene. Fe knew the skinheads had moved towards this new punk trend coming along, but he did not see Beast as the type of guy to socialise with skinheads. Then again, when a man is as big as Beast was, you assume he can do whatever the fuck he wants. Walking into Beast's studio, which doubled as his kitchen, you would always experience the thick clouds of cannabis smoke in the air. It was here, at thirteen years old, that Fe would have his first introduction to drugs. This would not be his last.

Scanning the playground during first break, Fe ensured that any appearance from him and his boys depicted a show of strength. Him, Sanny and Tam could handle themselves easily, and while their reputation proceeded them, it did not mean enemies did not exist. The religious undertones of Glasgow had now made its way into the smaller surrounding towns, including Falkirk. With all three boys being known Celtic fans, in what was a predominantly protestant village of Camelon, many boys in the school took offence to the presence of Fe and his gang. The playground was more enclosed to what they had known at primary school, and the sense that freedom had been sucked from them in this new big brother style environment made the prying eyes of teachers even more obvious. It made having a battle in the school grounds an arduous task, as too often it would be broken up just as Fe was getting into the swing of things. The enemies they had accrued over the years were forced to battle within the same constraints. One of those enemies included the McDonald twins, Barry and Stevie. In Fe's opinion, these boys came from an extensive line of idiots.

Each boy had a sturdy frame. The look was far from muscular, yet not particularly overweight. It would be difficult to highlight any definition on them, but those large frames offered natural genetic strength. The boys had always been bigger than most of their peers growing up, and the fact that every attribute they had was multiplied by two, they would become a big problem for lots of young men of similar age. Both boys rounded heads had been coated in freckles from a small age. It was as if the accumulation of marks increased with every passing summer. The short black hair cut to the bone on both boys, not quite to that of the skinheads of the day. The lack of hygiene obvious from both boys had probably left the task of clearing various bouts of head-lice more difficult with fuller heads of hair and to the point that their mother had simply given up and decided that short hair made the battle far easier.

Their dad was also a prominent member of the local orange lodge, the same lodge Fe's dad had joined a few years earlier. Both boys also played for the local football team, a team which had a local rivalry with Fe's team, Gurnoch United. The boys had initially approached a young Fe to join their team, the Camelon Mariners, a few years earlier after seeing him during a kick about down the park. But Fe remained loyal to the Gurnoch, with the boys taking offence to Fe's rejection of a place in the team.

The McDonald twins had the usual hangers on to the group. Boys who played in the team, as well as boys whose dads went to the same lodge. "Wee orange bastards" as Fe would refer to them. A term he never shared around his father for fear of a certain beating. Fe was not religious in any way, it just grated him every time someone would tag him a "wee Fenian". The tension between the McDonald gang and that of Fe's would simmer for weeks, then erupt into violence either in the playground or at pre planned meetings between the two gangs down the local park area known as the Easter park.

Fe was listening to Sanny explaining how he could get them access to the local shop once it closed, when Barry McDonald caught his eye. He could see a group of girls walking past the McDonald gang, when an argument broke out. Barry was notoriously cruel to young girls due to years of having his advancements declined, no doubt because he was ugly as sin. It was the kind of face only a mother could love. Fe stood, choosing not to react and help, as this was not the kind of fight he would normally get involved with when suddenly, his heart started kicking like crazy. As Barry moved to get physical with one of the girls, he could see the intended target step back, exposing herself from the earlier shielding offered by the volume of bodies around her.

At that moment, Fe knew. When a grown man falls in love, he falls in love hard, but when a young man falls in love, logic goes out the window. Fe burst across the playground, the eighty yards between them covered in seconds. Normally he would not dream of approaching the full McDonald gang without his boys behind him, but his logic was now out the window.

"Here you ya fat bastard, is the only cunt you can get a victory against a bird, aye" Fe roared, as he put every fibre of energy and conviction into his display.

By this point his boys had caught up with him and stood guard behind, still unsure as to what was going on, but offering absolute back up none the less. In their eyes, Fe could explain himself later, they had shit to deal with first.

"What the fuck's this wee scruffy cow got to do with you McAfee, ya Fenian bastard" Barry questioned, genuinely interested as to why Fe would suddenly show interest in the practice of him berating young girls, when this was something Fe had witnessed a hundred times and said nothing. "Awe you got a wee hard on for her McAfee" Barry said as he tried to belittle his enemy.

While both aggressors fired insults at each other, Daisy asked herself what was going on. Was this boy here to help me or was she just caught in the middle of another civil war between the two rival gangs. The conflict between both factions was well known by most pupils. Daisy had seen McAfee in the passing, and often had a laugh with herself at his bleach blonde/ ginger hair. He had never spoken to her before, why would he?

Daisy had managed to lose the unwanted attention from Barry, whose eyes were now firmly focused on McAfee.

"You're just angry because that's another lassie that wouldn't let you touch her ya ugly bastard" Fe chuckled loudly, now clearly ensuring a fight was inevitable. By this point the group of girls had moved away from the immediate area, but still close enough to see the inevitable gang fight about to unfold.

Fe's boys were clearly outnumbered, as a couple of the other gang members, George and Butch, were stuck in detention that week. As the seven strong McDonald gang walked towards Fe, Sanny and Tam, the collective thoughts inside the head of the three young men matched. "This should be fucking fun," they thought rhetorically, knowing the odds stacked against them. About twenty feet between both factions, the seven McDonald members started slowly and menacingly advancing.

Turning to Sanny and looking for some sort of plan, one of the McDonald's suddenly dropped to the ground, screaming in agony. As shock and confusion filled the air, another of the McDonald gang fell. Again, the young lad reeled in agony from the assault of a yet unknown source.

"What the fuck is going on?" Fe pondered, as the opposing gang stood, still eighteen feet away. "Argh ya bastard" the shriek of raw pain filled the air, as a third McDonald dropped to his knees.

During that look of concern and panic between Fe and Sanny, the bold Tam had other ideas. You see Tam, despite his lack of height or strength, had one ace up his sleeve. Tam could hit a fucking bird out a nest from fifty feet with a pebble. The guy was a mean shot. While all the other boys had air rifles growing up, Tam could only wait and hope someone would give him a shot. He knew his mum and dad could not afford to buy him a gun, but rather than feel sorry for himself, Tam taught himself to throw stones when others shot pellets.

For as long as Fe could remember, Tam always had a pocket full of stones. He did often wonder why Tam walked around with them, and after all these years of friendship, he was just finding out for the first time. Within the space of ten seconds, Tam had dropped three of the McDonald boys with stones, or as the boys would all later call them, his fucking concrete missiles! The odds still sitting with the McDonalds, Fe and his men fancied their chances.

Taking one final approving glance at his fellow warriors Tam and Sanny, Fe glared at the McDonald gang and roared from the top of his voice "We are the Mob!"

The two factions charged at each other, with Fe, as always leading with a head butt. Since that day six years ago when he proudly watched his dad deal with Harris, Fe always started every fight with a head butt. It was his token, and something more people would remember him by.

As a handful of teachers rushed to split the battle up, Fe lifted his now bloodied face to see Daisy's gaze locked on his. Not a single word spoken in that moment, but both new. In that instant Fe made the decision he was going to win Daisy's heart. And for the first time in Daisy's young life, she had a hero!

The following day, Daisy was miles away as she walked down the street with her older sister, her initial euphoria over the episode with Kevin dampened by her own self-doubt and low opinion of herself.

Daisy felt embarrassed that she had little to offer and impress a boy with, especially important now that someone was interested in her. She was sure he would lose interest once he could see through her and realise she was nobody, from a family that had nothing. No one had ever shown an interest in Daisy, and now she had her own knight in shining armour, someone who had just saved her from the ridicule and cruelty of two of the biggest bullies in the area.

"You're quiet, anything wrong?" questioned Morag, Daisy's older sister, concern etched in her voice.

"There's nothing wrong with me! Just leave it!" Daisy snapped, almost shouting.

"Who rattled your cage?" Morag asked, taken aback by the sheer strength of Daisy's outburst.

Daisy was almost tearful. "Nobody did! I am just fed up being the only teenager at school with nothing nice to wear and looking like shit most of the time. Why couldn't we just come from a normal family and at least have decent clothes to wear?"

Morag put her arm around Daisy's shoulders and offered her a sympathetic hug, examining her tormented expression. "Right, the games up, who is he?" Morag asked, the smile peaking at each corner of her rosy cheeks.

Daisy relaxed, looked at Morag and laughed. "What do you mean who is he?"

"I'm no buttered up the back hen somebody's got your knickers in a twist," her sister replied.

Daisy gave Morag an account of recent events and explained how she was feeling about herself and life at home. It was hard for all the family, especially their mother who had to contend with both children, as good as the two girls had been growing up. Add to the mix an alcoholic, violent husband and father, as well as poor health and little in the way of money coming into the home.

"Well stop feeling sorry for yourself hen, how do you think I used to feel when we had to walk up the road like a couple of knitted twins wearing a green and white skirt and jumper for fuck's sake! And I was older than you and a teenager! It was bad enough trying to start a new double-knit fashion craze, but to top it off it was a crime against Rangers!" Both girls roared with laughter, they loved their mum dearly and wished they could give her the world but having to wear the clothes she knitted for them could only be described as torturous and embarrassing. They were both aware that the garments were knitted due to a lack of money to buy new clothes. Their friends and peers, as well as their enemies, took great

34

delight in the hilarity of the situation and it made the girls an even easier target for ridicule.

Morag looked at her more solemnly and cautioned, "Daisy, just be careful and don't do anything stupid, he has got a bit of a reputation." She could see Daisy's mood changing again, so quickly added, "And as for everything else, just use your model good looks, shining personality and perky wee arse!"

Chapter 6

Bring home the cream

"He is still your dad Kevin" Daisy offered softly, as she sat perched on the end of the bench. It had been twelve of the most memorable months for a young Fe since that battle in the playground with the McDonald's, now both him and Daisy spent every waking moment together. However, this last year had also brought its own share of issues.

Jackie and Billy, after years of pretending normal was what they had, finally called it a day. It was an outcome few found surprise in, but for a young Fe, the pain stayed the same. The past few years with his dad had brought newfound respect for him. Fe, now understanding better than ever the turmoil that sits in the mind of a man, could only imagine what his dad, now alone in a small flat around the corner from the family home, was going through. The issue for Fe, was that the first time in his life, he had experienced the financial strain affected from an adult unwilling to take the slack.

His dad, through bitterness and ignorance, decided to punish Jackie and the kids for refusing to stand by his side and remain loyal, despite his behaviour. In his eyes, a woman stood by her man regardless. The insult of having to even discuss the potential of a divorce was a disgrace to him and his reputation. Having raised the family single-handedly for the last fourteen years, Jackie had only ever managed small part time jobs with the spare time she had. Cleaning jobs, which came few and far between, had always offered the pocket money to spend on the kids, or maybe a little something for the house.

This had never been an issue before, as despite Billy's erratic behaviour, he always made sure the money went in the pot once arriving home on a Friday night, and his drinking money for the weekend kept separate.

But now Billy was refusing to offer any form of financial support to Jackie or the two boys. "They are fuckin men now" Billy raged in his drunken display outside the family home. "Let the bastards start filling that pot on a Friday, cos I am done." The bastards he was referring to had been his fourteen and eleven-year-old boys. Not taking in just how ridiculous a statement this was, Fe viewed this as an expectation.

He was aware Tam, now living with a girl three years his senior in an old council flat, was making decent money working on the milk delivery vans. Tam, who was now head over heels in love with this older girl, was doing ok for himself. On the rare occasion he did turn up to school, he would make sure the money in his pocket came out at least a dozen times. For a boy who had spent his full short life with fuck all, these were good times for Tam. And he wanted to make sure those tormentors who had hounded him in primary school, knew he was a "something" now, and not the "absolutely nothing" he had been made to feel for so long.

"I am going to bounce down and see our Tam" Fe told Daisy, as they sat sharing a glass bottle of Irn Bru on the park bench. It was lunchtime, and the gang sat sprawled over the grass at the feet of Fe and Daisy. She was now a firm part of the gang. Any hero that had ever tried to slate or humiliate her in the past was now a distant memory. Nobody fucked with Daisy now, not while she was Fe's girl. That would be suicide. Even the McDonald boys knew to avoid that one, as it was certain a fight would follow any throw away comments made. This was her new family, and in the eyes of all the boys, she was their queen.

Sanny held a soft spot for Daisy, knowing the shite she had to put up with in the past, she was now safe with his brother. Make no mistake, different mums and dads did not stop the feeling and belief that Fe and Sanny were brothers. Sanny, with his coat draped over his shoulders to battle against the wind, was trying to roll a joint, with Butch and George both trying to offer added shelter.

"Aye fuckin go for it Fe" Butch declared, as he offered an added flame from his lighter to the collective efforts of trying to burn the hash.

Butch was a character. A few sandwiches short of a picnic, Butch was the joker of the group. With his trademark Doc Martens paired with a wax jacket, Butch was a standout. His thick jet-black hair sat in an erratic state on top of his head. You could never quite be sure if Butch intended this style, or if it were the product of zero fucks given when Butch had woken up that day. His biggest feature, the most unmistakable part of Butch, was his laugh. It was the hearty laugh that belonged to a man three times his age and one that started from the bottom of his soul and exploded with the sincerity inside this young man. As people often try to hide failings, Butch celebrated his. He knew he was thick as shit, and not on the same level of those around him. But what Butch lacked in intellect, he made up for in loyalty. Like most of the boys around them, Butch had a tough home life.

His old man had used him as a punch bag for the best part of his short life. And the result was a young guy who was almost invincible. You could not hurt Butch physically. This boy could take a set of size ten steel capped rigger boots straight to the balls and look at you and laugh. Was he completely incapable of feeling pain? Or was he just too stupid for it to register. Regardless of the answer, the boys loved him. This was not just a gang; this was a family.

George completed the family of outlaws. If Butch was the comedian of the group, then George was the connoisseur. By far the smallest of the group, sitting similar height to Fe, but without the physical strength and obvious shoulders and arms. Despite the physical restrictions, George was a dangerous young man. Fighting was not only about brute strength, you had to be clever, and none more so than George. His face was complimented by a sharp jaw line and his nose looked almost misplaced on his small head as it sat proud and thin beyond his eyes. Fe would often say George could "pick peas out a fucking wellie boot with that nose." George had swept back thin brown hair, looking to emulate the look of various rock stars he had adorned all over his bedroom walls.

All new things introduced to the gang came via George. He loved his music and was also crazy about motorbikes. He would often have the team round at his house while they listened to Pink Floyd or Led Zeppelin. His favourite party piece was having the boys all put a crash helmet on, have them do a handstand holding it against the wall upside down. He would then open the screen of the helmet, fill it with cannabis smoke, then close it over. This was all played out to the soundtrack of Pink Floyd's dark side of the moon. For most of the boys this was an amazing experience, but for Fe, who really did not enjoy cannabis at the best of times, this experience was hell.

A promising football career was still on the cards as well for fourteen-year-old Fe, who by this point was playing for his county alongside his efforts with Gurnoch. Trying to avoid the many temptations around him, he ensured he kept himself in top physical condition. The occasional joint would not hinder him, the young right winger assumed.

Standing up from the bench, Fe looked at Daisy and suggested she follow the boys back to school, as he was going to give the second part of the day a miss, instead intending to join Tam for a catch up.

"Is that wise Kevin?" Daisy questioned, knowing how much Fe struggled with school as it was. Despite being universally known as Fe to all in the community, Daisy insisted on calling him Kevin. The name Fe angered her, as she felt it sat hand in hand with the brute status her man was beginning to collect from the locals. She'd seen the different side of Kevin, the soft side, the side of a young man deeply tormented with the demons in his head.

"I need to sort this out somehow Daisy, my mam is stressed out of her mind" Fe snapped back, as if forgetting the recipient of that outburst had only his best interests at heart. "Sorry doll, I didn't mean to bark there" Fe said, knowing he was out of order. Daisy did not respond, knowing the genuine nature of the apology, matched with the obvious stress her man was under.

"Come and get me tonight then" Daisy suggested, as she got to her feet and joined the boys standing in wait.

"Tell Tam we are asking for him Fe" Butch offered, knowing the sentiment was reciprocated throughout the group. "Aye, a will do Butch pal."

Making his way down Glasgow road, Fe could feel the weight of the world on his shoulders. Surely Tam would come good and sort him with some shifts delivering the milk? No doubt his dad was just angry at the minute, and once he'd calmed down, he would come to his senses and help the family financially. He was also smart enough to realise that the world does not always work on "what ifs."

As he made his way into the communal area of the flats, the smell of cat's piss hit him hard. The walls on both sides littered with the ravings of drunken young men and women, some declaring their love for one another, with others offering full on threats of violence should two paths cross. This was the first time he had been down to the new house Tam called home. Despite the clear happiness Tam found himself in, he had been reluctant to let any of the boys meet his new girl, Sandra. She was not from round these parts, having recently moved to Falkirk with her mum. The flat was officially her mum's, but Tam told them the drink had long taken over the mum's mind and body, and that Sandra did as she pleased, which included moving in a fourteen-year-old boy. Fe knew what the door number was, a number Tam and he had shared as the age they first agreed they would be friends forever, as kids do. Tam proudly shared this point with him when he shacked up with Sandra. It was a number Fe rarely forgot as he arrived on the second floor.

Standing outside the door, he could not help but take notice of the noise coming from across the landing. Punk music escaped from every gap in the door as it swirled round his head. The volume was extreme, clearly the tenants did not have much regard for the public opinion of them. Carved into the door were the letters "SS" with the phrase "white power" underneath it. Sitting proudly above these engravings was the swastika emblem, something Fe remembered from history lessons at school.

He had seen the gang of skinheads walking around the streets the last few weeks, harassing the locals. The average age for the group pitched at twenty-one or twenty-two, Fe knew this was a fight that he and his boys were not yet ready for. This did not stop the already developing hatred he had for them simmering in his head. "One day ya cunts, one day" he told himself.

Chapping Tam's door: Fe took a step back waiting for a response. At that point, he heard the heavy door of the close entrance downstairs crashing shut. He knew someone had just come in. At only fourteen, a young Fe was by now battle hardened, and smart enough to know every unfamiliar environment was a potential danger for him. Had one of McDonald boys clocked him alone and decided to follow? Was the slashing promised many times by his enemies about to unfold.

Watching the figure make way to the second floor, a sigh of relief washed over Fe. This was not an enemy, at least not yet anyway. It was one of the skinheads. A lot of the skinhead gang had been boys from around the Stirlingshire area coming together through the joint hatred of outsiders in their country. Stealing jobs, stealing the money, fuck, even stealing the women in the eyes of these radicals. But Fe recognised this one. This was a Kemlin boy in front of him.

Camelon village was referred to as 'Kemlin' by the locals. The only people who called it Camelon were the lawyers and the judges when discussing the place in court. This boy in front of him was big Conner. Fe was not sure of his first name, Conner being his surname, he just knew everyone referred to him as Conner. He had been pals with one of Sanny's older brothers years ago. "Must be about twenty-one now," Fe said to himself. Conner was well built, with a physique refined from a spell or two in prison, a fact Fe had recalled from an earlier encounter, at which Conner had publicly boasted about his battles behind bars with boys from Glasgow. Tales which had been shared in public, with the younger Fe catching details as he stood in the background.

Conner's hair had long gone, and the raw cut to the head with the clippers had now allowed the sunshine a clear path to the young man's scalp, now bronzed from days spent stalking the streets with his comrades. A series of tattoo's littered Conner's arms, many detailing the Nazi ideology and the linking of episodes in central Europe thirty years ago holding some significance to this young man's efforts and focus. His tight light denim jeans were tucked around the neck of his Doc Marten boots and a chequered shirt was carved around the sculptured prison body. A part of Fe admired the look of Conner. There was a self-assurance and arrogance emanating from the man that appealed to young Fe.

"What are you after wee man?" Conner questioned, wondering who had dared to step on his patch uninvited. Now making his way up the second flight of stairs, only feet away from Fe on the landing. Fe's first thought was to drill his size eight right into Connor's jaw as he made his way up the stairs, but with war raging between him and the McDonalds, another enemy was the last thing a young Fe needed.

"I'm here to see ma pal" Fe replied, fake confidence oozing out of every visible part of him, trying to show this older villain if he wanted it, he could fucking have it!

"Wee Tam?" Conner questioned. Clearly Tam had been making friends in his new world. Fe responded with a nod of the head, still ready for an explosion of violence should it be required. "You're needing to have a word with him wee man, that's a fucking roaster that lives in there. She is bad news wee man" Conner said, almost as if genuine concern sat in his voice. As Conner made his way into the skinhead flat, he turned to offer a parting nod of the head to Fe.

Behind him, he could hear the various locks and bolts coming undone as the barricade behind the oak door let down its guard. As the door opened, the surprise from Tam was clear.

"What's happening Fe ya mad bastard, what are you doing down here?" Tam declared, with genuine curiosity in his mind.

"I am needing to have a word Tam, about a gig on the milk with you" Fe responded, wondering why Tam still stood guard at the door like an inadequate bouncer. "You going to fucking invite me in, or are we standing out here like a pair of spare pricks until the weather turns?" Fe questioned.

Tam, now visibly nervous, shifting back and forth, looking perplexed. "Eh, aye sweet, Fe c'mon in."

Stepping over the threshold, the attack to his senses came from an enclosed area clearly housing too many Tom cats. He had just found the source of the spray smell he had met as he walked into the close downstairs. "Fuck me Tam, it's a bit fucking nippy in here is it not?" Fe declared, now struggling to hold his lunch down.

"Fuck up Fe, fuck sake man, Sandra will hear you" Tam responded, pleading for Fe to behave himself.

"She fucking needs to Tam, that's fucking howling like" Fe said, now with a grin on his face as he could see his brother twist with nerves. Tam knew Fe was a wind-up merchant, and not afraid to mix his words up. If Fe felt Sandra was a dirty cow, he would have no qualms in telling her.

This was the beauty of Fe, and why the people admired and hated him in equal measure. He simply did not have a filter. While others have an opinion regarding every situation they come across in life, ninety-nine per cent would likely keep many opinions harboured to avoid an insult to others. Fe, a proud member of the one per cent club, had no such control. If a thought or notion popped into his head, you can be sure as shite you were going to know about it.

The décor in the hall left a lot to be desired. Old wallpaper no doubt supplied by the earlier tenants had seen better days. Strips of it had raced down the walls looking for a new home on the littered floor, falling away due to the lack of heating in the property. Old boxes stacked along each side as if the homeowners had still been undecided on the possibility of staying or moving on to pastures new. As they made their way down the long hall towards the living room, Fe stopped as he caught sight of something through the gap in the bedroom door.

Slumped over her knees, as if sleeping whilst sitting up, was Sandra's mum. Fe could see, even with the reduced view offered by the door's obstruction, that a lifetime of abuse had ravaged the lady. Bones sticking out of her skin, the scent from the room offered an unwelcome change from that aroma the cats had given. Her hair looked as though the last time it had seen water was during the last heavy downpour of rain which was a good few months ago.

42

The smell was a mixture of well worked feet, exposed from the chamber of working boots they had existed in, paired with stale sex you could find four days into a camping holiday. Fe looked at Tam, who ushered him to move on. As they made their way into the living room, Sandra glared up, quickly placing the tray which she had perched on her knees under the gap between the sofa and the tattered carpet. Fe nodded, still struggling to take in his surroundings. The main room in the property looked as bad as anything Fe had ever seen. Despite Tam's fights over the years, the one thing he had never been was dirty. The same could clearly not be said for his new love, Sandra. Rubbish lay strewn across the area, as if all efforts of a normal human existence and behaviour had long gone, swapped instead for a scavenger lifestyle, hoarding all objects that entered the vicinity.

"This is Fe hen, the boy I told you about, the one I grew up with" Tam said firmly, as to highlight to Sandra the audience they now had would struggle to understand the behaviours which could potentially be playing out in front of them.

Sandra was painfully thin, and Fe was already struggling to comprehend the sexual attraction between his young, virile friend, and this mess sat in front of him. Her hair tangled, as if some sort of protest between her locks and a hairbrush had long been in place. The leggings she had on were torn in several places, with what looked like holes from the burning drops of hash which had fallen from poorly rolled joints.

Sandra glared with eyes deep in their sockets and offered a rough "hiya pal" to the now tense Fe. As the words left her mouth, she nudged the tray on the floor further under with the base of her heel. "Take a seat pal" Sandra gestured, now picking her stance up with a puff of the shoulders as if it were time to show the best of herself. Fe wondered if this had been a test, as he tried hard to find anything to sit on which did not pose a potential health hazard as he scanned the room.

Lowering himself down on the couch, which looked thick with a mixture of dead skin, cat hair and tobacco, Fe sat level with the contents of the tray. He could see the old spoon, discoloured from the heat of the lighter which had not long since sat underneath it. Next to this, was the needle still sitting full of the poison that Fe had no doubt Sandra was just about to pump into her veins when he interrupted her. Fury filled Fe's brain. He was certainly no saint, and none of the boys in the gang ever pretended

43

or professed to be either. But the absolute promise each of them had always made to each other was that "no cunt touches the smack."

His eyes scanned Tam, now looking at him with detective precision, looking for any track marks or holes from a recent dig.

"So, what was it you were after Fe" Tam said, nervously sitting beside Sandra as if to show a vision of normality in this clearly fucked up scenario.

"My old man is coming the cunt" Fe explained, now remembering why he was there in the first place, "And I am needing to make some money for the house." Tam, who had seen Jackie as a mum to him most of his life, dropped his guard to offer genuine concern.

"Fuck sake man, I heard about them splitting up, but that's shite like." Tam looked at his brother sitting across from him and thought about what he must have been going through. "We will need to bounce up and see Big Smithy" Tam offered, knowing that this would be the best avenue for him to secure a job for his friend.

Sensing that Fe was uncomfortable with the surroundings, Tam had a quick word in Sandra's ear, then lifted himself to his feet. "Right Fe. C'mon and we will get this sorted for you. Smithy will be heading to the pub soon for the darts, and we want to catch him before he does." The two young men began to make their way to the living room door. Before Fe could even get out the room, Sandra was reaching for the tray. Clearly the temptation of that warm blanket covering her once the heroin kicked in was too much of a temptation.

Both men made their way down the stairs, not a single word shared between them. Walking back into the outside world, Fe's lungs began to celebrate as they were filled with clean air. An awkward feeling had now firmly lodged itself between the two boys. An alien feeling never experienced before from two people who had shared every feeling together in life up to this point. Tam was just waiting for it. He knew Fe had seen the contents of the tray, and he knew the stance his brother would take.

"You want to fucking explain that back there to me then Tam?" A now visibly upset Fe demanded.

"It's not what it looks like Fe, honestly man" Tam protested, knowing it would take more than that to regain the respect of his dear friend.

"Then what was it then Tam, you tell me pal, as it looked like a wee fucking smack heed to me" Fe roared, now clearly allowing his raw emotions to take over. "And don't fucking lie to me Tam and try to make a cunt of me." By this point Fe wanted nothing more than to land a straight right hand on Tam's chin to knock the fucking stupidity out of him.

"She is a good lassie Fe, honestly, but she just got herself a wee habit over the last year" Tam explained, trying to allow Fe an insight to the world he now found himself in. "Her auld man used to knock fuck out of her and her mam, and the two of them are fucked up". Tam was now showing the passion of a man trying to save his true love from the monsters of the world.

"Her mam is heavy with the drink, but Sandra just likes a wee dig to take the pain away." Tam's voice now lowering as he takes in the size of the task ahead of him now living with an addict.

"Tam a couldn't give two fucks about the world she comes from, how the fuck did you end up having to deal with it. You're a fucking fourteen-year-old laddie for fuck sake." Before Tam could respond, he was going to need to answer the inevitable question. The only question that mattered in the eyes of Fe. "Have you touched it yourself?"

"A swear down Fe, I have not touched it. I am trying like fuck to get her off it. Av been stealing Valium from my mam to try and get her to rattle off it with some sleepers." Tam's explanations seemed surprisingly genuine.

"I will be keeping a fucking eye on you Tam, am telling you sir. And if I find out you are on that shite; I will punch your cunt in straight after I have punched her cunt in." Fe gesturing back towards the direction of the flat, giving a clear warning to Tam that first impressions of his new girl had not exactly been great.

"I understand Fe, I understand"

Chapter 7

On your bike

"That's half four Fe" Davie said softly, knowing the chance of a back hander for waking his big brother up at this time of the morning was fifty/fifty. It had been ten months since his first shift on the milk, and things were going well. Apart from the early rises, Fe loved the job. The feeling of handing his wages over to his mum each week was up there with anything else he had experienced in life. The look of pride on her face, almost impossible for her to play down, would light Fe up.

He would always keep a couple of quid for himself, for that "rainy day" as his mum always taught him, but the bulk of the wage went to the family. His mum had also managed to get a wee permanent part time job at the local bus depot, just a cleaning gig at the minute, but it offered a consistent wage for the house. They had slowly been adjusting to new life without the permanent figure of Billy around the house.

The break-up of the family still hurt Billy hard. His drinking had now escalated, and the episodes of violence at the local pub now increasing at the weekends. In the point of a person's life when slowing things down should be the general direction, Billy was more out of control than ever.

At fifteen years old, Fe had now firmly established himself as the man of the house. As he hopped on to the back of the milk van, Tam offered a slight nod of the head. "Morning Fe, fuckin cold one the day is it not?" The boys had managed to build up quite a reputation on the milk van. Big Smithy, who had held this local run for the best part of twenty years, had never seen two boys that worked this well together. He would pay the young lads well, and knowing the reputation a young Fe was now developing, he did not want to have to answer one day the question of "why did you think it was ok to rip me off." Work hard, earn well, that's what he instructed the boys.

"How is she getting on?" Fe pondered, giving his monthly check in to see how Tam was getting on with the addict at home.

"She is down to three bags a day Fe, we are getting their bro" Tam declared, as if this were some sort of victory. Fe made sure to check on Tam's physical appearance as often as he could. Was he losing weight?

Did he look tired? Was he stinking? He knew the effect heroin was having on the community and losing his brother to this was unthinkable.

It was eight am, and the milk run was just ending. As Smithy pulled up outside Fe's house, he tossed over his weekly wage pack from the front of the van. "Cheers big man" Fe gestured, as he nodded his head to the gaffer.

"Nae hassle Fe, you tell your mam am asking for her son" Smithy replied, with genuine heartfelt care in mind.

"I will do Smithy." Fe then turned his attention to Tam, perched on the back of the van waiting to get off at his destination. "You coming to school today?" Fe asked, already laughing before the reply had landed. It had been a while since Tam attended school. Not long after he had hooked up with Sandra, he gave up on the idea of education.

"Aye very good Fe" Tam replied, now giggling at the thought of it.

"Take it easy man, and I will see you tomorrow morning." Today was Friday, and pay day, but Fe and Tam always picked up the wee extra Saturday shift. "Double time, fucking right" the boys would tell themselves. Fe stepped away from the van and allowed Smithy to set off, turning to see his mum just opening the curtains, however the usual smile she shared was missing today.

"You ok mam?" Fe enquired, as his mum slumped over the kitchen table.

"I am fine son, how was your shift?" Jackie responded. Fe could tell something was wrong with his mum. For all the shite she had to put up with in her life, she very rarely showed any sign of weakness. So, when something was wrong, it stood out.

"C'mon mam what's wrong with you. You know am not going to let it go until you tell me. Is it dad?" Fe asked.

"No son it's not your dad" Jackie hit back, quickly ending any thoughts in her young son's mind which would cause further friction between him and his dad. "It's your brothers' birthday on Tuesday, and I couldn't get the bike I promised him on Christmas day last year."

The first Christmas without Billy had been a tough one. Fe, now fifteen, had no expectations of gifts at this time of the year, but young Davie was just turning twelve on Tuesday. So, a few months earlier, for an eleven-year-old to wake up on Christmas day, and the one present he had asked for not being there, it was tough for Jackie to take. She had promised Davie on Christmas day that Santa had just forgot, and that the bike would be ready for his birthday. Davie was not silly. The notion of Santa had long gone since the age of six, but he had pinned his hopes on the bike arriving on his birthday. "I just cannot afford it Kevin, am so sorry son" Jackie pleaded, as if she had failed not just one son, but both.

"Don't be fuckin silly mam, Davie will understand, he knows how tight things are just now" Fe said trying to reassure his mum that this was not a failing.

"Aye a' suppose" his mum replied softly, as if the life had drained out her. She glared out into the back garden, deep in thought.

"A need to get ready for school, but don't you worry about a bike. Our Davie has no doubt forgot all about it anyway. Whatever you get him will be fine. He knows the script." Jackie did not respond.

Standing outside Daisy's house waiting for her, his goal was clear. "I need to get Davie a bike" he told himself. In the ten months since starting on the milk, he had managed to save just over £50 from the wee bit of money he kept separate each week from the house pot. "Surely £50 would be enough for the bike Davie wanted" Fe told himself, realising he had no idea how much it cost. As Daisy came to the gate, she looked at Fe, who was standing with his denim jeans and leather jacket on.

"Why are you not wearing your uniform" Daisy enquired, clearly caught off guard by Fe's dress code today.

"I am patching school today," he explained "and going up the toon to try and get our Davie a bike for his birthday on Tuesday." Daisy knew what Fe was saying. She knew the strain the family had been under since the departure of Billy.

"Fuck sake Kevin if you get caught stealing, that's your football career over before it started" Daisy protested, as if trying to remind her man the weight a criminal conviction can have around a person's neck.

"I am no fucking stealing it Daisy, am going to buy it. I have been saving the money up for the last while from my milk run."

Daisy's heart fluttered, as if she needed another reason to fall in love with the man in front of her. "Oh my god Kevin that is so sweet, but what about school?" Daisy offered with genuine concern.

"It's one day Daisy, and it's hardly like I learn fuck all when am there anyway." Fe snapped back. "I am only here to make sure you get to school ok, then am going to bounce up the toon." Daisy knew by now that when Kevin had made his mind up about something, it was happening.

Kissing her cheek at the side of the smoker's corner, Fe turned and made his way up the back of the flats, and back on to the main road. As he passed the whiskey distillery, he could see the workers sitting on the wall having one last fag before entering the premises for a day's graft. He looked at the worn-out faces on the workers, battered and beaten from years of manual labour. The distillery was one of the decent gigs within the town, but Fe just could not see himself working in this environment. The same thing, day after day.

No chance, this was not the life of a footballer, the only career path Fe could see himself having. He had local interest ramping up in recent months. His coach made him aware every time he reckoned a scout was at the game that day. A lot of the time it turned out to be the paranoia of the coach, but Fe told himself he must have been right some of the time. It made no difference to Fe, who played his heart out every week, regardless of the audience on the side-lines.

Standing outside the bike shop, Fe was met with an array of different options. None of that mattered to the young man, as he knew exactly which bike he was after. The bike his younger brother had spoken about for the last two years non-stop. 'The Raleigh Chopper Mark2 five speed.' As the owner of the shop looked out the large front window, he could see Fe staring at his choice of merchandise. With the leather jacket on and obvious tattoos creeping out of the top of his T shirt, the shop owner questioned if this young man had designs on stealing one of the bikes.

"Can I help you son" the owner offered, this point standing outside the shop. He had baggy brown corduroy trousers on, reminding Fe of Harris all those years ago, only a more relaxed version. The shop owner's shirt worked well with the trousers, as the white freshly pressed long sleeves offered a professional look. The thick Scandinavian features reminded Fe of Bjorn Borg, a fact which he wanted to point out, but nerves put stop to this.

As the gentleman walked towards Fe, he repeated the earlier question. With this, Fe looked up nervously as the encounter started to play out.

He had never considered spending this much money in his life, and at fifteen, his body suddenly filled with unexpected nerves.

"Eh, I am after a cross, mark 2, needs to be five speed" Fe responded, fidgeting with and adjusting in his leather jacket.

"Ah the Raleigh cross" the shop owner said, as if celebrating the success of the bike. "Is it for you son?" the owner queried.

"Eh no sir, it's for my wee brother, it's his birthday on Tuesday" Fe replied, still unsure as to how this process should play out.

"Very nice son, and I take it your mum and dad have sent you up with the money to buy it then" the owner bounced back, now relaxing to the fact a genuine sale could be on the cards, and not the initial fear of having to wrestle a five-speed bike out the arms of a young, fit biker.

"How much is it sir" Fe asked, praying the fifty pounds in his pocket would be enough to cover it.

"Well for the Raleigh Cross mark 2 - five speed you're after, it will set you back sixty-seven pounds ninety-five," said the shop owner as the lump in Fe's throat sank to the bottom of his chest.

"Fuck sake" Fe declared, not even realising he was talking aloud.

"You ok son" the owner responded, noticing the young boy in front of him was in some sort of turmoil. Fe turned and sat down on the curb below him. All emotions of the previous twelve months finally falling away from him, as the white flag in his young mind began to wave in surrender. Now intrigued as to what the circumstances of the young man in front of him had been, the shop owner, completely out of character, took a seat next to the young man.

"You ok son" the shop owner asked again, now in a significantly softer tone, treading carefully as he inspected the troubles sitting with this boy.

While explaining the situation to the man sitting next to him, the shop owner could see this young lad was hurting. Not just from the inability to afford the bike, but to the full situation in general. Several moments passed as both men sat in silence, as if each of them had been weighing up the details from each respective life.

"You know son, I lost my dad in the war." The shop owner said, opening himself up to the young man in leather sitting next to him. "It was tough. I had to become the man of my house at an early age, just like you have..." He continued, "...but I will tell you one thing son, days like these are teaching you how to become a better man. What you are doing for your brother, not everyone would do something like this."

Fe looked up, the words from this stranger wrapping round his heart like a thousand arms. As if sunlight had been rewarded to a room long imprisoned in darkness.

"I will tell you what we will do son. You give me that fifty pounds, and I'll give you the bike. And then one day, when you can afford it, you settle your bill. How does that sound." Fe looked on in shock. Was this a joke? Was this guy serious? Why would anyone do this? Before he had the chance to respond, Fe could feel the tear roll down his cheek as it crossed into the corner of his mouth. His heart felt heavy. Heavier than he had felt in a long time. But the weight of this, the load normally causing such pain and turmoil, it felt different. This was a happy burden. Fe looked up to the man, disbelief still gripping him with this incredible gesture.

"I promise I will pay you the rest as soon as I have it" Fe declared, praying his words would be taken in the genuine manner in which he meant them.

"I know you will son, I know you will."

Walking with the bike, Fe took one final look back at the man who would have such an impact on his life and the value it would create, he offered a nod of the head. The shop owner responded to this with a nod of his own. Fe realised he did not even have the money for the bus home. As he set off on his brothers' new bike, a smile lit up his face. Despite all the bad days that had led up to this one, this was a good day. As Fe went off on his journey, the shop owner watched, and just as he was about to make his way back into the shop, he noticed Fe do a turn in the middle of the road, now making his way back to the shop.

As the owner made his way to the curb, Fe stopped beside him. He looked in the eyes of his new friend and smiled "I am Kevin, but my pals all call me Fe."

The shop owner laughed and responded, "My name is Alec, and all my friends call me Alec." Both laughed in unison as Fe began to turn the bike. "Take care Fe," Alec offered jokingly, as the two men parted ways once again.

Tuesday morning and Davie burst down the stairs like a bat out of hell. Excitement from the young boy filling the air. Jackie followed, dread filling her as the certain disappointment which would shortly follow was too much for her to take. As Fe met her at the top of the stairs, both looking to keep up with Davie, he offered her a simple "morning mam." This followed up by a soft kiss on the forehead. As they made their way in the living room, they found a statue of a young Davie, by this point filled with disappointment as he scanned the room, clearly unable to find the shape of a bike from the few presents in front of him.

The room now offered proper comfort to the family, as Jackie had worked hard at it over the years to offer the family a proper home. The sofas on either side, offering ample room for them to cosy up on and share tales of their day's events each evening. At the end of the room was a series of shelving units, all holding Jackie's collection of teapots, all in different shapes and sizes. On the wall opposite sitting pride of place was a picture of the two boys taken when both toddlers during the village parade. Both young men dressed as sailors, outfits Jackie had saved hard for to create that special memory in her mind.

Opening the last present, a pair of socks that Jackie said would be "great for the fishing," Davie put on a brave front and looked at his mum.

"Thanks mam, a love you to bits." Her heart melted, the guilt of failure now consuming her. There was no tantrum from her youngest. Davie understood the situation the family had been in, and he knew the last thing his mum needed was him kicking off. Jackie's failure to get the bike promised to her youngest on the earlier Christmas cut hard. Despite Jackie knowing it was not her fault, that fact did nothing to subside the pain she felt in her heart, a pain which was now amplified by the fact her youngest son had taken it so well, a point in her mind making him even more deserving of the bike.

"Aren't we forgetting something mam?" Fe asked, looking at his mum as if she were part of the joke. Jackie looked back with genuine confusion. She was wondering if she had missed the start of a conversation, with the grief and guilt consuming her potentially causing her to miss something.

"You better go check the kitchen Davie" Fe shouted, as the energy in the room began to rise. A young Davie sprung to his feet; knowing today's proceedings had not yet concluded. Panic and curiosity filled the house. He ran to the kitchen, with Jackie and Fe both unable to keep up the pace. As Jackie passed the threshold of the living room, she could hear her youngest screaming.

"A fucking Raleigh Cross mam, a fuckin Raleigh Cross!" The words hit Jackie like a steam train. Had it not been for Davie repeating the fact during his outburst, she would forgive herself for mishearing him.

Jackie's heart sank. The final piece of the puzzle in her brain had just locked into place. She realised what her eldest son had done. As she stepped into the kitchen, Davie launched himself at her, lifting her off her feet with a sign of affection so raw, you could feel the emotion in the air.

"Thank you so much mam, a love it" Davie declared, clearly ecstatic that his mum had kept her word.

"Well, away up and get yourself dressed then" his mum roared. "The bike isn't going to ride itself now, is it?" Jackie declared, pride and emotion now causing her voice to ripple. Davie burst out the room and up the stairs at a speed that would challenge the great Jesse Owens in his prime.

Standing across from his mum, Fe could see the emotion was taking over. As the tears streamed down her face, she offered just one question.

"Please tell me it's not stolen for fuck sake" Jackie asked, now a complete wreck of emotion.

A now visibly emotional Fe burst out laughing, tears now mixing with those on his mum's cheek. He pulled her to him, and in a tight embrace whispered in her ear "no mam, it's all his."

Jackie didn't have to say how proud she was of her son at that moment. With family, sometimes words are simply not required. Her heart filled with acknowledgement. The acknowledgement that her son was turning into a man. And in a world filled with bad men, she realised she had raised a good one. A gentleman. It was all any mother would ever ask of the world when shaping their offspring. Money, wealth, status, fame, and all that comes with it, it is all secondary to the most fundamental need for our children. The most important fact from any parent. That our children, they grow into good people.

Mother and son finally gave up the embrace from what felt like an eternity. Suddenly, the phone rang. Jackie answered it, and after a few minutes of taking in the information from the other end of the line, looked over to Kevin and said, "it's for you son."

Chapter 8

A big call

"Is that Kevin McAfee I am speaking to" The voice on the other end of the phone enquired.

"It is. And who is this?" Fe responded, caught out by the strange accent on the other end of the phone. It was an accent Fe struggled to identify.

"Good morning Kevin. My name is Phill Owen and I am calling on behalf of Sunderland football club. Are you ok to have a quick chat son?" Fe, clearly not buying into the possibility of a phone call from one of the biggest clubs in Britain, responded in the only way he knew.

"Is that you Sanny ya big wanker! Aye very funny ya cunt. That is some fucking accent though a will give you that, you sound like a fucking farmer sir!" The voice on the end of the phone did not reply. By this point Jackie was looking at her son with great interest. She nodded to the phone as if instructing her boy that this was genuine.

"That's no you Sanny, is it?" The voice at the other end of the phone began to laugh. "No son this is not Sanny, although it sounds like you two have quite the friendship." Suddenly the magnitude of the fuck up Fe had just made hit him.

"I am so sorry sir, for using that language in front of you. I thought it was my big pal on the noise up" Fe explained, now firmly adapting to his best phone voice in order to excuse his earlier outburst and show he was not a scum bag on the end of the phone.

"The reason I am calling you Kevin, is we have had a scout watching you over the last month, and I must say the reports coming back have been very impressive." Fe listened intently, offering the occasional sounds to indicate he was still on the other end of the line. "I am not sure if you are aware, but we recently lost our position in division one, and are looking to bounce back up with promotion this season. In order to do that, we are looking to invest in some quality youth prospects. Your name is one which sits highly on our list." Fe was trying to process all this information in.

He had long known his ability could lead to the phone call from a big club one day, but he did not expect it to happen from a team in England.

"We have spoken to your coach at Gurnoch United, who passed us your contact number. We would be looking for you to come down on a three-week trial, which we have no doubt would be successful after what we have seen, which would be followed by you moving down here on a permanent basis."

Fe, now starting to take in the gravity of the offer in front of him responded "do you mean to live down there?" The voice at the other end of the phone began to laugh.

"Yes Kevin, you would need to live down here. As much as Scotland and Sunderland are not a million miles apart, the expectation would be you coming to training daily, and the commute across the border each day would be too much son."

Fe sat with the phone to his ear, silence flooding the room as his mum looked on at him. The caller had briefly explained the situation to Mrs McAfee before she handed the phone to Fe, so she was aware of the offer her son had just received.

"I will tell you what Kevin," the scout explained, clearly realising the massive decision sitting on this young lads' shoulders. "How about I call you back on Friday, give you a few days to speak to your family and see what they think. I know it is a big decision son, and one you need to think about."

"I would really appreciate that sir" Fe responded, knowing there was no way he could offer an answer just now.

"Well you take care son and keep the training up, and I will speak to you on Friday. Bye son." The line went dead. Fe placed the phone down and looked up at his mum.

"What do you think mam?" Fe questioned, gauging how his mum felt about the prospect of him leaving the family home to move to another country.

"The decision sits with you son, and I will support you whatever you go with" Jackie said firmly, as the thought of losing her boy sank in. Silence filled the room again, as both tried to process the potential outcome each decision would create. As Jackie made her way out the room to get ready for the day ahead, she turned to Fe and insisted "you better let your dad know."

With the phone ringing, Fe wondered what kind of state his dad would be in at the other end. Eventually the ringing stopped as a voice met Fe at the other end of the line.

"Who the fuck is phoning at this time of the fuckin morning?" The voice enquired with an aggressive tone, clearly upset at being disturbed before midday.

"It's me dad, Kevin."

A few moments passed before Billy responded, "the fuck is it you're after... money no doubt?" Fe, now filling with rage, a common emotion these days whenever dealing with his dad, responded harshly.

"No, I don't need your fucking money, I was phoning to let you know Sunderland have offered me trials." Billy gave no response. "Did you hear me dad? ... "They want me to go to Sunderland for a few weeks and trial for the first team." The phone line went dead.

Making his way to Daisy's house, Fe tried to work out in his head the best way to tell her, knowing that a decision to move would no doubt be the end to any future they had together. As he turned into the street, he could see Sanny, Butch and George all waiting outside Daisy's garden.

"The fuck are you boys doing here" Fe asked, knowing the usual meeting spot was the lane just up from them.

"We thought we would meet you love birds here", Sanny declared. The truth was, they had been out scoring a bit of hash before the dealer started his shift on the bins and had been passing this way.

"You ok Fe" Butch questioned, noticing his friend looked agitated.

"Aye am sound Butch pal, just a lot on my mind buddy eh."

Butch responded, "aye a' know what you mean Fe, I do that pal." George and Sanny both started laughing, to the surprise of Butch.

"Fuck off Butch, you are as bright as a fucking blackout sir, you've never had a stressful thought in your fucking life... Fuck me, it's a fucking effort for you to walk in a straight line without falling on your arse" Sanny declared, as the full gang started laughing, including Fe.

"Aye you're not wrong Sanny, you're not wrong" Butch replied, still not fully understanding what Sanny was trying to say, thus hitting home his point.

Just as the boys composed themselves, Daisy walked out the front door and along the path.

"Morning boys" she said, as the sight of the gang caused little surprise. "You ok?" Daisy questioned, looking at Fe as his usual bright smile when greeting her was missing today. Before he had the chance to offer a response, which would no doubt be a twist on the truth, as now was not the time to mention anything, the gang spun round to the reaction of an almighty roar at the end of the street.

"Fe!" The voice screamed, as if this had been the last attempt available to catch the attention of the intended target. "Fe!" Again, the voice bellowed to land with the gang.

"Is that Tam?" Sanny enquired, still unsure as to what was going on. The figure got close enough for the boys to realise it was one of their own. But something was wrong. As they made their way towards Tam, they could see he was struggling. As he moved between the fence on his left-hand side, and the parked cars on his right, he looked like a pinball in motion as he staggered from side to side.

"The cunt is steaming drunk" Butch offered, assuming the struggles with balance had been the result of a wet breakfast. Fe knew that was not the case. His friend was hurt. As they got within a couple of feet of Tam, they could see the damage inflicted to his face, and the bruising already starting to show on various parts of his body.

"The cunts taxed us Fe," Tam pleaded, as if still in shock at what had just happened, "and they ripped my fucking jaw open with a blade Fe." By this point the extent of the injuries had been clear. Tam was in a bad way.

"Who did this Tam, and what do you mean they taxed you? The fuck does that mean?" a now visibly enraged Fe roared, now furious that someone had taken this liberty with one of his brothers while they had been alone.

Before Tam could respond, Sanny declared "was it they fucking McDonald bastards that did this Tam?" Fe's attention swung to Tam, waiting for an answer to Sanny's question.

"None of that matters just now" Daisy intervened, "Look at the state of him. We need to get him inside and cleaned up."

Fe reserved his Investigation until they had gotten their friend patched up and calmed down.

"He is going to need to go to the hospital and get stitched for this slash on the face" Daisy declared worriedly. "I have stopped the bleeding just now, but it needs proper medical attention to avoid infection." Fe, who had been observing the patch up job from the other side of his mum's kitchen, stepped out to hold the attention of the gang.

"He isn't going anywhere until we find out what happened. It is time to start fucking talking Tam." Since the walk back to Fe's house and the chance to take in reassurance from those around him, Tam had calmed down.

"They taxed me and Sandra." Tam said, by this point reiterating the statement from earlier at a much lower level. However, the drop in volume from Tam was blown away by the explosion of emotion from Fe.

"You have fucking told us that already you silly cunt, what the fuck does it mean. And who the fuck done it!"

The full gang, taken aback by Fe's outburst, struggled to understand his mind-set. It was clear to all of them that the man they all adored had something he was harbouring from the rest of them. Fe, despite his fierce reputation, would never speak to any of them like that. Tam, shocked by the response, sat himself up in the chair and began to explain.

"Me and Sandra have been selling a wee bit heroin for the last two months, just to try and make it a bit easier to fund her habit. Nothing big like." As the words left Tam's mouth; the announcement destroyed Fe inside.

He knew Tam could be an idiot at times, and most of his decisions were questionable to say the least. But fifteen years old and selling smack. How did this happen? The one path he didn't want any of his friends to go down was playing out in front of him and he had no idea. Fighting the internal urge to lunge at Tam and show him how he felt with his fists was difficult for Fe to control.

"So, what happened?" Fe responded as calmly as possible, utilising every ounce of self-control he had in his body. "They taxed us Fe. They came into the house, stole all the fucking drugs, took all the money I had been banking and gave the both of us a good kicking." The only question left to answer was one they all wanted to scream at the same time, but before they had the chance, Tam shared it with the group. And the one thing Fe did not want to hear, the one enemy Fe really did not need this moment in time, was the one Tam confirmed.

"The fucking skinheads Fe, they dirty bald bastards fuckin turned us over good."

As the words left Tam's mouth; every head turned to Fe. This was his team. This was his gang. He was the unofficial head of the family. Sanny had always been top boy in the group when it came to having a scrap. That was a given. That hard bastard inside him as a seven-year-old boy was still just as strong in the now fifteen-year-old young man. But battles are not won with brawn alone, a fact the boys now understood. Leaders need to be thinkers. And none thought more in this world than Fe.

They had met several situations in the past where potential threats had come at them. When Sanny had been completely invested in the fight, but Fe, with tactical awareness growing by the year, made the decision to walk, and attack another day. This mentality worked well for the boys, with unwavering faith in Fe to keep them right.

"How many was there Tam?" Fe asked softly, now realising a calm head is what the team required, casting away any earlier aggression that had been displayed.

"They fuckin rushed me at the front door Fe and started melting me in the hall. Sandra ran at them with a fuckin high heel, but they dropped her before she could even land a shot. It's fucking hard to say Fe but am guessing seven or eight."

Fe looked around the room, minus Daisy, his soldiers, the only ones that he could rely on to fight stood in front of him. They had had many other members in the gang over the years, but the hard-core members, the members he knew would be willing to fight against much older enemies, stood in front of him at this moment. For a lot of the boys who had fallen away over the years, the ability to talk a good game came easy. False tales of glory which had been shared, quickly blown to pieces when faced with a real battle. But these boys in front of him, these were the real deal.

"Was Conner there?" Fe asked, now laying out the battle plan in his mind.

"The fuck would that matter Fe" Sanny snarled, not interested in the details of the attack, instead only wanting retribution for his friend.

59

"It fuckin matters Sanny as I need to know if he gave the green light for it, or if his boys fancied chancing it against some random." Tam was a stranger to most of the skinheads, but Fe knew Tam was known to Conner. Had Conner disregarded this fact and made the move on Tam, knowing Fe would potentially come back at him with retaliation? It mattered more than the gang realised!

"I am honestly no sure Fe; it all happened that quick" Tam answered, wishing he could tell Fe more, but he was clearly still shaken by the earlier events as well as being in pain from his injuries.

"It's fine Tam, don't worry pal." Fe said to his friend consolingly.

Fe instructed Butch and George to get Tam up to the hospital on the back of George's motorbike, with Butch following behind on his bike to ensure safe arrival. "Is it ok if I come and catch up with you later Daisy, me and Sanny need to sort some things out" Fe enquired gently, as if to remove any concern Daisy might have for her man.

"Please don't do anything stupid Kevin" Daisy pleaded, knowing her love could not allow this act to stand.

"I promise everything will be ok" Fe reassured, as if believing his own words to be true, when the reality could not be further from the truth.

He landed a soft kiss on Daisy's cheek and walked her to the door. Before she could leave, he scanned the areas surrounding his home, making sure there was no threat to his precious Daisy.

"Go straight home, and phone me as soon as you get there, as soon as Daisy!" The tone from Fe now stern, to ensure she understood the expectations, raising some level of fear and concern from Daisy who reassured him

"I will do, I love you."

Chapter 9

Decisions must be made

"What are you thinking Fe?" Sanny enquired, as the two young men stood in the kitchen, both contemplating the next steps.

"I am thinking we are totally fucking outnumbered Sanny" Fe responded. Back in the day, a fight in the playground or down the park between five of Fe's boys and eight of the McDonald clan would not have been an issue. If anything, the boys would enjoy the extra challenge, as the reward was greater. But this was different. These were grown men they were going against, grown men who clearly had no hesitation about either using weapons or beating up women into the bargain, as Tam's jaw would testify.

"If Tam reckons seven or eight, and he's not one hundred per cent sure Conner was there, then let's call it a full team of nine, and we have fucking five!" Fe raged, as the situation became clear in his mind.

"Fucking four to be honest Fe, as Tam is no good to any cunt in that condition. He will fucking open after the first dig to his face." As blunt as Sanny's response had been, Fe knew he was right. Tam was in no condition to retaliate yet. And it would take weeks for him to heal.

"We need back up, and it needs to be boys willing to go head on with grown men." Fe explained calmly, his thinking cap now firmly placed on his head. "Only one of these bastards comes from Kemlin, and that's big Conner, and we don't even know if he was part of this...". Sanny, wondering what Fe was suggesting, looked on with intrigue. "How many of the older boys are going to be happy when they find out eight fucking random cunts came into our toon, ripped the fucking jaw off one of our boys, and the fact he was only fucking fifteen" Fe offered passionately, as the war plan now started to unfold.

"Aye your fucking not wrong Fe, most Kemlin cunts would not be happy. Who are you thinking?" Sanny asked, knowing the respect for Fe by the older generation had been picking up pace over the last few years.

Fe reiterated, "This is still our fucking fight Sanny, but I reckon another two bodies."

The plan was simple. Get Tam away from the flat he and Sandra had been sharing. Tam could move back in with him. In Fe's eyes Sandra had outstayed her welcome anyway, so her and her mum needed to fuck off. Allow Tam time to heal up and get a couple of the older boys to join the fight. Attacking now would be silly, as the skinheads would be waiting for it. And Fe knew Tam wanted to be part of any counterattack. You do not slash a man's face and expect to get away with it. Let the skinheads think Fe and his boys had bottled it and allowed the episode to playout without retribution. Fe was patient, he could wait.

"Stix and Mercer" Fe announced, as Sanny looked at him in surprise.

"Not a chance Stix will help us Fe, he is boxing for Scotland at the minute am sure, no chance is he going to risk losing his boxing licence for a few young team boys." Sanny, resigned to the fact that Stix would want no part of it, advised his best friend on the unlikeliness of any help from him.

Fe retorted, "I know he is doing well with the boxing, but I also know there is no fucking danger he is going to allow that shit in his toon." It had long been known that Stix was the hardest man in Kemlin, with only one or two others who could have a go at that title.

One of those others had been Mercer. The outcome of such a battle should it ever take place, had been topic of many discussions, but with both young men being good friends, the battle had never materialised. A firm friendship between the two men, and mutual respect of eithers ability to have a scrap had always prevented this. Mercer had recently returned from the army and was quickly making his name as one of the best street fighters in Falkirk.

The standout factor of his ability was the absolute refusal to ever put the boot in anyone when on the floor. Mercer would demand the individual get back on their feet to continue the fight, until the life had drained out of them, and the refusal to rise would cement victory for a young Mercer.

"Just leave it to me Sanny" Fe advised, now firmly invested in creating a team worthy of taking on the skinheads.

"Nae hassle Fe" said Sanny who was still unsure if Mercer and Stix would help despite the confidence he had in his brother. As Sanny made his way out the front door, he turned to Fe, as if the morning's events had not actually happened, and asked "is everything ok with you? Before Tam turned up this morning, you didn't look yourself."

Fe, now reminded of the earlier phone calls from the scout and his dad, looked at Sanny and replied, "I am sound bro, just the usual man eh." Sanny nodded his head, knowing if his friend did not want to elaborate, then the task of digging for information was pointless.

"Sound Fe." Sanny turned and left.

Making his way down the street, Fe struggled to find comfort from the hammer digging into the base of his back. Since this morning's episode had played out, Fe ensured the team knew he wanted them tooled up to try and help should any further attacks take place. He knew it was unlikely, as they were only fifteen-year-old boys, but this was war, and they had to conduct themselves accordingly. A hammer tucked in the back of his Levis jeans would offer some additional aid should it be required.

While he stood outside the gym, a second thought came to his mind, as if the pressure he was under was not enough. Tam said they had taxed all the drugs. Had Tam payed for the drugs upfront or had they been distributed prior to sale? Was Tam now in debt to the distributors and who were they? What additional danger did this pose? Fe told himself "fuck me Tam, this is some fucking mess you have got us all into."

The minutes passed as Fe stood outside the gym, waiting for Stix to finish his session, he asked himself the inevitable question. "How can I up and leave everyone to live in Sunderland with all this going on?" He was not just referring to the issues with Tam. He knew his mum was still having issues with his dad, and that his mum needed him around the house to help raise Davie.

He also knew Daisy needed him. She loved him. And he knew the reality of them lasting with him so far away was unlikely. This was an amazing opportunity for him, he loved his football, but surely other opportunities would come up. Surely Celtic would hear about his efforts, just how good he was and eventually come knocking? Then there would be no reason to leave Kemlin and the family home. He would even be happy pulling over the colours of Glasgow Rangers if it meant he could stay at home.

With all the potential outcomes playing out in his mind like a bad movie, the doors to the gym opened. As the flow of fighters passed by, some of whom offered an interesting gaze as to who this young guy was, he was met with the sight of Stix at the back of the pack.

"Is that you young Fe?" Stix declared, knowing the answer to his question, but offering in a cheerful sense.

"How are you doing big man, how was your session?" Fe replied.

"Aye all good son, all good. Are you thinking of joining up?" Stix questioned, now curious as to the motives of the young man in front of him.

"Sadly, not today Stix. I am not wanting to have to show you up" Fe joked, knowing the likelihood of that actually happening was one in a million. "Can I have a word with you Stix?"

Stix was in phenomenal shape, a young boxer moving into the best years of his life. His thin athletic body carefully sculptured through training to ensure every kilo or pound on him was part of his arsenal for a fight. No room for any wasted weight on this finely tuned weapon. His dark hair contrasted with those sharp bright eyes. The cheeky grin he would offer, leaving recipients unsure if he were about to kiss them or blitz them with a flurry of punches. His reputation within the boxing world was higher than ever, and he had the world at his feet.

With Fe explaining the situation, Stix listened without offering any response. Once the details of the event had been shared, silence sat between the two young men. After a good moment had passed Stix finally asked,

"And they are twenty-one you said Fe? The same age as me?" making sure he had all the details correct.

"Aye around that age Stix, a might even say a couple of them are older," Fe confirmed.

Stix looked on into the distance, as his brain started to digest the facts recently delivered to it.

"And how many boys has your team got, and a mean proper boys Fe, not wee carboard gangsters that want to talk the talk. How many fighters do you have?" Fe, knowing Stix was asking too many questions to then deliver an instant no, was now needing to sell the fight to his older friend.

"Once Tam has healed, I have five good men, including me." Fe declared with pride, knowing the announcement was not one which offered a particularly promising sales pitch.

"And how many men are you wanting behind you when you go to war?" Stix replied, as if the earlier announcement had not phased him in the slightest.

"I want to run at them with seven soldiers!" replied Fe enthusiastically.

"I reckon running at the nine of them with seven of us should be enough." Before Stix could reply to the audacious plan delivered to him, Fe continued.

"And this is our fight Stix, my team need to do this. I am only wanting you to help build the numbers, no disrespect intended." Stix looked at the young lad in front of him, under no illusion every word just spoken was meant.

"You have got some fucking balls wee man, I will give you that." Fe did not respond. "Let me speak to big Mercer and I will see what I can do. Are you going to be in tonight?" Stix asked, now almost on side to the point Fe could taste it.

"We will be in all night," Fe declared, already daring to feel a sense of optimism creeping in.

Chapter 10

You want it?

Making his way back to the house, his mind emptied of all thoughts. By the time he reached his front door, he had to question how he had gotten here. The walk home was missing from his memory bank. He made his way inside and cleaned up the mess in the kitchen. The trail of blood from the front door was still visible and he knew his mum would be home shortly.

Once finished, he placed the mop away in the cupboard, happy with the job he had done. He instantly felt his back go up as he heard a noise in the back garden. The first thought that entered his head was "skinheads." He drew the hammer from the back of his tight jeans and gripped on to it, the fear that should be all consuming for a normal person in a situation like this, missing in action for Fe. He wanted this, even if it meant nine skinheads versus only him, he was spoiling for a fight.

Making his way to the backdoor, Fe slowly unlocked it. Taking one final look out the window to see just who was waiting on the other side, he swung the door open and burst out on to the breezed block patio, instantly scanning the area to look for the enemy, ready to smash the claw hammer into the shaven heads of some young radicals. But instead of a tool handed mob of skinheads; he was met with a familiar face.

"You ok Dad?" Fe could see his dad had been drinking.

"So, you are a big fucking football player now are you, awe geared up to go down and play for Sunderland are you. Fucking lucky laddie you are eh."

"Your drunk dad, so let's just leave it and we can speak again when your sober" Fe suggested, knowing any reasonable conversation was pointless at this moment in time.

"Is that right son, is your old man no good enough to fucking talk to now? You always were a wee shite house bastard." Fe looked on.

"A still remember that time a' had to burst your teacher's face cos you were too fucking scared to do it yourself." His father now choosing to sully the one proud moment Fe had of him.

"I was fuckin seven-years-old ya daft cunt" Fe offered in return, knowing any form of response was pointless, but still having the urge to fight back.

"Daft cunt, daft cunt is it?" Billy started to move forward towards Fe. During fifteen tough years Fe had taken countless beatings from his dad, but never once responded with any form of physical retaliation. He just took it, as had his mum on all those occasions.

"I am fucking warning you dad, today isn't the day. It's no playing out how you think it is!" Fe growled, attempting to stop his father's advances.

"Oh, you're a fucking big man now are you" Billy growled back. At that moment, the back door swung open and both men were greeted by the sight of Jackie.

"You don't touch him Billy McAfee, I am warning you, enough is enough" Jackie snarled, resembling a lioness protecting her cubs from the threat of attack. As if the years of mental and physical abuse were finally ending.

"You keep your fucking mouth shut and I will deal with you after I have fucking dealt with this fairy" Billy drunkenly declared, making his intentions clear. Fe turned to look at his mum. In a moment that would define him as a young boy now becoming a man, his mum looked at him, and with not a word spoken, gave a nod of the head.

With that clearance, Fe looked at his dad, the drunken man in front of him whom he had once adored. As Billy continued his advance, Fe lifted the size eight samba off the ground and planted it right between Billy's legs. The shot hit Billy clean in the balls. The drunken attack Billy had planned for his son and ex-wife had suddenly and abruptly come to an end. As he fell to his knees, Billy looked up to his son.

"You have a good think while you are down there. And if you want more once the pain has passed, you fucking step back up." As the words left Fe's mouth; he made his way inside. Billy, now crumpled on the ground as he twisted in pain, watched his son as he walked away.

As they closed the back door, Fe looked at his mum and said "I am sorry mam, a' couldn't punch him, he is still ma dad, and a boot to the balls was the only thing I could bring myself to give him."

"I understand son, and it was a long time coming," Jackie admitted resignedly.

A few moments passed as they sat at the kitchen table waiting for round two, but nothing happened. Jackie got up off the chair and walked to the window, but Billy was gone. Clearly during the shoots of pain a kick in the balls tends to deliver, his estimates of his son had obviously grown. The game was up. Billy would never lay a hand on Fe or any of the family again.

"A will get it mam" Fe shouted, as he made his way to the front door which had just knocked. As Fe opened the door, Stix stood below him on the bottom step. Behind him was a figure that would confirm the fight was on. "How you are doing Mercer" Fe gestured trying not to show his excitement, as the thought of having two of Kemlin's best behind him suddenly started to look real.

"I hear you have got yourself into a wee bit of bother Fe" Mercer laughed, as if the problem was a minor one and nothing to worry about.

"Something like that", Fe laughed back, wishfully buying in to the harmless nature of the full situation. "C'mon in boys, we will bounce up to ma room." Mercer nodded his head in agreement. Around the same height as Stix, Mercer looked the more masculine of the two. Years of training in the army, and natural genetics offering stronger arms, Mercer was an impressive specimen of a man. His wild red hair matched that of every Mercer before him, his filled strong jaw and chin matching that of his brothers and father. He was sharply dressed, cleanly shaven and every bit proud of the man he had become. Both he and Stix typified the term alpha male and were a force to be reckoned with.

With the three men making their way into the hallway, Jackie walked through to greet the visitors.

"Ah Mr Mercer, is that you back from the army now son." Jackie smiled at her new visitor.

Mercer looked up smiling back at her friendly face and replied, "I am that Mrs McAfee."

Jackie coaxed, "ah c'mon now son, you call me Jackie, you know that."

Despite being one hard bastard, Mercer was a gentleman before anything else. The years in the army had added to this and taught him proper values, the same values he would share in his civilian life. This was one of the reasons he refused to put the boot into someone when they were down when fighting. That's how thugs reacted, and Mercer was not a thug!

68

"And how is your family keeping Stix son?" Jackie enquired of her other visitor, showing the familiar nature of the group of individuals brought together by these unnecessary times.

"Aye they are doing well Jackie, just getting on with it" Stix replied.

"Nothing else for it son, nothing else for it" Jackie replied, the full room sighed in acknowledgement of this.

This was the reason Mercer and Stix stood in the hallway of Fe's house at this very moment. For all the downsides and negative comments people made about the area they lived in, this was their home, their community. This was Camelon. This was Kemlin! It might have been viewed as a shithole, but it was their shithole, and god help anyone who would hurt any of their own.

"We are just going upstairs mam", Fe instructed. Despite the age gap between her boy and the two men, Jackie had no concerns. She knew Stix and Mercer were good boys and could only be a good influence for her young son.

Walking into the shared room between Fe and young Davie, they were met by the sight of the young lad sitting on the end of the bed. "You pulling the heed off it wee man?" Mercer joked, as if suggesting they had caught young Davie in a compromising position with himself. The group laughed, and Davie turned scarlet.

"Do me a favour Davie and go and give us some privacy for a wee minute pal" Fe requested, assuming the following chat was too much for his younger brother.

"He is fine Fe; he needs to learn how big boys do it" Stix advised, as if highlighting the fact that twelve years old was age enough to learn how this world is not all butterflies and sparkles.

At that point, the front door went again, this time immediately opening after the chap. Sanny and Tam had been family long enough to know they did not need to wait for an invitation, they were family, they could chap and enter. As they walked in, Jackie got her first look at Tam's face. Now stitched up, it was still a mess.

"In the name of god, what happened to you Thomas?" Jackie asked, with deep concern in her voice. Tam knew better than to lie to the lady he seen as a mum most of his life.

After explaining the situation to Jackie, she turned and made her way up the stairs in the direction of the boy's room. Tam, Sanny, Butch and George followed behind. Jackie had now worked out why Stix and Mercer had decided to visit her home.

With Jackie walking into the room, silence fell upon the group. "I am going to make this clear to everyone of you. Number one, Davie is not involved. He is too young. Number two, you make those bastards pay for what they have done to our Thomas. And number three, you all come home safe."

This was not the response Fe expected from his mum, but she clearly felt her son was old enough to defend himself after seeing him dealing with his dad a brief time earlier. No response to Jackie was required. Everyone in the room knew the score.

As Jackie turned to leave the room, she turned her head back, and reiterated her last point "I mean it boys, you all come home safe."

Taking seats in various areas of the room, Mercer took his role and held court with the group.

"Here is the fucking script. These bastards will be geared up for a battle tonight, no doubt about that. So, we sit and do fuck all today. We play it as defeat. Do you all understand?" The room nodded in agreement. "Tam, what recovery time are they giving you pal?" Mercer questioned.

"They are trying to tell me I could be weeks away from getting stiches out, and fucking months of healing time before the skin looks normal. Fuck that though Mercer. I am going in there tooled up, and no cunt will get near me. I am ready to go bro!" The full room burst into laughter, including young Davie. The bold Tam giving zero fucks to the scar now covering most of his cheek.

"You sure" Mercer asked, to the shock of the room.

"Tam canny be fighting in that state Mercer, for fuck sake" Fe protested. Mercer stood up, with rage filling his face.

"You think a fucking soldier calls it half time when he gets wounded on the battlefield? You think the fucking enemy pack up their guns and stop for the day? This is a fucking war Fe, and that man is a soldier. If he says he ready, he is fucking ready."

A shocked Fe did not respond, as the full room took in the outburst.

70

"Nae cunt comes into our toon and fucking opens up one of our own. It's no fucking happening. So, tomorrow morning we hit these bastards. They will have their guard down and you can be fucking sure of it they will not be expecting us."

Mercers initial crazy talk now starting to make sense. As the boys looked around each other, Stix stood up and took over the platform. "I will head in first, and your team behind me Fe, and Mercer can hold the rear." With this Mercer nodded the head as if agreeing with the course of action.

"Are we going in tooled up?" Sanny asked, wondering if this was going to be a good old school beating for the skinheads, or if they were going in to open them up.

"Would you remember the cunt that ripped your jaw Tam?" Stix enquired. "Hundred per cent Stix" Tam responded, positive in his ability to identify the man who had changed his appearance forever.

"Then the only cunt that goes in tooled up is Tam, and you repay the compliment. Are we all clear?" The group nodded in synchronised waves. It was on!

Chapter 11

Retribution

"That's 5am Fe", said Davie this time with no fear of a back hander as his brother was wide awake, looking at the ceiling from his bed as if weighing up the world in his mind.

"That's fine Davie pal, I have been up a wee while now. You get yourself back to sleep son." Lifting himself up, Fe looked down at Tam, also awake, wrapped up in his sleeping bag on the floor.

"You sleep well Tam?" Fe asked, knowing it was unlikely his brother got much sleep.

"Did a fuck Fe, ma face is stinging like a bastard" said Tam as he motioned to the scar on his face with his hand. "You reckon she will still be there Fe?" Tam questioned, referring to Sandra. After the boys all left last night, Fe forced Tam to instruct Sandra to get the fuck out Camelon. She had told him she intended to move in with an uncle down in Grangemouth, a few miles from and on the outskirts of Falkirk but far enough away from the skinheads.

"Tam, we have bigger things to worry about the day pal. And while we are on the subject, how much do you owe to her dealer?" Tam looked at Fe in shock, as if that massive part of proceedings had completely slipped his mind.

"Just shy of a ton Fe" Tam replied. Fe's head dropped back on to the pillow.

"Fuck sake Tam, well you better hope we get that smack and coin back the day, or we have another war on our hands after this!"

While the two boys got themselves ready, they heard a whistle from outside the house. As they looked out, the other five boys stood outside, ready for war! As Fe walked down the stairs, his mum was waiting at the bottom, looking like she had not slept a wink.

"You ok mam?" Fe asked softly, as if it were any other morning.

"Don't you worry about me son, how are you feeling?" Jackie was trying to gauge her son's mood and ability to handle the events that lay ahead.

No sooner had the words left her mouth, than she lifted her hand and slapped Fe firmly across the jaw. Fe and Tam stood in shock. Before Fe even had the chance to question his mum's actions, she lifted her hand and belted him again.

"What the fuck mam?" By this point Fe was totally confused by his mum's actions.

"Don't you worry son; they do this to all the boxers before a fight. It's meant to get you riled up to fight better." With this declaration, Tam and Fe both burst out laughing.

"Aye nae fucking bother mam, fucking ten past five in the morning and you're giving it fucking big licks!" The both off them looked at each other and smiled.

Jackie hugged her boy with the strength of ten men, leaving Fe with no doubt how much he meant to her.

"I don't think I will bother hitting your cheek Thomas, it looks like you have had enough punishment in that area son" Jackie joked, as she gave Tam a wink of the eye. As Tam went to walk past Jackie, she grabbed him and pulled him towards her, with a hug to match that of the one she had just given to Fe.

"I love you son" she whispered in his ear. Tam could feel his throat begin to swell as the rush of emotion caught him off guard. A tear started to roll from Tam's eye.

Making their way outside, the rest of the gang greeted them.

"Morning gentleman" Stix declared, keeping his voice down so as not to awaken the neighbours. As Tam got to the front of the garden, just before the gate, Mercer came to him as if looking to shake his hand. As Tam went in to reciprocate, Mercer handed him an open razor.

"You make sure you open up that bastard good Tam." The rest of the group looked at Tam, all in complete agreement of Mercers instructions. The group all began to walk in silence, there was no conversation that would be suitable at this precise moment. Each member readying themselves mentally for what was about to happen.

Once they arrived at the top of the skin heads' street, they could see the flats at the bottom of the road. The window from the skinheads flat had the curtains closed.

"No need for any stealth measures" Mercer declared, as his strategy for breaching the flat had obviously been planned out with precision in his military mind. Butch turned and agreed, as if this were something on his thoughts as well.

"Exactly Mercer, I was thinking the exact same." The full gang began to laugh breaking the tension slightly, with Butch oblivious to the joke which had caught their attention.

"What do we do if they are tooled up Mercer?" George asked, a question that all the gang had considered but hadn't verbalised.

"If any cunt comes at you tooled up, you take it off them and make sure they regret it," Mercer stipulated. He hated weapons, but the gang knew this was the green light for them to use the enemy's tools, without Mercer having to actually say it.

Gathered at the foot of the stairs leading up to the flats, the last one to enter was Tam. He knew the noise the door would make when it slammed shut, so he held it firmly until it had connected with the frame. It was clear everyone, despite the early hours of the day, was on the ball!

Fe stood behind Stix; he could feel the adrenaline coursing through his body. He was electric! He knew fear should be the overriding emotion just now, but all he could feel was the rush. That rush you get when a fight is about to begin. When your body begins to shake as you try to control the adrenaline. That first few seconds it takes for your body to get in line with your brain.

"Every cunt knows the script, let's do this" Stix whispered, as to avoid any detection.

Standing at the front door of the skinheads, Tam suddenly pulled away to enter his own flat.

"What the fuck Tam?" Fe said, at the lowest tone he could.

"I need to make sure Sandra is not here!" As Tam went into the unlocked flat, Mercer gestured Fe to follow him. As they scanned the flat, which had been smashed up, Fe joked in his mind that it probably now looked tidier than it did when he was last here. It was clear Sandra had left.

"Are you a fucking mad man" Fe fired at Tam, wondering what the fuck he was thinking breaking rank.

"I love her Fe" Tam replied, knowing how fucked up this situation was, but simply unable to control his feelings.

"C'mon ya crazy cunt, let's do this" Fe offered back, as he hugged his brother. Love works in mysterious ways, and who was Fe to tell Tam his logic was all fucked up, despite the clear fact it was. Brothers stick together, despite conflicting opinions.

The two men made their way back to the landing between the two flats... As they gently closed over the door, the rest of the boys nodded.

"All ok?" Stix asked, hoping the drama had not yet begun.

"Aye they have turned over the flat, but the lassie and her mam are away." Mercer looked at the soldiers surrounding him, each of them ready for war! "Let's fuckin do this boys."

Stix gently held the door handle, praying the skinheads had not locked the door. Having to gain entry by chapping the door was a nightmare and surely give warning to the oncoming threat. As he gently pulled the handle down, the door opened. As soon as Stix nudged it further, the gang were met with the sound of music. He could hear murmured conversations from the end of the hall, in the living room they assumed, matching the layout of this flat to that of Tams.

"These bastards have not been to bed yet" Stix declared quietly, as to inform the gang that attacking the group while they slept was no longer a possibility.

"They are all fucking speed freaks" Tam announced, a point he had failed to share with the boys earlier.

"Are you fucking kidding me on Tam?" Mercer snapped, rage now consuming him at the fact that one of his men had failed to warn him the enemy had probably been up all night high on amphetamines.

"Sorry Mercer" Tam replied sheepishly.

With the last of the gang moving over the step at the entrance, they gently closed the door behind them.

"Lock it" Mercer instructed, much to the surprise of the group. "No cunt is running from this, these bastards are going to pay, and we will be leaving when we are ready."

George locked the bolt on the door, before stepping in front of Mercer to make the formation arrangement they had agreed to the previous evening. They had four doors to walk past before they arrived at the end of the hallway and into the living room. Mercer instructed the boys to check each room before moving on to the next. The last thing they wanted was for the skinheads to flank them. Mercer's military knowledge now in full effect!

"All clear," George announced quietly as he stepped out of the kitchen. This confirmed to the group that the full skinhead gang would be in the living room. Stix took one final look at his fellow comrades, with the knowledge that each individual present was willing to die for the man next to him. None of the boys knew what was on the other side of the closed living room door.

"C'mon you fuckin bastards!" Stix roared, as he burst through the door, charging across at the most distant enemy, allowing his fellow warriors a chance to get in the room. As they filed into the enclosed area, the skinheads, most of whom had been lying around on the floor, simply froze in shock. The violence exploded in every area. Stix, with hands like lighting, laced into multiple enemies on his own. It was simply too much for anyone to take. The gentleman reputation that Mercer held now parked out in the street, ready for him to collect once the job was done in here. This was revenge, and any rules he would normally set himself firmly put to one side. He drilled his samba deep into the jaw of his opponent.

Soon the skinheads began to fight back, now bought into the fact that they had picked on the wrong person, various weapons began to appear. As Butch struggled with one of the boys next to the television, one of the other skinheads made way for him, screwdriver in hand. Fe, who had just finished smashing in the face of a lifeless nemesis, caught sight of this. As the thug lifted the screwdriver ready to drive it into the side of Butch, Fe grabbed his wrist. Shocked by the intervention, the skinhead turned to look at Fe.

Without hesitation, Fe lunged at him, mouth open, and latched on to the side of his cheek. A shriek of pain filled the room, as Fe's jaw locked on the skin head's face. Like an animal released from a cage and ready to devour their prey, Fe snapped his head back with force, teeth still locked on. With that, a palm full of skin sat locked in his clenched teeth, blood now flowing down his face. The skinhead fell to his knees, as if

76

searching in vain for a piece of the puzzle removed from his face. As he looked up, He could see Fe standing over him, part of his face sitting in Fe's mouth like a bloodied trophy.

Fe looked down at him, and with pure rage coursing through his body, eyes bulging with the force of hatred behind them, spat the piece of flesh back down at his enemy, as if returning something once borrowed. The skinhead looked down, screaming in agony and his face dripping with blood, trying to find the chunk of flesh, as if somehow hoping he could return it to its rightful place, Fe volleyed him with a force he usually reserved for the ball during a Sunday morning game.

Behind Fe, George wrestled with one of the smaller enemies. Still bigger than George, the tactical intellect that the smaller combatant possessed became known. As George could feel the larger enemy pushing him down the wall, he slid to one side, pulling his foe off balance. With a swift pivot, George then returned with a sharp knee to the ribs of his enemy. The brute exchanging blows with him dropped to the ground, desperately fighting for the air which had been whipped from him. With this knee going down, George snatched the empty bottle of vodka sitting on the table opposite them and smashed it into the face of the fallen man. The bottle exploded, with George still holding on to the top of it. His weapon now cut in half, this only added to the potential damage it could cause. Without hesitation, George drove the shard remains of the bottle into the jaw of the now dazed and bloodied skinhead, who was near to unconsciousness. The bottle ripped at the jaw, with a large chunk forced out from its place of origin, leaving a gaping hole in its place. The crazed look on George's face only served to honour the work of art he had created with the skin canvas.

As Fe turned to observe the proceedings in the living room, he could see victory was theirs. Sanny was smashing a lifeless body with shots of combinations from both hands, ensuring the damage caused would make the recipient consider any future attacks. All his men still drilling into the enemy, as to ensure no change of direction was possible in the battle, his attention shifted to the bodies sprawled out around him.

"Conner" he roared, waiting for one of the skinheads to acknowledge his cry. No response. As he pulled over several of the lifeless radicals, some of whom had been knocked out during the battle, he could not find him. As he made his way to Butch, who was at this point about to smash the kneecap of one of the skinheads, with the skinhead's own hammer, Fe instructed him to stop.

"Where is Conner?" Fe enquired, looking at the enemy with deadly focus.

"Take yourself to fuck ya wee fanny" the skinhead responded.

"Take myself to fuck?" Fe laughed, as he looked at Butch, signaling him to hand over the hammer. "Take myself to fuck" Fe repeated, instantly followed by the swing of the hammer that landed on the Centre of the kneecap. The skinhead screamed in pain like that of a mother about to give birth. "Now we can play this fucking game awe day if you want, but I reckon you will get bored before I do. So, answer the fucking question, where is Conner?"

The skinhead, knowing his attacker meant every word he had just threatened, gave the game up.

"He is in remand for fuck sake." Fe stopped, surprise filling him as the announcement was made.

"How long has he been in custody?" asked Fe, wanting to know if the attack on Tam had been authorised by him.

"Three weeks now", the skinhead declared. Fe stepped back, as the updated circumstances made themselves clear in his head. Conner did not green light the attack. These wee bastards just chanced it while he was away. Which also meant Conner would find out his full team had just been turned inside out. Meaning this war, despite today's clear victory, was far from over.

"Is every cunt ok?" Mercer shouted, making sure all his soldiers had survived this battle. The only men still standing in the room being that of Fe's gang, making the answer clear.

"Right Tam, what one was it that opened you up?" Stix enquired, knowing that for one lucky punter, the fight was not yet over. "That bastard there" Tam replied, as he nodded to the boy Mercer had flattened a few moments earlier.

"Get him on his feet" Mercer instructed, requesting his men lift the fallen enemy for one final act of retribution. As the men lifted him to his feet, Tam pulled out the open razor, and made his way towards him. "Wait!" Fe declared, as he walked towards the intended target. The group stopped and offered Fe their attention, still unsure as to what he had planned.

"The money and gear, where is it?" Fe questioned the skinhead, who at this point was significantly smashed up. Before he had the chance to respond, Fe continued "And do not fucking lie to me, or you will be smiling from ear to ear for the rest of your life." The skinheads had only slashed one of Tam's cheeks, but Fe was promising failure to comply would result in double dose of the damage dished out to his brother.

"Biscuit tin" he replied, knowing any hope of help had long gone. In the time they had spent terrorizing the community, the skinheads had ensured any chance of anyone helping them was slim. They hadn't gathered any friends or allies, neither had they endeared themselves to the locals.

Fuck, nobody would even call the police when hearing the noise from the vicious battle and sustained assault that was taking place in the flat. In comparison to the amount of times the neighbors had been up all hours having to listen to the noise from the music and parties the skinheads had, this noise would offer a pleasant change and possibly some level of satisfaction, as twisted as the notion was. As Butch handed Tam the biscuit tin, he emptied the contents on to the partially smashed coffee table.

"It's all their Fe" Tam gushed, as if celebrating the fact of any potential war with his drug dealer was now off the cards.

Fe looked at Tam and nodded, as they both realized there was only one thing now left to do. As Tam made his way towards the boy who had changed his appearance forever, a smile lit up his face.

"Your turn" Tam told him, as he lifted the open razor towards the boy's cheek. As Fe walked out the room, the scream, despite the fact he knew it was coming, made him jump. As he made his way down the hall, Mercer and Stix followed.

"Are we good wee man?" Stix asked, wondering if the work here was now complete, or if the young man in front of him had other ideas.

"I owe you one boys," said Fe gratefully.

Making their way down the stairs, the door opened to the flat directly underneath that of the skinheads. An elderly gentleman stood at the door. He looked each of the gang members dead in the eye, and without saying a word, nodded his head. The number of times the skinheads had caused distress to this elderly man had been many. But victory on this morning was his. As the gang made their way outside into the chilly morning, Butch turned to them and casually questioned "so what are we all up to the day then boys?" The full gang erupted in laughter. As if the episode of ultra-violence they had just dished out moments earlier was just a starter.

The men all agreed to part ways for the rest of the day, keep it cool until this blew over. As Fe and Tam made their way back up to his house, Fe turned to him and advised "you need to fucking chill it out a bit sir, awe this man, it's nae life." Tam looked at his brother, and quietly responded.

"I know Fe, I know." Fe wrapped his arm around the shoulder of his friend as they made their way down the street.

Once the school bell rang, the gang greeted each other at the gates. As the group of fifteen-year-old students all stood chatting with school uniform on, it would be almost impossible to believe this same group of boys, only a few days earlier, had handed out a beating with such ferocious violence. As they started to walk home, with Daisy now part of the group once again, they began to laugh as they caught sight of Tam walking towards them.

"Nae fucking drama today Tam, I am warning you ya cunt" George roared, as all the gang began to laugh.

"You model pupils all learn a lot today then?" Tam fired back, as if to highlight the fact he no longer wasted his time at school.

"Better than spending a full day with that wee tadger of yours going soft in your hand." The conversation went back and forth, with the kind of patter only years of friendship could permit.

Standing at the top of the Easter Park, Fe suggested they all have a seat on the swings at the bottom of the hill. As they all got comfortable, Fe asked the gang if he could have their attention.

"Fuck sake Fe is this you coming out to us" George joked, as the gang all began to laugh. Daisy however could see something was wrong.

"Fuck up George ya fanny" Fe responded. As the gang all curbed their laughter, Fe looked at all of them with a straight face, firmly proving that the information he was about to share, was no joke.

He began to explain the offer of a potential football contract from Sunderland, and what that would mean for his place with the gang, and indeed with Daisy. Silence fell on the group. Each member, who had a special bond with Fe in their own way, began to work out what this would mean for them.

"You just need to tell them to fuck off then Fe, simple as that" Butch declared, as if he had just solved the problem. Fe laughed nervously, as he struggled to remove his gaze from Daisy, who since the announcement, had not lifted her head once, instead offering her complete silence and focus on the blades of grass at her feet.

"What are you thinking Daisy?" Fe asked nervously. No sooner had the words left his mouth, than Daisy got to her feet, tears now streaming down her face.

"You need to do what's best for you Kevin." With this piece of advice, Daisy then turned and began to walk off in the direction of her home.

"Daisy, Daisy. Fuck sake Daisy" Fe shouted, as he attempted to go after her. In that moment, Sanny stood up, preventing his best friend from chasing her.

"She just needs time Fe, let her have it" Sanny suggested, knowing Fe was not good in situations such as this.

"What am I going to do big man?" Fe pleaded to Sanny, with desperation now filling his eyes.

"Only you can decide that Fe" Sanny responded.

"I need to get up the road boys" Fe announced, knowing it was Friday and the call from the Sunderland scout would be coming soon. With his head in turmoil, that walk from the Easter Park to Fe's house would be the longest in his life.

Walking through the front door, Fe was caught with the sight of his mum sitting at the kitchen table, almost lost in thought.

"I don't need two guesses to find out what you're thinking about" Fe offered jokingly, to lighten the mood.

"Have you decided what you are going to do son?" Jackie asked, with the future of both lives sitting within the answer. Before Fe had a chance to respond, the phone rang.

"Hello" Fe introduced cautiously, knowing this was more than likely to be the biggest call of his life. The other end of the phone was silent. "Hello?" Fe offered again, this time wondering if the caller was still with him. "Listen son, your old man fucked up." The sound of that familiar voice caught Fe off-guard. It was his dad on the other end of the phone. "What do you want dad?" Fe asked sharply, as if his patience with his father had finally dried up.

"I want to tell you I am sorry son, and not just for that pish the other day, but for everything over the last few months. I have been a prized prick, that's no lie." Fe did not respond, as if taking in the unexpected apology would take time to process. In his fifteen years on earth, he had never seen or heard his dad apologize to anyone.

"It's fine dad. Don't worry about it, you just need to screw the nut moving forward." Fe knew the last thing his dad needed was a long-winded examination of his recent behavior.

"You are spot on son, and your dad is going to try his best to be a better man, a promise you that. Have you made the decision about moving down south yet?" Billy queried, knowing this was the chance he had prayed for so long would come to his son. All those Celtic matches, despite Billy's own beliefs and views. This was it!

"Am still no sure Dad, the guy will be phoning shortly." The line again fell silent, as if Billy were weighing up the situation in his head.

"You need to follow your heart son and do what is right for you. Don't worry about the people around you, they will move on, and you can always visit if you do decide to move away. This is your decision son, and your auld man supports you whatever decision you go with." This was parenting! This was Billy being the father his son needed.

"Thanks dad, love you."

Fe put down the phone and turned to see his mum smiling at him. Despite everything, Jackie only wanted her boys to have a normal life, and that would need to include their dad. If Billy were on self-destruct mode, the boys would always have something playing on their mind.

Jackie and Fe sat at the table exchanging small talk, purposely avoiding the topic of conversation which sat between them like a double decker bus. Suddenly, the phone rang. Jackie looked at Fe and offered a smile as genuine as that first hug from a mother to a newborn child. As Fe lifted the phone, he knew the next few minutes would determine the path of his life.

Part 2

Chapter 12

The style icons

It had been almost four years since the decision to spurn the football contract, and Fe had battled with that choice ever since. He had the maternal logic of trouble never being too far away from the people he loved, and with that in mind, the distance accepting the football contract would create was just too much to risk.

Daisy and Fe had been almost inseparable since leaving school. Fe was happy, things with Daisy were going well, but he still couldn't believe he had agreed to go to the Key club of all places. He preferred to stay closer to home and just go to the Mariner bar in Kemlin with his boys. The faces within the Mariner offered security and peace, with most individuals aware of the pecking order, with the need to test this stance arising on the very rare occasion. But the Town Centre was a free for all. Sanny and Davie were equally unhappy about being dragged along but there was no way Fe was going to enter that place without moral support, and more importantly, a bit of back up. He knew the bear pit the club would potentially create, with each faction of testosterone enraged youth vying for that immortal glory of being a name. If you wanted to be a young fighter, with the respect of the other areas in the town knowing of that ability, then battles must be fought on a grander stage.

Despite what seemed like universal disdain at the thought of going into Falkirk, Butch readily agreed and much to Fe's dismay, was visibly excited by the prospect! Fe only agreeing to it as Daisy's sister had put that much pressure on. Fe would do anything for Daisy of course, but this really was stretching it. To top it off, Daisy's older sister Morag was going; a punk rocker of all things, as well as being just a wee bit scary into the bargain in Fe's opinion! "Make sure you and boys look smart for the dancing on Friday night" Daisy had said to him, "I don't want you turned away at the door and I want you to impress my big sister."

Fe felt like he was preparing for a major battle and was out of his comfort zone. "Why the fuck can't we just wear jeans and a T shirt for fuck's sake!" he said angrily to no one in particular whilst adjusting his new clothes in the mirror and feeling like a proper fanny, as Davie returned from the bathroom. "Fuck me Davie, you look like you've fuckin French combed your hair with Bellair hairspray, and fuck me sir, you smell like a tarts handbag, why don't you finish the look with some lipstick pal!" Fe roared with laughter at his younger brother but was still envious of his good looks and stature. Davie answered slightly dolefully,

"C'mon Fe, a bit of Bryl Cream on ma hair hides ma ears a wee bit."

"The boys are here Kevin!" Jackie roared upstairs, as Sanny and Butch followed her into the kitchen. "Well don't you boys look smart; I don't think I've ever seen either of you in shirt and trousers."

"And a' don't think you'll be seeing it again Jackie, am only doing this for Fe and his big night out with Daisy and her sister!" exclaimed Sanny, who was shifting about uncomfortably and pulling at the collar of his shirt. His chino's rubbing the crotch and causing him to shift around like he had caught a fresh dose.

"Fuck me Butch, you look like a cross between a fucking shortbread tin and a set eh fucking bagpipes" Fe declared as he walked into the kitchen, Davie following behind him. Butch stood across from him with his full head to toe tartan style attire. The tartan shirt, the tartan trousers, fuck the boys would have wagered that he had a wee pair of tartan Y fronts on underneath! He even had a wee tartan bonnet to top it off. "You do realise that look went out with the fucking 70's Butch pal eh, and even then, you wouldn't find any sane cunt with it on over the age of fucking thirteen?" the full kitchen, including Jackie erupting into fits of laughter, with Butch joining in the hilarity.

"I am no giving two fucks Fe, I asked the boy in the shop what the young teams are wearing these days, and he handed me this. So, with the greatest respect Fe, you can ram your fashion advice straight up your arse pal. I look the fucking part so a do, and there is fucking zero chance that boy was just trying to make me look daft. You will need to get up earlier than that to fool me, I will tell you that for fuck all." the declaration from Butch doing nothing to subside the laughter, if anything the words stoked the flames even higher!

"Aye, fashionable for wee fuckin yappy dugs and for keeping your granny's knees warm!" Fe carried on laughing with the others until Sanny pointed out,

"To be fair Fe, you could easily pass for a wee skinhead in a pair of stay press dressed like that yourself!"

Fe growled under his breath as he looked down at himself, then crossly adjusted his manhood and retorted, "Lets down a couple before we go boys, we fuckin need it. A hope nae fucker from Kemlin see's us when we walk doon the street, let's go the back way to Daisy's or else all respect for us will be gone!"

The love in the room was clear. This was Fe's mob. This was Fe's family!

All the boys laughed at the irony of the situation, wishing they'd never agreed to go to the Key club in the first place, except Butch of course and perhaps just a little bit of Davie. As they started walking up the street, not wishing to leave Sanny out of the equation, Fe quipped, "Hey big brother, is that just the way you walk or are those trousers too tight? John Travolta eat your fuckin heart out!" he shouted while walking doubled up with laughter.

"Fuck off Fe" retorted Sanny, "or you'll be going your fuckin self, and with a fucking sore face if I get my hands on yeah!" Sanny clearly unimpressed.

"I would fucking pay to see you chase some cunt in those bad boys, fuck me man it would be a sight, big baws swaying in all directions as Sanny puts his game face on!" Fe ensuring he finished with the final word.

Jackie watched the boys leaving and thought just how smart they all looked. Jackie was a proud mother and felt very emotional as the boys walked into the distance, she could almost hear the sound of the Bee Gees playing in the background!

Daisy was in her element; she couldn't believe she was going into the town dancing. She'd been wanting to go to the Key club forever and was so pleased that Fe had agreed to go with her so she could show him off. Daisy loved Fe with a passion and always felt safe when he was around. She just hoped her sister Morag liked him more. Daisy thought that Morag could be a bit stand offish at times, but as a sister she had always looked after her and Daisy knew she only wanted what was in her best interest.

"How did you get all of those tickets for the dancing Morag?" asked Daisy.

"Two weird Irish blokes in the record shop in Falkirk kept asking me and Grace to listen to the record they'd brought out and said they'd give us free tickets to the Key club if we bought it, where they were playing! I didn't really like the record, plus I was saving my money to see The Jam; I knew you had talked about going up the Key club so I just bought the bloody record and they gave me the tickets," Morag answered a little indignantly.

"Awe am so grateful Morag, it'll give you time to get to know Kevin and his pals a bit better, I know you'll like them. What are you wearing the night?"

Morag looked across at Daisy questioningly. "Why what is it you want to borrow now?"

"Well, could I borrow your grandad shirt and your pencil skirt if you're no wearing them? And what about your black leather jacket?" Daisy added quickly, knowing the latter was Morag's prized possession.

"What about ma knickers, do you want them as well? Wait and I'll quickly take them off" Morag said sarcastically.

"Don't be funny Morag, you know I don't get as much money as you," Daisy answered dejectedly. Morag looked across at Daisy, she loved her sister dearly and would do anything for her but did get angry at the liberties Daisy took at times with her stuff. They were both used to having nothing, so to be able to even buy and wear new clothes and not have hand me downs, was something to be grateful for. To put make-up and perfume on was a real treat and it was always a surprise to both how it transformed their looks and made them feel both attractive as well as important. To feel like somebody and not just nobody.

"Unless you've turned into a punk rocker to emulate your big sister hen, a' would say that the grandad shirt's out of the question, have you not seen it lately?" laughed Morag. "I've punked it up with a few rips and sewed on some chains…look," said Morag as she held up the shirt. Daisy looked on in absolute horror and found it incomprehensible that Morag could rip up and destroy perfectly good clothes, new ones at that. She really liked that shirt and wondered what on earth she was going to wear now. It had always shocked Daisy that Morag was into punk rock because she was always a lot more reserved than Daisy and usually not as outgoing. Daisy on the other hand liked to live life to the full and could be a bit of a party animal, but they complimented each other with their differences and had some good laughs.

Morag could tell what Daisy was thinking, sometimes she was like an open book. She was worried about Daisy and didn't want her to get hurt by Fe, whom she had nothing against except his reputation. He made Daisy happy though and she deserved all the happiness she could get. "Here" said Morag, taking a top out of the cupboard, "this is brand new and a haven't even worn it, so I'm warning you hen, nae drink stains or fag burns or you'll buy me another one! As for ma leather jacket, I saved for ages to go to the Barras and buy that, so just this once right!"

Daisy was over the moon and gave her sister a big hug as Morag pretended to act indifferent, then asked, "Morag, you haven't got one of those little head scarves to match have you?"

Morag glared and with fake irritation snarled "In the drawer!"

"Where did you say you'd meet Fe and the others? And what time?" asked Morag.

"Just up the top of the road around eight cause we're going to get a few drinks before the dancing" advised Daisy.

"Is the Mariner bar still doing karaoke, as I wouldny mind a wee sing song to get us all in the mood?"

Daisy smiled at the thought of this "I spoke to Liz yesterday and she promised the place would be bouncing. They still had a lot of drink left over from Mariners' day, so she promised a good deal if we bring a crowd in, and I know my Kevin prefers that place anyway."

As Fe and the boys approached Daisy, Morag and her friend Grace, Sanny exclaimed quietly, "Fuck me Fe, look at Morag. She looks like a fucking Zulu with that make-up on her face and her hair spiked like a dead hedgehog! And she's only wearing half a fuckin shirt!" Fe and the others could hardly contain themselves; Fe was physically hurting by trying to hold in his laughter. Offending Daisy's sister before they even went up the town would be a disaster.

"Come on boys, best behaviour and mind your fuckin manners towards the young ladies" he forewarned them in a lighthearted manner.

"Hello Morag, you look gorgeous doll, spectacular even" Butch said in earnest. Morag simply glared at Butch; no doubt amused by his choice of evening wear. The others sniggered but Butch wasn't to be put off, he had always fancied Morag and welcomed any attention from her, he simply relished the opportunity to be in her company.

"You look lovely Daisy; it's good to see you again Morag and nice to meet your friend" said Fe respectfully. "Shall we make a move then?"

"Are you sure they'll let us all in at the Key club?" asked Davie.

"Don't worry" replied Fe, "Big Kempy's on the door and he owes me a few favours if you know what I mean."

After a few rounds in the Mariner, the group ordered two taxis to take them into town. Daisy and Morag jumping in one taxi, with Morag's friend Grace adding to the giggles that filled the air in the back of the car. Butch took it upon himself to jump into the passenger seat and join the girls for the journey. He looked out of the window of the car and offered a subtle nod of the head to Fe, Sanny and Davie, as if indicating to the boys that he was probably in there with Morag, the truth couldn't have been any further away. The boys all filled the second car as they shared the usual pleasantries with the driver, the same pleasantries he would listen to with every passenger before and after Fe's crowd. The weekends were a tough gig on the mind for the reliable taxi fraternity of Falkirk. Drunk after drunk sharing stories of glory and love, with the occasional clown deciding he would do a runner before paying the fair.

As Big Kempy looked around at the clientele, he was checking out any potential sources of trouble in order to give his lads a heads up and make sure they kept a close eye on any problem areas. Big Kempy was a reasonable man but he wasn't one to stand for any trouble from any of the little tickets or would be 'gangsters' that came to the club. He'd grown up in some of the roughest parts of Glasgow before he moved to Falkirk, so as far as Big Kempy was concerned, the little 'pups' that came to his club grew up in heaven in comparison. Big Kempy had good instincts, it was those instincts that helped him survive over the years. By the time the head bouncer gig came along, he was a seasoned veteran when dealing with drunken clowns.

"Ah young Fe, how are we doing son?" the question catching Daisy out as she assumed her man would be alien to this world, so for a familiar face to be found before they even got inside, she struggled to decide if this was a good thing or bad.

"Aye all good big man, although I would rather be fucking anywhere than here!" Fe quipped in a jovial fashion but meaning every word he said.

"Aye, I was surprised when you phoned, didny picture this as your thing. Well as long as you guys are here for a good time and not a wild time, we will all be happy." Kempy winking at Fe with the expectations he had.

"My boys know the script big man, no worries from us." As the group made their way into the entrance, handing over jackets and filtering up the stairs to the entrance of the main room area, Kempy tugged at Fe and asked him if he could have a quick word. Daisy looked at Fe, who gestured for her to go on ahead and he would catch up.

"Listen Fe, a few decent sized mobs up there the night son. My boys are always on the ball, but if it kicks off, the numbers don't sit well for us tonight. The gaffer has been at us to keep the head count up, but it fucking takes control away from us a bit. Can you keep a leash on your boys the night? I know you boys don't fuck around, and you have my respect. But I want a fucking easy night, and no dealing with police statements until the sun comes up." Fe looked at Kempy, knowing that trouble must have been a regular thing for him to say that.

"Any mobs in particular causing issues?" Fe questioned, genuinely out of touch with the workings of the Falkirk night life.

"Awe the usual, your Bog boys, the Y mob and that Valley young team. These boys don't even attempt to come in here tool handed, but they will use fucking anything in there as a weapon when it all kicks off. And I am the daft cunt left to help with the housework when it all calms down." Fe nodded his head and firmly shook Kempy by the hand. With a pat on the back from his friend, he made his way up the stairs to join his party.

As Fe made his way into the main room, he was immediately attacked by the volume of the music. He had never set foot in a club before, and the volume of the anthem chasing him as he walked around the dancefloor looking for his group was deafening. As he passed the first group of tables, every eye from every man stood nursing the drinks in hand attacked him. This was exactly why he didn't put himself in these situations. He knew these teams were like fucking piranhas when shit kicked off. He held his head high, holding gaze with every one of them. They might not know who he was, but he was fucking happy to share with them should they keep that patter up. Making his way up the stairs, the second faction offered the same welcome. Growling and snarling spread over every face. Fe knew he looked like a handy wee cunt, and normally that would be enough to scare these wee fannies off. But when they are all teamed up, and tanked up with the drink, the wee boy bravery inside them likes to come out to play. As he passed the bar, relief washed over him as a friendly group of faces waved in his direction.

As he joined Daisy and the gang at the table, she handed him a bottle of beer. "You ok?" Daisy questioned; she could see her man looked tense.

"Aye all good, where is Davie and Butch?" Fe now starting to panic.

"Oh, they are with Morag and Grace on the dancefloor." As Fe stepped over to the bannister above the dancefloor, he was shocked at the sight playing out in front of him.

"In the name of fucking god, what the fuck do they look like" The question fired to Daisy as they both broke out into fits of laughter. Down on the dancefloor, Davie and Butch had been throwing shapes from every piece of dance they had ever seen. Despite Butch looking like the top shelf of a Scottish tourist shop, the big man was loving life as Donna Summer serenaded them from the free-standing speakers. Indeed, we could all feel love!!

"We going for a dance then?" Daisy looking at Fe expectantly.

"Daisy, I adore you sweetheart, I really do, but if you think I am bouncing around like a dafty while everyone looks on, your sadly mistaken doll. Away you go and join your sister, and me and Sanny will get another round in"

Daisy smiled at this suggestion, quickly landing a kiss on Fe's cleanly shaven cheek before darting down the stairs and falling into the drunken hug that Morag offered. Fe smiled. Daisy was happy. This might just be what he would have to endure every now and again to keep his Daisy sweet.

As he turned to catch up with Sanny, three men began to advance towards him. Fe had no need to panic, as these were comrades. Kemlin boys. And some of the top boys from the feared Y mob. "There he is" The welcome fired across the club as the men got closer. "Evening boys, didny expect to see you in here" Fe looking at his old friends with secret relief, now knowing should things turn south, he had some of the best Kemlin could offer behind him. Wee Higgy and Inchy both went to school with Fe, and despite being loyal Rangers men, had no issues with the young Fe. They knew Fe couldn't give two fucks about football or religious loyalties; he was just a good lad.

Wee Higgy was as short as Fe, with not nearly the same build. However, the lack of intimidating features would be a costly thing to underestimate. Wee Higgy was a hard-little bastard. Much like the generation they came from, defeat was not something that registered easily, so to beat Wee

Higgy, you had to make sure the coffin nail was drilled home. Short dark hair with the clean-shaven complexion, Wee Higgy was a young warrior. The single letter G tattooed on his neck to avoid any confusion with his sibling. Next to him was Inchy. The opposite to Wee Higgy, Inchy was a giant of a man. He had that solid frame like every Inch before him. Sharp features despite his giant frame. Inchy had some experience fighting in the local boxing club, however his love of a tear up outside the ring had led to various problems retaining his credentials as a serious boxer. Inchy would burst people then ask questions.

And to make up the trio of approaching allies was that old familiar face. The face of the Y mob. Stix. Fe and his friend had come across each other a couple of times since the battle with the skinheads. Stix, despite his unquestionable ability in the ring, could not stay away from the lights of the night life. His dancing in the ring matching his dancing on the sticky dancefloor. "What brings you here wee man?" Stix questioning Fe being in an environment most knew didn't sit well with him.

"Out with the bird and her sister. Sanny is cutting about somewhere, and Butch and Davie are making cunts of themselves behind me. And for fucks sake, dinny look. I am trying to pretend I am imagining it all, but if you confirm it, then fuck me it must be true!"

The group burst into laughter once the sight of Butch in his regatta was made. "Ah the big bold Butch, not a single fuck given." Stix laughing away before turning to Fe with a serious expression taking over. "You see who is in here the night?" Stix nodding to the first corner Fe had been introduced to when he entered the main room. "The YVT. Valley boys. Fucking animals. Like these cunts eat their own wains. Bad bastards. Will cut you from ear to ear as quick as they would shake your hand. A few good Stenny men behind them as well." Stix then shifted his eyes to the corner opposite them, at the other side of the bar.

"Bog boys. They reckon they run the show in here. If trouble does kick off, you can be sure as shite these bastards will be in the middle of it." Stix then looked around the room. "A few other wee teams but nothing worth talking about. Keep your eye on these two though. Just avoid they corners, and you should be sweet. And if anything does kick off, us Kemlin boys will light these bastards up like a fucking cheap Christmas tree. You understand Fe?" As Stix shared his expectations with Fe, it was obvious he could not turn him down. Stix had helped them overcome the skinheads, and despite Fe promising Daisy there would be no drama tonight, Fe knew if it kicked off and the Kemlin boys were involved, it would be his fight also.

About an hour passed with no trouble, Daisy, Grace and Morag blowing the dancefloor up with the moves they had. Butch and Davie both trying to offer similar moves. As the droplets of sweat began to run down Morag's soft cheek, she caught sight of two young girls aiming the deathly stare they wore at her. Morag attempted to ignore it, however when she would turn to review the updated stance of the potential threat, the glance was still locked on. "Who are they?" Daisy questioned, noticing her sister was clearly rattled.

"Couple of wee cows from the Bog. The one on the right, her man Craigy had tried it on with me last year, but I told him to bolt. She is convinced I led him on. Her name is Kerry. A right bitch." As Daisy looked over, she could see Kerry with eyes locked on her direction. Next to her was Claire, a notorious tough girl from the Bog. She could see the girls deep in conversation, clearly the topic of chat being the young sisters. Both Kerry and Claire had natural beauty in abundance, however that aggressive vibe that sat with them detracted from this, instead the natural beauty swapped with a gurning mess of rage.

As Daisy and Morag left the dancefloor, with Butch and Davie following, they joined Fe at the table with the rest of the Kemlin mob. Grace, a natural beauty herself with soft brown hair riding her cheeks, perched with the puffed shoulder pads holding her slender frame to the world, told Morag she didn't want to be part of any trouble, and hastily made her way out the club. Fe noticed this exit, and questioned Daisy as to Grace and her sudden departure. Daisy updated Fe on the proceedings, to which Fe moved his gaze to the direction of the Bog boys. In response, Craigy, head of the Bog boys, growled back.

"We might just have ourselves a wee boogie tonight boy's" Fe said, informing his soldiers on the potential change of events. When Butch found out about the hostility directed towards Morag, he offered to single handedly go over and wipe out the full Bog team. "Slow doon Butch for fuck sake" Fe laughed at his valiant friends' intentions. As Fe started discussing potential issues with Stix, Cocky, the leader of the Young Valley team joined them.

"I know we have had our issues in the past, but these Bog boys are getting out of control." Cocky opening himself up with stark honesty, knowing even attempting to approach the Y mob without his team behind him was suicide. However, the chance to hold court and speak to Fe and Stix would have been impossible had he approached them with his boys behind him.

"What is it your saying?" said Stix firing back at Cocky, still measuring up if he should blow this guy away as he stands. Cocky was no fool. And even with the craziness of the Valley boys, Cocky had a level of maturity about him, hence his ability to run the firm. Dark short hair and strong shoulders, Cocky stood impressively in front of the enemy or allies, the outcome of that yet to be decided. "Any of your boys try anything funny and we will fucking run right through you", Stix refusing to blink as he offered his assessment of the event. "But if you keep your word, then we take these bastards out, and we can deal with our troubles another day." The handshake between Cocky and Stix sealed this uneasy alliance.

No sooner had the handshake been shared, did the Bog boys rise to their feet. About twenty deep, this was a mob! They had some top boys in the ranks, and this would be a test of who really ran Falkirk! No sooner had the Bog army got to their feet, testosterone simmering above the gang as the sweat chasing down the side of the macho collection of jaw lines glistened under the spinning disco ball, Big Kempy gave the nod to his bouncers to make way to his location.

"What's the plan gaffer?" a question which fell at Kempy's feet as he looked around at his team. Kempy knew the Bog boys would continue to cause him problems down the line. He had no doubt the Y mob could mix it up with them, but the addition of Fe and his men signified they might get a proper lesson served tonight.

"Let them dance" Kempy ordered, his gaze locked on both factions.

"Are you serious? They will turn the fuckin place inside out by the time they are finished" one of the junior bouncers suggested. Kempy's gaze now shifting to his colleague.

"Are you hard of fuckin hearing, or do I need to repeat myself?" The response from Kempy reminded everyone in the group who ran this fucking show!

As the Face-off between both groups began, Stix, Inchy and Wee Higgy formed the snake's head of the Y mob, a good ten men stood like brothers in arms behind them. With Fe and Sanny standing firm, flanked by Davie and Butch. "The Kemlin Boys are in the house" a chant which landed at the feet of the Bog boys.

Daisy and Morag ensured proper distance sat between them and the battle about to begin. Daisy knew any attempt to stop Fe from being part of this would prove futile. More than anything else, he was defending the honour of her sister, Morag. Daisy turned to look at Morag, who could not hide the sense of excitement which had washed over her. This was the Fe she had been told about. This was the reputation that preceded him. But at this moment in time, this was exactly what she needed. For tonight only, it was time for Morag to have Fe as her hero.

As both teams got closer to the main event, hands began to dive into pockets. The lackluster security checks at the front door had clearly missed the array of knuckle dusters as the tense fingers set themselves in place. Fe didn't bother packing a weapon. As he stood looking at the DIY dusters from the Bog boys, Fe's face lit up with a perverted smile at the thought of a proper war! The foreplay was indeed something to behold, but Fe was now ready to get down to some serious fucking.

"Cmon then ya fucking bastards!" The roar from Stix instinctively bringing his soldiers to life, as the Kemlin loyal charged the Bog team. Within seconds the violence erupted, the volume of the speakers now being drowned out by the sound of violence. Missiles glided with elegance as they crash landed on unsuspecting heads, slices instantly removed from skin as the claret exposed went to the task of changing the visual landscape of the recipient. As the battle raged, The Valley boys charged at the rear of the Bog army, as if tactical planning had been played out in advance of the chaos. This move welcomed by the Y mob who played out every promise of hurt and pain made over the previous months. This battle had been brewing for a while, and Stix knew Fe and his boys being here tonight was fate.

As the shard of metal broke away from the duster attached to Craigy's hand, Fe knew he had a new guest within his anatomy. The shrapnel from the poorly designed DIY duster had lodged itself within Fe's cheek. Craigy stepped back, admiring his work, waiting for his victim to drop and surrender. He knew the reputation of Stix and the rest of the Y mob well, but Fe was a random. A stranger. A nobody. At least in his eyes. As the blood ran into the corner of Fe's mouth, he slowly lifted his head. A smile lit his face as bright as a shining star. The crazy in his eyes clear as his mouth opened, his tongue whipping round as he licked and tasted the blood. The smile of madness causing Craigy to drop his lower lip in surprise. Fe exploded from his static position, his head crashing into Craigy. The blood from Craigy landing sweet on the other side of Fe's face. Again, imitating a lizard who had recently devoured its prey, that tongue appeared and cleared the blood, the smile from Fe crazier than ever!

Wee Higgy gripped the bar stool, eyes scanning as he stalked the enemy. As the unsuspecting Bog boy stood back, dodging the punch from Inchy, Wee Higgy crashed the stool into the back of his head. As the injured man staggered forward, Inchy lifted him a good couple of inches of the ground with a sweet right uppercut. As the human obstruction between Wee Higgy and Inchy cleared, both men walked to each other and shared a hug, not something you usually see in the middle of a fight, but these two crazy bastards didn't follow rules.

As the amateur violence played out around him, Stix stood out like a different breed. A new species. That lightning speed was impossible to defend. Impossible to beat. Resistance was simply a wasted venture offered only by the ignorant. The flashes of brilliance as he would pivot between several enemies at the same time, mirroring the thousand drills he had performed time and time again in the gym. Absolutely nothing amateur about Stix. If anything, the inclusion of him slightly unfair.

The Bog boys fought with everything they had, with pride and heads held high from the offering. However, the addition of the new union between the Valley team and Fe's faction proved too much to contest with.

When Big Kempy thought they'd had enough, he got his men to start breaking up the fight. "Well young Fe, I'm glad you enjoyed your first and probably your last visit to my club as I can see you're not much of a dancer and like to keep a low profile." Big Kempy laughed as he looked on at the state of Fe's face, which was still surprisingly attractive despite the damage. "It would be better if you lot took your leave now Fe," he instructed. Nodding towards an extremely bloodied Craigy and his gang Big Kempy continued, "Your friends here will stay behind until we've worked out the bill they'll be paying for the damages they've caused here" winking at Fe.

As they left the club, Daisy and her sister looked over at the Bog girls who had suddenly become very quiet and looked away quickly. Morag put her arm around Daisy and despite the fact she hated violence, burst out laughing. Daisy, who could not help but feel anger towards Fe for getting in a fight, was taken aback and said, "What's so funny? Our night was ruined, and I thought you hated fighting?"

Through her laughter Morag highlighted to Daisy "You do realise those cows will never bother me again, not now they know I am part of the Y mob!" Morag mocked Daisy, "We are the mob!" she continued laughing, "I suppose being a Kemlin lassie does have its perks."

Realisation struck and Daisy cracked up with laughter as well and said, "Love you sis"

"Aye, me too hen" answered Morag. They both laughed as they quietly reflected on the events of the evening, walking together away from the club.

"Are you girls okay" enquired Fe as he and the boys caught up expecting a real tongue lashing from Daisy and an even bigger one from Morag. Daisy looked at him and kept walking in silence with the others. Fe couldn't interpret what the silence meant and didn't know whether this was a good or a bad sign.

However, the silence was swiftly broken by Butch who shouted, "Awe fuck, stop!" as he threw both hands up to his head, exclaiming loudly "I must have lost ma tartan bonnet during the scrap!" The whole group exploded with laughter as Butch glanced over embarrassingly but adoringly at Morag, he could have sworn she smiled and winked at him.

Chapter 13

The future is here

The sound of the bell horn roared, signaling home time for the battered workers. As the men filled out into the yard, the air filled with talk of matters relating to anything other than the last eight hours of work they had just undertaken. Any danger of taking your work home with you in this world had been limited to the foreman and above at best. With manually demanding jobs, it would be easy to allow the brain to shut off, stimulation becoming a hopeless chase. You left your work at the foundry door and picked it up at eight am the following morning along with your "piece".

Making his way along the cobble road, Fe could see young Davie perched against the side of the car, in the process of rolling a cigarette while he waited for his older brother to catch up. Both boys had found stable work within the iron works. It was a physically demanding job but ensured stability within the family home for Jackie and the boys. At twenty years old, the outcome of historical decisions Fe had made were now abundantly clear. With all that had been going on back then, and him ultimately rejecting the opportunity to go to Sunderland for trials, the dream which multiple McAfee's had held for the young Kevin had long diminished. That follow up call from Celtic football club never did materialize. Truth be told, once the decision to not follow his dreams to England had been made, the love affair between football and young Fe had slowly started to die, just like a part of him buried deep inside, which would never re-surface.

Like so many young men before him, and indeed after, the fairytale pathway that footballers often take had been scattered and laid open by the bare truths of reality and the real world they lived in. At sixteen Fe had left school with no qualifications. The only thing close to any form of criminal record had been a few assault charges in the years following the battle of the skinheads. Indeed, even the prospect of a return battle had died long ago. It had made its way to Fe that upon Conner's release from prison, the once hardened gang of young radicals he had commanded had diminished to nothing more than a couple of speed freaks, who wore the scars of the first battle like unwelcome medals. The message Fe and his gang had delivered that day had been a brutal one.

Word of the attack spread, and the reputation of each young man involved elevated in the eyes of the local community.

The only positive Fe could find from the drudgery of working in the foundry had been the personal effect it had been having on his body. He looked strong. His arms thickened from the manual labour, and his collection of tattoos added to the masculine presence he had. His hair was crew cut short, the style he felt offered the least amount of contribution from him. This would allow his focus to sit with the beautifully sculpted moustache that had now grown well since the early days of puberty. The thin slug that once graced over his top lip was now a strong thick brown masterpiece. His cheeks and jawline shaved to the bone, washed over by Brut aftershave to finish off the effect.

It was 1984 and the world looked a vastly different place from that Fe remembered as a child. Movies and popular culture would see the once hardened young street gangs bearing razor blades and chains, now replaced by an Americanized society. Kids no longer wanted to emulate the hard men depicted in the stories from the streets and tales of violence. Instead, heroes such as Indiana Jones had taken over, as young boys now looked at the journeys people like him would make into the temple of doom, with the Ghostbusters offering equally fabricated imaginations to the younger generation. It was an alien environment to Fe, who had well and truly shunned any form of adolescence he might have held on to.

One thing that had remained the same was the circle of love Fe surrounded himself with. Daisy was still by his side, the hollow victory she had yielded when Fe decided against a move down south, now a double-edged sword between them, as she often sensed that this decision was the biggest mistake of her young loves' life.

And the gang was still as strong as ever. Sandra and Tam had resumed life within that squalid flat opposite the skinheads, Fe satisfied that the safety of both had been secured by the level of violence dished out that day. Tam's usage of heroin was often debated particularly when he appeared disheveled, but nothing had been proven, and he was still a brother after all. Big Sanny had now settled down, with one of the many women he would share his heart with during his young life. George and Butch both plodding away, jumping in and out of various forms of employment.

Fe also found extra income selling hash. It was a small-scale operation. Beast the tattooist had picked up on the stellar reputation a young Fe had earned and decided to set the young man up with men from Glasgow who could keep a steady stream coming into the Falkirk area. Fe had been advised to keep his full-time job in place to avoid any suspicion from the Feds, not that this worried him in the slightest. He was still living with his mum and Davie, often using his younger brother as a runner when delivering hash during the evening. A young Davie always willing to help his big brother out, making a few extra quid in the process. Jackie was oblivious to this and would have single handedly executed Fe had she ever found out about the blocks of cannabis hidden expertly at the back of her loft.

"I am needing to make a run through to Glasgow tonight Davie, you fancy coming through with me?" Davie was sitting on the end of his bed, flicking through one of his comics. Davie had always been obsessed with comic books, but at seventeen years old, Fe struggled to understand the continued fascination.

"Aye Fe I am up for that, we going to pick up hash like?" asked Davie in a voice a little too loud for Fe's liking.

"Fuck sake Davie, I don't think the cunt heard you three miles down the fucking road!" snarled Fe, throwing a scowling look at Davie for his lazy outburst, knowing his mum was downstairs cleaning.

"Sorry Fe, I wasn't thinking." By now Davie had grown into a fine young man, a fair bit taller than Fe, he had also inherited his Dad's strong physique. Fe's battle with acne over the years had left him scarred from various battles with the mountain like boils that had covered the landscape of his face.

Davie however looked sharp. His movie star features often annoyed Fe. How did this young boy, who had ears like Dumbo the elephant, turn into this sturdy young lad, who had the dark brooding look of Sylvester Stallone, a point the female admirer often highlighted. With the massive popularity in rocky movies, Davie had inadvertently even managed to style his hair to match that of a young Rocky Balboa. The resemblance was uncanny. And Davie, covered with his black leather biker jacket, did nothing to persuade people otherwise. The once ugly duckling had grown into a beautiful swan, much to Fe's annoyance.

The boys' room now perfectly illustrated the two young men. Davie's side draped with posters of his musical fancy, Madness, and T Rex, with

Bolan and Suggs each looking as progressive as possible. Fe's side simply asserting that love he had for Celtic, with the occasional small photo strewn around of him and Daisy from various episodes of the years they had spent together. A few group photos of the boys drinking in a threadbare flat, a property no more than an established off grid club.

With the car making its way through the side streets, Davie felt his hand fall down the side of him, impulsively checking if the fat end of the pool cue he had placed there on the previous journey was still at hand. The task of collecting the hash had always been a straightforward one, but Davie and Fe knew the suppliers could decide to rip them off and smash them up anytime they saw fit. Business was business, and the regulations within the drug world had been thin at best.

Joining the motorway, Fe began to pick up speed, really opening the Opel Manta and sharing that sharp growl it made with the world. Fe loved this car, bought in cash by the rewards of good business. He knew it could be seen as a tad flash, rolling up to the foundry with his two litre engine roaring, but the link between a hard-working young man and a potential drug empire was well off the mark, at least at this point of his life.

"Now remember Davie, you stay in the motor and let me do the talking. If anything kicks off, you bounce out and start opening cunts up with the fat end of that BCE pool cue." Davie nodded his head, knowing Fe gave the same instructions on every journey, but still displaying the same attention as the first time that they discussed it. He knew his big brother could be robotic with procedures, facts always becoming the most important part. That tactical awareness would ensure drug dealers had as little chance as possible of turning them over.

Pulling up the old dirt track, with swirls of dust waving over each curve of the vehicle, Davie could feel the adrenaline begin to disperse around his body. This was a good thing Fe had always taught him. "Be scared and stay alert." These words had been as honestly sold as anything Fe had ever taught him. When we become lazy and trusting, mistakes will no doubt rear their ugly head. The winding road came to a head at an old abandoned car park, long since populated by various farming machinery since the farmyard ahead had fallen into disrepair.

Holding centre stage was a beautiful new BMW, looking every part the getaway vehicle for any would-be drug kingpin. Davie looked on in envy at the vehicle, which would no doubt cost three or four-years wages from the foundry. The beautiful royal blue accentuated by the warm summers evening shining off it, an image that would not be out of place in one of the new Hollywood blockbusters, Davie told himself.

Chapter 14

A new rush

"Ah young Fe, how are we doing today son, was the journey through ok?" Fe could not help but feel the patronising tone grate him as the man in front, only a couple of years older than him, saw fit to talk to him like he was some fucking schoolboy looking to buy a fag off a senior.

Pedro was small but well built, with that Glasgow arrogance Fe found tough to stomach. His arms solid from years of training, Fe was aware Pedro was one of the top kickboxing prospects in Scotland, a point Pedro shared each meeting, just to ensure Fe was under no illusion of his alpha male status. His arms perfectly decorated with tattoos; the standard of which Fe had never seen before. The old school sailor tattoos Beast had shared with the gang were a million miles away from the work Pedro had emblazoned across him. His short legs reminded Fe of the tree branches he had struggled to cut during many a fishing trip, legs he had no doubt could snap a man in half during an attack. His swept dark hair mirrored that of the Fonz from Happy Days, and his cauliflower ears honoured battles past.

Fe knew Pedro could easily man handle him if required, but he also knew the probable choice of attack from him would more likely come from a firearm, than a well tattooed arm. Pedro oozed the desire to be a gangster more than anything else, but clearly not at the level he desired yet, since he was in a fucking deserted car park about to sell a bag full of nine bars to Fe, hardly cartel stuff now is it, Fe thought to himself.

He had been surprised when first introduced to Pedro, as he could not imagine Beast ever associating with someone like this. After the first meeting, he had returned to Beast to discuss his encounter, at which point Beast realised Pedro was just a middleman for the bigger boys he had known in an earlier part of his life.

"All good Pedro, just wanting to get home and into my bed." This declaration did not sit well with Pedro, clearly unhappy that his presence had not been celebrated as a weekly highlight in anyone's eyes.

"How long you been punting our stuff now Fe?" Fe was unsure the direction this conversation was taking.

"Just over three years now Pedro, give or take pal," Fe answered suspiciously.

"And your still only punting five bar a week, you're a fuckin mad man sir. You could be trebling your coin by pushing a bit Brown." The grin on Pedro's face lit as if he had just entrusted a friend with the secrets of the world.

"I am not interested in any of that crap, its fucking destroying our wee toon, a' hate the fuckin stuff!" This announcement from Fe instantly ending any opportunity for Pedro to expand his heroin arm in the community.

Fe could see Pedro was not impressed, and he could tell it was a rare occasion when someone declined a proposition from him. The thought of Davie with the pool cue crept into his head, all the good it would do should Pedro or one of his goons tucked away inside the BMW pull a gun.

"Tell you what Fe, and I don't extend this kind of offer to just any cunt off the street. How about I sub you an ounce of speed for the week? In fact, fuck it, let's call it a fucking early Christmas present, my gift to you. Am that much of a good fucking guy!" Before Fe could decline the offer, Pedro had produced the bag of amphetamine and placed in the palm of Fe's hand. "Trust me Fe, your punters will have a fucking hard on over this gear. It's fucking electric!"

Fe knew better than to reject Pedro a second time, and the fact it was free, before anything else, Fe was a businessman. Free product always equals good business. With the usual pleasantries, they handed over the matching Adidas bags in opposite directions, one holding the carefully counted cost of five bar, and the other with the soft black gold seal hash, from which Fe had been making a tidy profit from. As Fe turned to walk away, Pedro gestured back to him stating that the same time next week, the Adidas bag would have the same ounce of speed in it, charged at full price this time, obviously.

Making their way back along the motorway, heading to the town they called home, Davie questioned Fe about the second product Pedro had given him. Fe explained the speed, and that it could be a new avenue to drive up custom. Davie warned him to be careful.

"I have seen plenty cunts turn into space cadets on that stuff Fe, that's no joke sir. It will fry your brain after about three days." Fe had never tried speed before, in fact the only drug he had ever experienced was cannabis, and he was not overly fond of it. The paranoia which ran with it did not hold great appeal for Fe. This was a money product in his eyes, and easy profit.

Once they pulled up outside the house, Davie went to open his door, before Fe instructed him to hold off for two minutes while he had a word with him. Fe had long been the biggest father figure in young Davie's life, and often found himself dishing out advice to the younger McAfee lad.

"How are things anyway Davie pal?" Fe looked at his younger brother, acknowledging they were both men now, and any fears held as young boys long gone.

"I am good Fe, really good. The gig at the foundry is tough going, but the banter makes it easier. And mam seems happy enough with the money we are bringing in." Fe smiled at this, happy that his brother had similar thoughts and concerns as him.

"Listen Davie, I was speaking to a boy I went to school with, who said he passed you and a few of your pals up the canal." Davie looked on without responding, wondering what direction his brother was going with this. Fe continued "He said you had your heed stuck in a glue bag, that you were fucking away with-it Davie. I thought you were finished with awe that shite? For fuck sake Davie, that's a fucking wee boy's gig the glue." Davie began to laugh, knowing his big brother was only looking out for him but failing to see the issue with him and his friends buzzing the glue.

"Fuck sake Fe, cunts my age firing that shite in their veins, stealing off their own, and you're giving me it tight for a fucking glue bag. C'mon Fe, play the fucking game!" Davie was letting his older brother know he had it under control and he needn't worry.

Fe looked on into the distance for a minute as he processed Davie's stark honesty. "Just fucking look after yourself Davie, the last thing I need is you causing mam any grief." Davie nodded and assured him the use of Glue would not escalate to harder drugs. As the boys made their way inside, Fe launched an arm round the neck of his younger brother, pulling him in for an embrace, ending with a kiss to the top of his head. The boys went straight upstairs, with Davie hopping into the loft to drop the newly acquired batch of cannabis in the secret stash area.

The following day, Fe had a well-earned additional hour in bed. It was Saturday, and no overtime this weekend due to the recent drop in orders at the foundry. Davie was still sound to the world, and Fe could identify his mum by her singing in the room directly below them. As he made his way downstairs, the volume of chanting increased. His mother jumped as she turned to find her son staring at her. Despite the additional years on the clock, his mum looked better than ever.

While the physical and mental drain of being in an abusive relationship with Billy had taken its toll, now free from that world, Jackie was like a new person. Her hair curled from a recent visit to the hairdressers, a trip funded by her eldest son. Fe made a point of treating his mum as often as possible. The bulk of the funds coming from drug money, a fact Jackie would no doubt directly refuse if she only knew. Her physique now much shapelier, complimentary of a better all-round diet. Jackie was healthy and glowing.

"And what are the plans today then son?" Jackie pondered, genuinely interested in her son's movements for the day.

"Daisy is still away at her friends down South, so I am meeting up with the boys and heading out for a few pints." Jackie stopped in her tracks and laid down the law.

"I want nae trouble today then Kevin, I mean that! The last thing we need is you in the fucking cells all weekend again. And that goes for the rest of them as well, you tell them Jackie will foot their arse if she finds out any nonsense took place." Fe broke out in laughter, joy filling him with his mother's self-placed matriarchal role within his life. She was the queen, and all the boys knew it.

"Aye mam you just settle yourself back inside they wee socks of yours, fuck sake, you're going to give yourself a fucking hernia."

Both mother and son began to laugh at this comment, Fe knowing his mum had little resistance to his unique vocabulary. As she leaned in to offer him a kiss on his unshaven cheek, he turned and wrapped his strong arms around her. Fe loved Daisy, but there was only one true woman in his world. Only one woman who would always stand behind him, despite his failings, and that was his mum. The relationship between the two was like no other. A mother and her first born, especially a son, is a special bond. As Jackie closed the front door behind her, Fe turned and placed the contents of his pocket on the floral kitchen table. Seven fags left from a ten pack, an old gas key, Fe still unsure how that even got there, and two grams of amphetamine.

Fe knew the only person selling speed in Kemlin had been big Risky, and he knew a war with Risky would be a walk in the park. Risky was a good guy, but he was no match for Fe. He was an old school stoner, who had seen his best days involving a few tabs of acid and a walk along the canal. Risky was always being ripped off by his good intentions of offering people tick, who then failed to pay him back. Fe knew that was no way to run a drug business, and in all honesty, Risky was on his way out. The only requirement for Fe stepping up and taking over would be informing Risky that it was time to hang up his boots. In return for moving to one side, Fe would keep the flow of free drugs to Risky plentiful enough for the older boy to have one less worry of the direction his giro would take him. The protective backing from Fe offered him the chance to sit back and enjoy the later years of his life. Almost fifty and tormenting his body with chemicals the way Risky had, it would hopefully be a welcome change.

Knocking on Risky's door, his eyes became tranced by the swirling dream catchers mesmerising in motion at either side of the front door. A peace sign sticker with the two fingered salute, which had been decorated by the colours of the Jamaican flag, only emphasised to Fe that Risky was no threat.

"Ah Fe, c'mon in young man, what can I do for you?" Risky said as he ushered Fe through the front door. Although almost six feet tall when standing straight, Risky now walked with a hunch which was no doubt induced by the various chemicals circulating his body. He had the look of an old reggae Rasta man. Skin darkened from years of sitting in the garden with his can of super lager, the various tattoos now faded after years of attack from the ultraviolet rays. As Fe sat down on the old rickety chair next to a table holding a variety of different bongs, he wondered why Risky had never actually bought hash from him. "Grow my own son, only way for it" Risky declared, as if reading young Fe's mind.

Fe sat down and explained the situation to him, and his likelihood of moving into the amphetamine distribution business. Risky looked on into the distance, processing the information.

"You are telling me I need to get out?" Risky questioned, in the most non-threatening manner he could create.

"Listen Risky, boys are ripping you off left right and centre. You are too old for this game sir. And you have no crew to back you up. When everyone knows you are onside with me, fuck you will be an untouchable man!" He continued, "And you will never pay for a thing again." As the words left Fe's mouth, he knew this still didn't pose a particularly appealing deal for Risky. "I will tell you what Risky, you let me bank the gear in this house, and I will pay you forty pounds a week. Forty pounds a week for doing fuck all, just babysitting, and nobody will come near you when they know you're working with me." Fe made it carefully clear to Risky that he would be working "with" him and not "for" him.

Knowing any point of resistance was probably futile, Risky nodded his head while stretching out his long thin arm, and Fe shook his hand with the firmness his father had always insisted on as being important. You instantly show the recipient what you are worth with a firm handshake. "Different class Risky" Fe declared, as he knew that it could have been a lot more awkward than it was.

"You been taking it yourself young man?" Risky enquired, gauging how deep his young protégé was.

"Nah it holds no appeal to me Risky, nae interest pal." Fe could see Risky was not impressed by this admission.

"Kind of a drug dealer doesn't understand the drug he is selling. No passion in that son. You need to appreciate the chemical balance in the product. You need to understand the customer need." Fe knew Risky was right, and with it, he dug into his pocket and removed the speed which had been wrapped up in a small envelope constructed from one of his mum's magazines.

"Do I snort it?" Fe enquired, unsure of the optimum method for consumption.

"No son, stick a wee bit on a teaspoon and down the hatch with it." As Risky made his way from the kitchen, moving through the Kashmiri beads running the height of the room that had been hanging from the archway of the kitchen door, he handed Fe the teaspoon. Looking around Fe could see the contents of the room had been a lifetime collection for big Risky. Every item would tell a story of this man's well-travelled history. He knew it could take an age for Risky to explain the backdrop of each object, something Fe would one day be happy to listen to. As Fe nudged the head of the spoon into the makeshift envelope, he returned with a small firm scoop of amphetamine.

"That enough?" Fe enquired, still unsure about the expectant dosage for a first timer.

"Aye that will get you started young man!" Risky assured.

Placing the tip of the spoon to the edge of his mouth, the foul scent hit his nostrils. It reminded Fe of a soap powder like scent, something he was not expecting. As he placed the speed on to his tongue, that bitter taste matched the expectations the earlier scent test had offered. His face twisted as he swallowed down the drug. Risky laughed at Fe squirming and offered the dregs of his super lager to wash it down. Fe accepted without hesitation, but soon realised the characteristics of the super lager had not been much better.

"Fuck me that's rotten sir!" Fe declared.

"Just give it ten minutes son and you will be saying something pretty different," Risky declared confidently.

Sitting satisfied that everything here was sorted, and no backlash would be felt from Risky, Fe knew it would be rude to just get up and leave. So, he told himself he would sit for five minutes, listen to Risky's pish about conspiracy theories and how the government is watching us all, then he could bounce out of there and go meet the boys at the pub. As he offered the occasional response to Risky's ramblings, he could feel something changing. "What the fuck?" he asked himself. Suddenly a massive rush surged through his body, a surge he had only recognised just before releasing his seed during the throes of passion.

"Holy Fuck!" Fe felt electric!

Everything was alive. Every sense, every nerve in his body had just woken up for the first time. His breathing intensified as he attempted to control this orgasmic sensation.

"Fucking hell sir!" Fe roared, this time allowing his feelings to become vocal. Risky broke into laughter, realising his friend had just felt his first amphetamine rush.

"It's fucking something else is it not?" Risky shared, as if his friend had just entered the private room of the party for the first time.

"Holy fuck Risky, what a fucking feeling man!" Again, Risky struggled to contain his laughter. His mind cast back to that first experience for him with speed, many moons ago. Risky felt a pang of jealousy, knowing that feeling of the first hit would never completely be replicated, instead only chased with every hit afterwards.

Fe began speaking, with every word feeling like the most passionate he would ever share. Every topic they discussed held the most meaning, regardless of how insignificant it was. Both men began discussing the turmoil in the world today, Fe finding himself gripped with content he would never usually offer a second thought. It just felt right. He had never experienced anything like this. The amphetamine was filling Fe with euphoria, and it created the impression in his mind that he had just been born again. Like life up until this point had failed to offer the truths the speed he had just ingested, would offer. The five minutes he had intended to share with Risky soon turned into five hours, as both men poured out past experiences. Risky, simply happy with the company, while Fe brimming with thoughts, the same thoughts he was unable to share all at once. Electric. Pure electric.

Chapter 15

Keep up

"When I give out an instruction, I expect my workers to follow it, is that understood Kevin?" The heads of all other workers within the cutting shop turned to view the episode unravelling in front of them. For the second time today, Fe's boss had decided to read Fe the riot act. It had been well known that the line manager within Fe's section of the foundry had a real disdain for him. It was not that Fe was a bad worker, the complete opposite would be the truth when describing Fe's work ethic. It was just clear the gaffer did not like or appreciate him being part of the team. The reason for this would be the fact that beyond all else, Patrick felt threatened by Fe. Almost the same age, Patrick had landed the gig of supervisor due to his dad being one of the directors of the company. He was the kind of weasel little cunt that would rush to the teachers at school whenever one of the bad boys would swear, no doubt him and Harris would have gotten on like a house on fire! Fe and Patrick had nothing in common, apart from the same employer.

"I asked you a question Kevin, are you struggling with the words to answer?" Patrick stood, with his fat round head, sitting perfectly on his fat round body. Looking increasingly each day like an Easter egg with rigger boots on. His receding hair line offering no help to his clotted face, bright red as the blood vessels scattered over his cheeks, bursting each day with increased aggressiveness. He looked ill, clearly the product of junk food and no exercise.

Patrick assumed that this being his kingdom, the verbal assault he offered Fe daily would be allowed to stand, with no resistance or fight back from his victim. In his eyes, the tables had turned. All those bullies at school who tormented him, this was now Patrick's turn to dish it out. Fe never even went to the same schools as Patrick, but his alpha male status clearly symbolised all Patrick hated. Secretly, all Patrick wanted was to be like Fe, but that clearly would not happen! In his twisted mind, Fe needed this job. He would never dare do anything to jeopardise losing his job. Which in the eyes of Patrick, made him easy pickings! Everyone knew Patrick would not dare speak to Fe like that outside the confines of the foundry.

Fe looked Patrick dead in the eye, his patience for the abuse Patrick would deliver weekly clearly running low.

"Just settle it down a bit Patrick, you understand me pal. I know your old man is a big player in the company, but just watch your tongue." Silence flooded the workshop, as the energy of the room was beginning to peak. Nobody had ever answered Patrick back. Just as the words left Fe's mouth, young Davie was walking past the workshop window and could see the stand-off between his big brother and the foreman. He turned and made his way inside, with his brother offering him a nod of the head as he caught his attention

"I beg your pardon" Patrick hit back, still in disbelief someone had finally called him out on his bullshit.

"You heard what I fucking said Patrick, so don't come the cunt with me. You give plenty of us good men a tough time for fuck all on a daily basis. And I really need you to back the fuck off now, as I am struggling to put up with it."

Before Patrick could respond, Fe continued "And be fucking careful with your next words." As shock filled the room, the viewers stood hanging off every word Fe had uttered. Patrick looked round the room, aware that the episode would spread like wildfire, and he had to keep face, knowing his father would not tolerate weakness in any form.

"I think you have forgotten who it is you are speaking to? This is our company. You work for us." As the last words left Patrick's mouth; he drove his index finger into Fe's chest. You could hear the gasps bounce off every wall, the echo lingering for a good few seconds. Fe slowly looked down at the finger, still lodged into his pectoral muscle, and gradually lifted his head back up, drawing level gaze with Patrick. Without a word, Fe tilted his head slightly, then drove the full force of his cranial being into Patrick's fat nose. The crack of his nasal bone reached the far reaches of the room, with the collective "oohhh" the room made sitting steadily as Fe pulled his head back into standing position. Patrick's nose exploded, like a grenade long sat dormant, finally free after the removal of the pin. He floundered back, hitting his head off the side of the vice attached to the work bench. A couple of the older boys looked at Fe for permission to intervene, which Fe approved with the nod of the head.

Patrick was slowly lifted to his feet, his nose twisted out of shape. Already swelling in an effort to self-repair, his eyes instantly blackened due to the broken nose.

"Your fucking done here McAfee; you hear me! And you will be going down for fucking years for this, you mark my words. My daddy can get the best lawyers in the land. You are fucking finished boy!" As Fe made his way past Patrick, the men holding the disgrace of a man up helped turn him to watch the dramatic exit play out.

Patrick caught sight of Davie standing at the door. "And you too you scruffy bastard. Your fucking fired as well." Clearly the shock of the attack causing Patrick to forget who he was speaking to, as no sooner had the words left his mouth, Davie began removing his leather jacket and walking towards the once revered foreman. As Davie was only feet away, the two men aiding Patrick's efforts to remain standing peeled themselves away, clearly wanting no part of Davies intentions. "Look David that was out of order, and I am..."

Before Patrick could finish his sentence, Davie had smashed his head into Patrick's beaten face. Again, the battered foreman dropped to the ground like a sack of shit, however this time none of the colleagues could be found running to his aid. Instead, the occupants of the room slowly started to filter out on to the main floor of the foundry, leaving the disgraced Foreman the arduous task of lifting himself up.

As Fe and Davie made their way outside the large entrance to the workplace, both boys looked at each other and smiled. "I love you bro" Fe declared, showing his gratitude for Davie's loyalty. As the boys made their way home, Davie turned to look at Fe as he lit the roll up hanging out the side of his mouth and questioned:

"So, what is the plan now?" Laughter filled the car as both boys realised the next chapter of their life was about to begin, as they closed the previous one in spectacular fashion.

Sitting at the kitchen table, Jackie was surprised to see her boys' home early.

"They give you a half day today then son?" Jackie gestured to Davie, as he was reaching into the fridge to grab the bottle of milk. As they explained the events that had contributed to their early arrival home, Jackie held attention in the room and declared "Nobody fucks with my boys. Nobody!"

"What are we going to do about money then mam?" Davie questioned in genuine fashion, knowing Jackie would not accept a single penny from dirty drug money. Fe butted in quickly before Jackie could respond.

"I can get us a gig on the blocks with big Rab. He is always after strong boys to help with the mono-blocking."

Jackie nodded her head in agreement. "There you are then Davie, your big brother has it all worked out, he will keep you right son" Jackie gushed with pride as again her eldest displayed his ability to look after the family.

"I am heading down to see our Mandy, is anyone needing anything while I am out?" Jackie offered, as she turned to wait for response from her boys.

"We are fine mam; you tell Mandy we are asking for her." Jackie smiled as she draped her jacket over her shoulder. A gentle kiss placed on the side of each boys' head before she turned and left for the world outside.

Once Fe was confident his mum was out of sight, he explained to Davie that he would be increasing his sales with the full-time introduction of speed to the menu of drugs available. He failed to share his own experience with the drug, knowing how easily Davie could be swayed with the thought of a good stone, it was best to keep it to himself.

"Aye Fe whatever I can do to help, just let me know man." Davie said helpfully.

Chapter 16

Big news

"Happy birthday to you, happy birthday to you".

The chants rang out as the room was filled with those he loved. Fe was twenty-one today, and a "real man" now, as his dad had mentioned an hour earlier. The Mariner bar in Kemlin had been expertly decorated by Daisy in order to celebrate the coming of age of her loved one. It was a special day today, and they had more reason than one to celebrate.

"Well Fe you somehow managed to fucking survive to this point ya mad bastard" Sanny joked, as he pulled his best friend in for a warm, drunken embrace, a show of affection that would be replicated throughout the evening as the alcohol took effect.

The handmade decorations adorned on each wall, clearly showing a lot of time and attention had gone into this. It was also a rare occasion that saw Billy and Jackie in the same room. They had been making a real effort to put any troubles to one side and show the family unity for their boys.

The door opened, with Beast walking into the lounge area of the bar and nodding over to Fe.

"Is it ok if I bring the dogs in Fe" Beast enquired, gesturing to the two giants flanked either side of him.

"Of course, come here my best pals!" Fe motioned as he dropped to one knee as Lola and Loki charged over to him, clearly the bond between man and dog stronger than ever.

"How's business?" Beast questioned, knowing Fe was now making a name for himself in the underworld.

"I cannot complain Beast, shifting more speed than I ever imagined. Don't get me wrong, the hash is still the biggest earner, but people are going fucking daft for the speed at the minute." Beast looked on at his young friend, his mind casting back to that thirteen-year-old boy writhing on the table as he had his chest tattooed, now replaced by this confident grown man who looked fantastic.

"You have eyes on you like a pair of fucking space hoppers Fe, I hope your no getting high on your own supply, you know everything I warned you about" Beast stated in a jovial fashion, but Fe knew his old friend was being serious.

"It's all good Beast, I have it under control. Just a wee dabble on special occasions, you know how it is." Fe was not sure if he was trying to assure himself or Beast. His giant of a friend patted him on the back and instructed him of his plans to get a drink. "I will catch up with you later big man, have a great night."

Fe made his way across to the table housing the collection of drinks, all being manned by the collection of his closest people. Suddenly he was intercepted by big Smithy.

"Happy birthday Fe, I hope you are well son." Fe smiled. "All good big man, and I am glad you could make it today." Both men smiled.

"So, I take it my greatest ever milk boy isn't interested in a return to the back of my van?" Both men laughed at the thought of this.

"Sadly, not to be big man, but the memories will always be there, some good times we had Smithy, and you were always a fair man, I cannot thank you enough for that." Clearly the alcohol was now turning the bar into a love fest of memories and emotions.

"I was wondering if you were holding Fe?" Smithy questioned, taking the conversation into a darker place.

"Fuck sake Smithy, you only bought a quarter off me last week, you must be powering through that stuff sir." Smithy laughed nervously as Fe continued.

"And they say Ernie is the fastest milkman in the west? Clearly no cunt has heard about big Smithy from Kemlin on the speed!" Both men found the comical side of this reference.

"Tell you what, I am dry just now, but pop up and see me tomorrow, I will sort you with a few grams to get you back in the swing of things, how does that sound?"

Smithy's face lit up. "You are a fucking gentleman Fe, a gentleman!" Fe patted Smithy on the back and walked over to his table.

When Fe sat down, picking his pint up in the process, Daisy shuffled along on the padded oak chair, stained from years of spilled drinks. She held Fe by the hand and kissed him on the cheek.

"How are you enjoying your party?" she asked, already knowing her love was having a wonderful time being surrounded by the people that meant the most to him.

"Fucking magic, I cannot think of anything that would make this day any better!" Fe declared, clearly proud of all his beautiful Daisy had done for him.

"Is that so?" Daisy challenged, as if she had one ace still up her sleeve. Fe looked at her in confusion, wondering which direction the conversation was going.

"Let me guess, you have booked me a fucking stripper! Awe Daisy you shouldn't have, a mean am no saying no, but..." Daisy playfully slapped the side of his arm as the very notion made both break out a smile.

"Cheeky bastard, I don't think so!" Daisy retorted, still laughing at the potential look on Jackie's face had she attempted a stunt like that.

Daisy moved in closer, about to deliver a fact that would change Fe's life forever.

"I'm pregnant."

As the words passed through Fe's conscious, his body froze, stunned by the news he had never expected. He turned to look at Daisy, waiting to see if the back end of the joke was about to be delivered, but the look of honesty sat proudly on her gentle face.

"You serious?" Fe questioned, struggling to get the words out as the emotions began to tighten his throat. Daisy began to laugh as the tears jumped out from her eyes to join in the celebrations.

"Three months now. I didn't want to say anything until I knew everything was ok, then time just kind of ran away from me, so I guessed your birthday as good a time as any to let you know you're going to be a daddy."

Fe fell back into the chair, aware the normal reaction would be embracing his expectant girlfriend, but instead his thoughts shifted to his own dad. In that very moment, Fe was promising himself that his unborn child would never harbour the same thoughts Fe had been forced to have about his father.

"I am going to be the best dad in the world Daisy, you mark my fucking words on that, I won't let you or the wain down." The longing embrace

Daisy had been waiting for finally fell into touch, Fe squeezed her tight, then suddenly pulled himself away in fear of hurting the baby.

"Calm down Kevin, it's not a Fabergé egg, you won't break it." Daisy giggled, as the tears and emotion caused her voice to sit with a comedic tone.

"What the fuck is a Fabergé egg?" Fe replied, desperately unsure of Daisy's comparison. Daisy laughed and pulled herself into the embrace once again.

Fe realised he had to share the news. During her announcement, the rest of the bar had been captivated by Big Sanny's effort on the karaoke. Now the gang had been filled with some tough members, who had all been capable of dealing out some extreme punishment should the need ever arise. Smashing bottles into skinheads' faces, biting chunks out of cheeks. Crushing kneecaps with hammers... But it is safe to say that Sanny's singing would be one of the harshest punishments any member of the gang could dish out.

"Fucking hell sir, it sounds like he is ripping the head of a fucking cat, I thought the big man loved animals?" Fe declared, highlighting the fact that every person in the bar already knew. It was painful to anyone exposed to it. And what made it worse was the fact that big Sanny was loving it. You could see the passion exude from him. His eyes closed as he moved side to side, clearly under the impression he was offering a performance the public would normally expect to pay for. This one was on him, and you are all welcome!

"Crazy for trying and crazy for crying, and I'm crazy for loving...!" Before Sanny could finish the verse, Fe whipped the microphone out his hand, shock etched over Sanny's face as to the cause of the interference. No sooner had the microphone been removed and the singing stopped, did the full pub erupt into cheers of celebration. Sanny smiled and nodded, assuming the celebration was due to his flawless performance, when the reality was, the jubilation was offered to Fe's intervention, putting every punter out of their misery.

"You ok if I get a shot of the microphone for two minutes big man?" Fe enquired, smiling at Sanny as he ran his hand up his back to pull in for a hug.

"Right every cunt, we need your attention, as our Fe is about to declare his undying love for me. I am sorry Daisy, you needed to find out some

117

time, and it's a fucking sin it had to be like this." The full bar erupted in laughter, as attention was now firmly locked on the two best friends. The background music that had been aiding Sanny in killing a Patsy Cline classic, ended abruptly.

"First of all, I would like to thank you all for joining us here today to celebrate my twenty-first. Fuck me I didn't realise I still had this many people left in Kemlin who hadn't fallen out with me yet, but hey, give it time!" The friends and family in the bar joined in laughter as Fe held complete attention from the room. "The reason I had to jump into Sanny's, what will we call it, unique... Fuck me that was a fancy word for me! Yes, as Sanny's unique rendition of that dear Patsy Cline classic, which I know you were all gutted about by the way, was me and Daisy have a wee announcement to make." At this point Fe ushered Daisy to join him at the Karaoke station. Fe wrapped his strong arm around Daisy's shoulder and returned his attention to his audience. "Daisy has just informed me that I am going to be a dad in the not too distant future."

No sooner had the words left his mouth, the full bar erupted in raucous cheers. A prominent figure like Fe starting his own family in the community was fantastic news for these locals. Waves of loved ones began to make their way forward to the couple, offering congratulations and pleasantries associated with such news. As the kisses' and hugs flooded in, Fe was shocked to catch the sight of his mum still planted on her chair, looking deeply into the Bacardi and cola she had been nursing. As Fe allowed Daisy to celebrate the news with mutual friends, he peeled through the crowd and took a seat next to his mum.

"You ok Mam? I expected you to be the first person launching a hug at me, you are going to be a granny for the first time!"

Jackie looked at Fe, with Fe finding an expression alien to him. His mother had always been confident in Kevin's ability to manage most situations. Surely, she had no doubt over her grandchild being born to a great father.

"You don't have a job; you have nowhere for you and Daisy to live and to add a fucking cherry on this shit show, your selling drugs to every arsehole in this town." As the words left Jackie's mouth; Fe nearly spat his pint across the length of the room. "What the fuck are you talking about mam? Am no selling drugs?" Jackie looked at Fe with the kind of disdain he had only ever seen reserved for his dad. "Don't you ever

118

fucking lie to me boy, your mam might be a lot of things, but an arsehole she is not. Driving about in that car like that with fucking foundry wages. And that arsehole of a brother of yours making his detours up the loft every chance he gets. I went up their Kevin, and I did not find a fucking toy train set up, let's just make that fucking clear."

Fe looked on into the crowd of people all having the best night of their lives, oblivious to the conversation taking place only feet away from them.

"I will make a good dad! I am not going to make the same mistakes my old man made; I promise you that mam." Jackie did not reply, clearly holding judgement on the assurance her son had just offered. Daisy could see her partner and future mother in-law deep in conversation. Her relationship with Jackie had always been amicable at best. Not that Daisy had ever done anything to upset Jackie, it was just the type of love Jackie had for her son. The introduction of another lady in his life, vying for number one spot, it was something Jackie struggled to take. It would not have mattered who Fe had chosen to raise a family with, Jackie would have raised an eyebrow.

Daisy made her way over and took a seat next to Fe, offering a welcoming smile to Jackie despite knowing something had upset her. As if putting any news of the baby firmly to the back of her head, Jackie looked at Daisy with the precision of a sniper perched deep within the overgrown grass, all gaze pointed at the enemy.

"Did you know?" Jackie's question landing at the feet of Daisy, locking her in motion and forcing the subject for the three participants. Daisy turned to look at Fe, who offered a defeated nod of the head to indicate the game was up.

"He had always told me it was just to make enough money to get us started, get a wee house of our own and keep the wolves away from the door." Jackie looked on in disgust, the very thought of her grandchild being born into a world of drugs and the drama which comes hand in hand with that environment.

Jackie stood up, lifting the beautifully crafted leather handbag her eldest son had bought her for her birthday a few months earlier. "Drug money no doubt" Jackie queried, as she gestured to the handbag.

"Fuck sake mam settle down; you're making this something it's not." Jackie did not offer a response, instead marching out of the pub, heads following her every step, wondering what drama had just unfolded around them.

"You need to go after her and sort this" Daisy instructed, desperately hoping her man could rectify the void now sitting firmly between the family.

"No point, you cannot talk to her when she is like this, just let her cool off." Fe said somewhat sadly. Davie and Sanny walked over with a fresh round of drinks, and the obvious orange juice for Daisy as if to stamp home the fact that it was the good life only for her now. Davie offered Fe a curious glance.

"Everything ok with mam?" Fe looked at Davie and began to laugh. "Aye she found your train set in the loft, and she was not best pleased. Choo choo Davie, Choo choo." Both boys began to laugh at this, but both knew they would be returning to a war once they got home, a war none of them fancied their chances in.

Chapter 17

Face the music

"I am sorry mam?" The declaration bounced off each wall as a remorseful Fe began to struggle with the incident from the previous encounter. He expected to return home to a war, but instead a wall of silence had engulfed the property. It had been almost two days since the party and Jackie had refused to enter any form of communication with her son, Jackie sat, legs crossed under her as she watched "Take the high road" with a box of Black Magic. Jackie had given the silent treatment to her boys in the past, but this usually lasted a couple of hours before all hell was let loose by her, thus announcing the incident was over, victory sitting firmly with the queen of the family.

Sitting down on the recliner next to her, his eyes burned into his mother's back. She turned to hold his attention.

"I knew since you were a bairn Kevin, I have always known you were a bad yin. I love you dearly son, I really do. But this world, the drug world, I see on the TV what it does to families. You are going to be a dad. Your own son or daughter. Does that no bother you!" The room fell silent for a couple of seconds as both parties processed Jackie's words.

"I understand that mam, and I have it all under control. Look at me. Do I look like a fucking junkie? Look at the size of me. I am built like a fucking brick shit house. This is not the body of a junkie mam. It is all about the money for me. And it is not heroin; I am no destroying families. It's a wee bit hash or some speed. Fuck sake mam it is fucking businessmen that buy off me. With big fancy houses and fancier cars... You should see some of the people that buy from me." Fe clearly feeling that sharing a descriptive vision of his clientele would somehow get Jackie onside. "And don't worry about us finding somewhere to stay. Daisy phoned me yesterday and said she has been offered a wee two-bedroom house, front and back garden mam, fucking cracking wee place. From the council, so it is all legit, different class mam eh!"

"And where is this wee house of yours, in fucking Grangemouth or Shieldhill or some other village that is a million miles from your mam's house?" Jackie suddenly becoming vulnerable again at the thought of losing her eldest.

"No mam it's just round the fucking corner, Fairlie Street!" As the news landed at Jackie's feet, as hard as she tried, the fight against the smile that had formed on her face was impossible to hide. As soon as Fe caught sight of that smile, he knew it was game up for his mum.

"Come here ya daft old cunt that you are, I love you to bits mam." With that he lifted his mother off the couch with the confident strength of a grown man. "So, granny Jackie it is then!" Fe declared, with the joy of the thought causing both to become emotional.

"I don't care what it is son, as long as it's healthy, and I mean that!" Jackie reassured but continued. "But it would be rare to have another wee boy around us. Awe can you imagine it Kevin, a wee you running around our feet." Jackie paused for a second, her mind darting back to the adventures of Kevin as a child. And with an instant back step so precise, you had to be impressed. "With Daisy's nature mind you, another wee shite like you in one lifetime is more than enough punishment for any sane woman." Both mother and son began to laugh at the thought.

"Do me a favour mam, go and phone our Daisy, she is feeling rotten after what happened in the Mariner the other night there." Jackie knew she had to be the bigger person, suck up that pride, and make the first move. Despite her son's decisions in life, whatever they may be, he was still her son, and a mother sticks by her young regardless of what they do. That is the law of nature.

Jackie placed the phone back down on the receiver, offering a nod of the head to Fe, assuring him all was well with the two most important people in his world.

"She is on her way round" Jackie informed. "We are going to start planning what the wain needs, pram, cradle, car seat. I will get our Mandy to make a start on a baby box." Jackie's imagination came to light, suddenly the enthusiasm Fe had expected was present and taking over. "And we will need to start decorating the wain's room as soon as possible. When does Daisy get the keys?" Fe burst out laughing at the pace which Jackie had developed.

"Fuck sake mam, have you been dipping into my speed, slow down a bit." Jackie launched a snarling glance, as if to signify any jokes involving drugs were not yet ready to be shared in the family home.

Daisy made her way into the kitchen, with Fe getting up and landing a kiss on her forehead, before moving in to whisper in her ear "good luck" as if Daisy better be ready for Jackie's energy. As Jackie made her way into the kitchen, she curled her arms around Daisy in a motherly embrace and congratulated her, now offering the maternal knowledge she had a wealth of to the expectant young mother.

"The keys are ready for collection if you want to go down the council office and get them" Daisy instructed Fe, knowing Jackie would not allow her to leave with Fe before she had went over her grand plans for the baby.

"Away you go then Kevin, me and Daisy have a lot we need to discuss." As Fe turned to leave the room, with Jackie setting up two cups of tea for her and Daisy, Daisy turned and offered Fe a joking plea for help with her eyes.

Fe laughed as he made his way out the house, wrapping his leather jacket over him. As he made his way down Mariner Road, he caught sight of a Harley Davidson at the bottom of the street, both bike and biker in a static stance. The sight of motorbikes around the village was a common thing, but something stood out to Fe about this biker. It was as if he was staring directly at the property Fe had just vacated. As Fe crossed the road to be directly in the path of the Harley, the biker started the engine with the powerful roar this breed of bike was famous for. The biker had a vest on that Fe did not recognise, the distance making it difficult for him to identify. The biker had a hightail open-faced helmet on, eyes disguised by the thick dark sunglasses' Fe had thought a bit over the top considering the shit weather they had been experiencing, sun being a rare thing in these parts. The biker had faded dirty jeans on, stained with oil and other engine components shared with the environment. He looked dirty; arms covered with old tattoos Fe could not make out.

Fe refused to drop his gaze from that of the biker, who returned the compliment by keeping eye contact with Fe as he passed, head turning to avoid the eye contact being broken. It was only when the biker came within feet of Fe as he roared passed did his eyes focus on the road ahead as he opened up the bike's capability, growling away as if to create a show that Fe should remember. It was only as the biker passed did Fe's throat sink into his stomach. Emblazoned on the back of the biker's vest was that logo. The logo Fe had only been told about in stories of the infamous gang. That image of the Rottweiler with the old German helmet on. The K4 Rottweilers! "The fuck was that all about?" Fe asked himself as he puffed himself up to ensure he was looking every part the man he was should the biker return. Was it just a coincidence the biker had been looking in Fe's direction? Had he just been lost and was attempting to find his bearings? What issue would any biker gang have with young Fe? The questions ran through his mind.

Making his way out of the council office, keys to the new family home sitting pride of place in his leather jacket, he made the point of scanning the outside world for anymore two wheeled friends, but he could not see anyone. Walking up the road, Fe assured himself the earlier episode with the biker was simply a misunderstanding.

Chapter 18

Home sweet home

"Look at the size of you now hen!" Heidi declared, as she took in the sight of Daisy, now only weeks away from giving birth to her first child. "Have you found out the sex yet sweetheart?" Heidi continued "And how is your Kevin keeping, he is a good laddie, misunderstood I always said." Daisy, unsure which question to answer first or really if Heidi even wanted an answer, or if the process of being a nosey bastard didn't warrant a response, just smiled and nodded her head. "Well we are all really excited to have you and Kevin as neighbours, and if there is anything you ever need hen, you just let old Heidi know. We stick together in this street, look after each other. Any babysitting you need, I am here to help my wee darling." Daisy could feel Heidi's voice eat into her brain, as second thoughts of taking the property jokingly played out in her head.

Heidi was a small round woman, around mid-fifties Daisy reckoned. Her short brown hair tied back with as little effort as possible, Heidi kept it simple. Her face wrinkled from years of stressing over her own kids. Daisy could tell Heidi had no doubt been a looker once upon a time, however the effort of maintaining a standard simply seen as too much of a task for the mature woman. She was a nosey bastard, no doubt about it, but Daisy knew she was a good woman. A long-time friend of Fe's mum, Daisy had come across Heidi on many occasions, so the opportunity to have a close family friend next door was a welcoming one.

Arriving around twenty minutes later in the van borrowed from Sanny, Fe was met with the similar greeting from Heidi.

"Fuck me that cunt can talk. I thought I was going to have to pause her halfway through to change her batteries, but the cunt must be running on Duracell, fuck me sir." Daisy began to laugh as Fe shared his experience of Heidi with her. As Fe placed a box of plates down donated to them by Jackie, Daisy moved in for a hug.

"Still a lot of work to be done doll, but I think we might just have a wee home here!" The two of them scanned the room, taking in the environment they would raise a family in.

"I love it Kevin" Daisy declared, ignoring the volume of work still to be carried out, and appreciating the property for what it represented. That childhood romance at school had turned into two adults deeply in love, awaiting the arrival of their first born to introduce to the world.

The layout of the property was straightforward. A comfortable living room downstairs, decorated with magnolia paint, height of fashion at the time, with a delicate floral border hugging the room. The artexed ceiling painted off white, with the floor covered in a thick brown carpet, expertly laid by Davie a few days earlier. The living room flowed on to the dining room, with an artexed arch playing as a partition between both rooms. The dining room shared the same brown carpet, with mahogany furniture adorned in place to offer an area of comfort during family meals. The walls mirrored those in the living room, however a large rug with a tiger lazing over a group of rocks sat pride of place on the centre wall. It was a garish look, and one Daisy was not sure of. Fe loved it though and was insistent on it staying in place.

The kitchen had equally striking wallpaper, with various standard kitchen objects printed on it in a series of rows. The kettle followed by the toaster followed by the bread bin. The sight of it almost hypnotic, Fe told himself as he had pasted it up a few weeks earlier. Your standard kitchen utensils all in place around the room, each brand new, purchased with the profits of Fe's roaring drug trade within the world of narcotics.

Business was going well, and Fe ensured the family home reaped the rewards of this. They had a long back garden, sitting bare just now, but Fe knew it would be a great area for his young family to grow up in. The plans rushing through his head. A big shed for him to keep his motorbikes in. A swing set for his growing family to play on. It was his little slice of suburbia and normality, and something Fe had longed for. The endless incidents with his parents growing up, Fe promised himself this world would be different for his kids. They would not know of the drama the young lad had once been tormented with. This would be a clean world. A happy world. A gentle world.

Upstairs the influence from Jackie was clear. Despite the fact neither of the couple knew the gender of the baby, Jackie's desire for a grandson was apparent. The initial decision to go with a neutral soft yellow bedroom quickly descended into masculine ideas, with a football sat proudly in the corner, and more male orientated ideas dotted around.

The colour blue making more than one appearance in each corner you leaned to. The changing bag Jackie had bought; blue. The changing table that no doubt cost a small fortune; blue. Fe had to laugh. He understood in these times how important the family name had been. To have a son carry on that generational heritage, it was an important point. Daisy knew the pressure to deliver a healthy young baby boy was very real. This was something Fe made no effort to play down, as his desire for a son was made clear as well. In Fe's eyes, a boy could protect himself. Fe knew only too well the dangers in the world associated with women. There were bad men out there, and Fe would not always be present to protect his offspring.

The bathroom was basic, a bath set in place, with the rubber duck and other potential toys all waiting in line for the baby to play with once it comes of age. The wall a thick green colour, Kevin insistent on the green as a nod of the head to his love of Celtic. The master bedroom was Daisy's project. Any interference in this room had been harshly fought off from Daisy. She had spent her full life the youngest of two girls. Sharing rooms, hand me down clothes. This was her time. This was her room. And this was her world now. She was firmly in control. The peach walls had been beautifully painted by the decorator Daisy had hired. The beautifully crafted four poster bed, to which Fe gulped at the price, until Daisy gently pointed out the origins of the money in his pocket which paid for their slumber. The pair of oak drawers matched the style of the oak wardrobes, which held host to Daisy's ever-growing range of clothes. Again, years of growing up with nothing, Daisy was making sure people knew she was something now. Fe took good care of her. And despite the occasional outbursts from him, life was good for the young couple.

The family unit was completed by the car parked outside the small front garden. Fe's beloved Opel Manta would no doubt need updated once his tribe of children start to come along. The thought of a big clunky family vehicle did not appeal to Fe.

"Hello, is this the McAfee residence, we are the bailiffs, and we are here to take every piece of furniture in this house as you're a pair of thieving bastards." The small hallway at the bottom of the stairs which made welcome to the house erupted in laughter. The full gang was here. Sanny, Butch, Tam, Davie and George all made their way into the living room, each holding a case of beer in hand.

"Evening gentlemen, how are we all doing today?" Fe asked cheerily, clearly happy to see his boys. Sanny stood up and roared.

"Not bad Mr homeowner, Mr fucking daddy that you are. Fuck me Fe, who gave you permission to grow up?" Again, the room filled with laughter as the two friends hugged it out on the newly purchased tartan rug.

"Fuck me sir you smell like a fucking brewery, you boys been on it all day?" Fe questioned, laughter filling him as he knew the answer.

"We thought we would come and have a wee housewarming with our best pal before Miss Daisy here cuts his balls off completely and turns him into a boring bastard."

Daisy looked on and laughed. "Aye not much chance of that" Butch retorted, which was probably the most sensible thing he had said in the last ten years. "Listen, you boys have fun, I am going to pop round and see my mam for a couple of hours. Are you wanting me to bring anything on my way back?" The question aimed at the full gang by Daisy.

"We should be fine doll" Tam replied, knowing the gang had more than enough beers to go round. "You phone me if anything happens" Fe demanded, as he looked down at the ever-present bump sat firmly between them. Daisy agreed and planted a soft kiss on the cheek of her man. As she walked out the front door, the gang all wished her well and assured her they would still be there upon her return, a thought Daisy was elated with...

"So, what's been happening then Fe, not seen you in a good few days now man. I know you are busy with the wain and that coming, and the place is looking fucking cracking Fe, some effort sir!" The full gang agreed with George and his assessment of the house.

"Ah fuck all boys, just working away." Tam took a strong drink of the tin in his hand then enquired "you punting a lot these days?" The question caught the attention of the full room. "Aye things are going great. The fucking speed has far overtaken the hash as biggest product. Cunts cannot get enough of it. Nae hassle with the Glasgow cunts, well, the occasional smart comment from the wee prick that drops, but its par for the course with these arseholes. Always a fucking gangster with one of them." Tam smiled at this. Fe noticed Tam was beginning to look distant, as if the urge for something was pulling him away from the gang, the urge Fe knew only too well was difficult for him and the boys to compete against.

Fe had made the conscious decision not to involve any of his friends in his world of drug dealing. He knew how ruthless and dangerous it was, and he made sure it was his gig, and his alone. The gang made no secret of their love for Fe, and that if he ever had any hassle with anyone, they would back him up, but the need for any of that had never materialised. In return for their loyalty, Fe always flooded his best friends with as much drugs as they wanted. He would never charge any of the sacred five, the group he had grown up with. Sanny and George just liked a smoke more than anything else, but Tam and Butch loved amphetamine and the mind-set it offered.

The one point that Fe failed to share with his gang, through the fact he was unsure if it was just paranoia more than anything else, was the occasional sighting of the bikers. He would go weeks and even months sometimes not having had any sightings, then unexpectedly, he would be coming out a shop, or leaving a friend's house, and there they were. Always a single biker. He had identified several different riders, but all the same gang. The K4 Rottweilers. He initially assumed it was just a coincidence, however the pattern was the same: the engine of the bike turned off, the obvious glare from the rider, then the engine starting up and them opening the bike up with a roar when level with Fe. He would be lying if he said it hadn't occupied more than a few of his thoughts at night.

The men partied on through the evening, as Daisy returned and joined them briefly, sitting with her fish supper and bottle of Irn Bru. When she went to bed through exhaustion from carrying the weight of the young child inside her, the boys stepped up the party, introducing the speed into the mix. The conversations intensified as the amphetamine kicked in, the love in the room being amplified as the drug did the job intended. Friends for life, and now having the unique ability to share that love through the effects of the drug inside them. These were good times, times the boys would look back on years down the line and miss with a hint of sadness.

Chapter 19

Welcome to the world

"She's in labour, she's in labour!" Jackie screamed, head hanging out the driver's window as she tried to inform other cars at the traffic lights of the urgency required. In the back of the car, Daisy's contractions had become more aggressive. Fe, sitting next to her unsure of his role in the process, looked at his mum in the mirror for some guidance. "Hold her hand then ya daft cunt, sitting there with that glaikit look on your face." Fe nodded his head, as he took hold of Daisy's hand, of which she immediately began to crush. As they made their way to the hospital, Jackie's driving was something to behold. It was like Stirling Moss on the final stretch vying for first place.

"We can see the head Daisy, just one more big push and baby will be with us" said the nurses assuring Daisy it was almost over. The screams of childbirth filled the room with horrors Fe had never experienced. Even when he was biting the face off skinheads, or crushing kneecaps with hammers, he had never heard such vocal displays of pain. He had always insisted on being in the room during the birth, however this decision was coming into question as he struggled to control his emotions. He wanted to help Daisy, but only being able to offer a hand and the occasional "you are doing well doll" made him feel more like a spare prick than anything else.

Daisy offered one final push of heroic strength and finally, the baby was welcomed to the world. The room filled with the cry of a new-born, the sound hitting Fe like a train head on. As the nurse wrapped the baby in a small shawl and cradled it in her arms, she looked at both new parents, her smile etched from ear to ear, and declared "Let me introduce you both to your healthy new son." No sooner had the words left the nurse's mouth than Fe filled with emotion. This was emotion so raw it was like nothing he had ever felt before. Unable to control this, he burst into tears, something none of the nurses would have banked on when looking at the big hard man who had sat in front of them for the last seventeen hours of Daisy's labour. The heavily tattooed strongman let all the barriers down, and the absolute instinct of any good father kicked in. As Daisy was handed her son, Fe moved in, kissing his beautiful wife on the side of the head and telling her how fucking proud of her he was, then moving his attentions to his new-born son.

He was perfect. Like nothing Fe had ever seen before. His friends who had kids all informed him that being at the birth of your child is the single most amazing experience of your life. Fe took all those comments with a pinch of salt. But every one of them was spot on. This feeling was incredible. In that moment Fe found himself assessing every aspect of his life. As if judging himself on whether he was worthy enough to be a father to this young boy gifted to him by his beautiful Daisy. After a few minutes of mother and son embrace, Daisy looked at Fe and asked him if he would like to hold his new son? Panic suddenly filled his head, and the concern that he would somehow hurt his young son if he held him the wrong way or dropped him by accident. Absurd notions suddenly feeling very real. "Don't be silly" Daisy reassured, knowing how gentle her man could be.

Fe took his first child, his new-born son into his arms for the first time, with the emotions he had managed to reign under control suddenly attacking again. Tears streaming down his face as his throat fought with him, that lump swaying up and down like the coastal waters threatening the beach.

"Hiya wee pal, I am your daddy" Fe explained, half expecting the baby to reply with a handshake. "He is fucking perfect doll, and I am so fucking proud of you." Daisy smiled as she sank back in her hospital bed, the relief of the marathon labour now finally being over. It was a tough one for Daisy, who had clearly created that much of a haven for her young one, he did not want to come out.

As the various pain reduction methods, the one's the midwife had used to try and ease the process of childbirth continued to flow through Daisy's body, she nodded off to sleep. Fe looked at the nurse, unsure if this was a problem.

"After seventeen hours of labour Mr McAfee, I can assure you sleep is not frowned upon on this ward. Your wife did a remarkable job, and you should be very proud of her." As Fe looked down at his baby boy, he offered a simple response, "I am!"

The nurse smiled as she gathered up the bloodied towels scattered around the area.

"I will leave you to it just now Mr McAfee, give you some privacy. If your wife needs anything, you just let me know." Fe looked up at this point.

"What, you're leaving me with the wain?" Fe questioned, clearly worried about the very thought of being alone with a new-born.

"That's your son Mr McAfee, and you will be fine. Any issues and you just push that big red button, we will be along the corridor." Fe smiled nervously and offered a nod of the head.

The nurse left the room, with Fe's eyes falling to meet those of his son. Everyone had told him on the lead up to this that the baby would not be able to see anything for a few weeks, but in that moment, as the baby boy looked up to his father, Fe was sure both man and boy had looked into each other's souls. That connection, that bond, from that moment was instant. An hour or so passed and Daisy began to come around, still groggy with the chemicals inside her.

"How is he?" Daisy questioned with that soft tone. Fe looked up and replied, "Fucking perfect."

With the couple settled, Daisy eating half burnt toast one of the nurses had prepared for her, the midwife popped her head round the door and looked at both parents and asked, "time for visitors yet?" With this request, Fe bounced up out the chair, with baby almost launched into the air, and screamed "my fucking mam!"

During the seventeen hours of labour, Jackie had spent the full time in the hospital waiting room, holding vigil for her young family and awaiting the new arrival. Fe had completely forgot, and had it not been for Jackie questioning how Daisy was getting on, there is a good chance she would have been left there for another seventeen hours! Fe handed the baby over to Daisy, then charged down the corridor, swinging open the waiting room double doors.

Jackie stood up at the sight of her first born, waiting for the news. As Fe locked eyes with his mum, he declared the words "it's a boy!" Jackie let out an emotional roar, like nothing Fe had ever heard before. She held her young son for what felt like an eternity. For anything that had ever caused friction between both in the past, the unity between mother and son at that moment was stronger than anything on the planet!

As Jackie stared down at her new grandson, she was completely overwhelmed by the sheer strength of emotion engulfing every part of her heart, body and soul. Yes, Jackie's boys were her world, and she would fight to her last breath to protect Kevin and Davie, but this was different, and difficult for Jackie to comprehend. This was her grandson, her first grandchild. This beautiful, precious, vulnerable little human being whose tiny little fingers she now held in her hand, was both a part of her and her own first born. Jackie was turned inside out and blown away by the sheer magnitude of her feelings as she continued to hold and stare in awe at the bundle of joy, frightened to blink in case he might disappear. As if sensing the love and security being conveyed from his Gran, the baby boy wrapped his tiny fingers around Jackie's thumb, and tears of happiness began to flow freely and abundantly down Jackie's cheeks. Although she loved her son, looking down at the newest McAfee, Jackie vowed that she would do her utmost to protect and shield him from the lifestyle chosen by his father and consequently accepted by his mother.

Once the hospital had given the family the green light to go home, they made their way to the new life waiting for them. As they pulled up into the street, Fe, who had been sitting in the passenger seat as Daisy cradled the baby in the back of the car, felt his heart tense like a vice had been clamped around it. Sitting in front of his Opel Manta, staring at the house, was a Harley Davidson. Fe asked his mum to stop the car, Jackie looking at him unsure of the request due to the fact they were not yet at the property. "Stop the fucking car mam!" Fe roared, in a style which Jackie had never once been spoken to by her young son. Without response Jackie stopped the car, with Fe springing out of the passenger side.

"Right ya cunt what the fuck are you doing here and what the fuck do you want with my family?" Fe shouted as he charged at the biker; this time assured that any previous paranoia was justified. The biker did not respond, instead starting the bike and taking off in the opposite direction. Fe began to chase after the new enemy, sprinting out of the junction leading to the main road, but unable to keep pace with that of the bike. As he watched the biker roar off into the distance, he turned to make his way back to the house. At this point Jackie was out of the car but had instructed Daisy to stay in it until Kevin had returned, fearful of the events playing out.

"You want to tell me what that was all about?" Jackie shot at Fe, clearly unimpressed with the scene she had just witnessed. Fe looked at his mum with desperation

133

"I don't know mam; I honestly don't know." Jackie knew the genuine plea from her son was sincere, and that he was clearly spooked by the unwelcome visitor. As the family made their way inside, Fe informed them of the sporadic sightings of the lone biker, each always acting in the same manner. Never once opening any form of dialogue, instead just staring at him behind those glasses.

"You both need to come and stay with me!" Jackie declared, adamant she could protect her family.

"We will be fine mam, they know where your house is, so it wouldn't make a difference. And I have plenty soldiers if I need them. We will be fine," said Fe attempting to play down any potential threat. He could tell Daisy was scared and he assured her all would be ok.

Once they got the wee man settled, Jackie brought the conversation back to the new arrival.

"And all the names you could have given the wee man, you go and call him Kevin!" The room filled with laughter, as the notion of another small Kevin terrorising the family became a reality.

"Hey, it worked of me" Fe declared, with Jackie offering a derisory glance at him. Any concern regarding the biker seemed to have passed, and Jackie made the decision to go home and leave the family to get to grips with their first evening as a new mum and dad.

Chapter 20

Big time

Daisy found it hard adapting to being a new mum and was constantly reminded of her parenting inadequacies when observing the ease in which Jackie was able to nurture and cope with baby Kevin. While Daisy loved little Kevin with all her heart, she had no hesitation in allowing Jackie to provide her with an abundance of support, although at times this did raise a certain level of jealousy and resentment from Daisy. She knew that she could never share the same type of special bond that Jackie enjoyed with Fe and baby Kevin, despite the immense love she felt for both. Fe idolised his mother and vice versa, and it looked as though history was about to repeat itself in the form of baby Kevin.

The situation was only exacerbated by Fe's increasing absence in their lives, and his lack of consistent and regular input as a father and husband. As far as Daisy was concerned, the initial adoration that Fe had expressed when his son was born towards both wife and new son, had all but disappeared. Daisy was starting to feel dejected as a wife, lover, friend and mother. The money, new clothes and shiny new trinkets no longer held the same appeal and status for Daisy a she was exiled to the background, no longer a key figure or one of the 'gang'.

By 1987 the twenty-three-year-old Fe was now firmly established as the biggest hash and amphetamine dealer in Falkirk. All the cannabis and speed that moved through Falkirk and its smaller villages went through him first. He had set up smaller dealers in each village to help with distribution. A small network of dealers who would buy in bulk from Fe and keep control of their patch. Any violence or moves made on these people would be down to them to manage, and if a patch were lost, Fe would assess the new top boys of that area, and if he trusted them, a new business link would be created.

Fe never got involved in the turf wars of the communities outside Kemlin. It brought too much heat with it and exposure was bad for business. Everyone wanted to be a gangster, but Fe was a businessman in his eyes. Fe still maintained his dealing in Kemlin on a personal level, enjoying the interaction with his long-term customers. The landscape of his portfolio looked a lot different. He would no longer make the tedious runs to Glasgow, instead paying one of his many young followers to take the trip, and ultimately take the fall should they come across any trouble during the journey. Everyone knew, you get caught holding any stuff, you take the fall. The understanding would be Fe would look after you and your family should you receive time for the incident. And you would be well rewarded following your return from any prison spell. The one thing nobody did was grass. The cardinal sin for a world like this was to become a grass. It was effectively a death sentence.

On a personal level, life was better than ever. The incident with the biker outside the new house was the last time Fe caught sight of any member of the K4 gang. He was under no illusion that he was the intended object of interest, however with no interaction in well over a year, Fe assumed he was obviously not the big fish they expected. He was aware the biker gangs had made moves on dealers throughout Scotland, looking to either take over the customer base they had, or tax the dealers and make them do all the demanding work. Life at home was good. He had the most beautiful young son, wee Kevin, who had really brought the family even closer, while his relationship with Daisy was still strong, the arguments over his personal use of speed had become more regular as well as the lack of time he spent at home. Fe had reignited his love of fishing and would often be gone for two or three days at a time. The condition he would return home in would tell Daisy he probably hadn't slept much during the time away, his body consumed by the effects of the amphetamine.

But Fe couldn't understand why Daisy was always complaining. What more did she want? He was working hard to give her absolutely everything and make sure both she and baby Kevin wanted for nothing. Only the best for his family, his son. He wasn't Billy, and his family would never go without or be subjected to the same treatment his own father put Jackie and the family through. He made sure all his family and friends benefited from his business dealings, he was a generous and loyal man.

Fe considered the amount of time he spent at home after Daisy had complained. What else was he supposed to do? He couldn't be there every five minutes when he had a business to run and soldiers to protect and keep in line. Daisy knew it was a tough business and Fe had to be on top of his game, he had been honest with her from the start. Didn't she understand the hassle he was having to deal with on a daily basis just to provide for her and the wain? He couldn't do that sitting at home. And he needed his outlets as well, like his fishing and a wee bit of something extra now and again to keep himself going. No, Daisy needed to get real – she should be grateful, he treated her like a queen, and she was able to drive around like one, dress like one and spend like one.

Fe still had concerns on a personal level. Tam's behaviour had become more erratic, with the grips of heroin appearing to be taking over, Tam no longer attempted to hide it. The frequency in which he would look to Fe for money was more common. Tam had never been one to ask for anything in his life, being an immensely proud young man. This Tam was different. The desperation for the fix becoming more apparent. What made matters worse for Fe, was the fact that the biggest heroin dealers in Falkirk had been his childhood enemies. The McDonalds.

The battles of adolescence had long since gone, with grown men now looking to make money in the murky depths of the Scottish underworld. Fe had always thought the uncomplicated way to get Tam clean would be to go round to the dealers and smash them up, warning off the prospect of selling anything to Tam again. But the McDonalds had also grown up. The days of carrying a small switch blade had turned into large machetes with no qualms of taking the head off an enemy. Fe had learned of stories of punishment handed out by the McDonalds. They were the real deal now. Not wee boys any longer.

"Morning Tam, how are you today then pal." Tam looked up; face distorted as he struggled to hold the lids of his eyes up, clearly the grip the recent hit was having on him forcing his body into the state of unresponsive euphoria. Fe had been walking to the shop for the morning paper when he came across Tam, slumped against the metal barrier cordoning off the newly built house next to the kids play park.

"Is that you Fe my best pal?" Tam responded, his words slurred and accent almost different to the normal one Tam would use. The very response destroyed Fe inside. His mind cast back to the bold young Tam sitting inside the chip van smiling out at him, victory for both in those easy days as kids.

"Fuck sake Tam, look at the fucking state of you sir, your needing to get your fucking act together pal." Tam's face winced at the very thought or assumption that he was under any foreign influence.

"What the fuck are you talking about Fe? I have been off the kit for four month now. I am just no sleeping very well at the minute, I hurt my back, and the doctor gave me these painkillers." The bare faced lie cut Fe to the bone, knowing that the brother he once had in Tam had been stolen by the heroin coursing through his body.

"When you want help getting off this shit, you come and see me Tam, you know I would do anything for you brother, but I am struggling like fuck to deal with you lately in this mess. And before you give me anymore of your lies, just save it Tam." Fe walked on before Tam could respond, but the words sat with Tam as he slowly lifted his hand to stroke his face, knowing every word his brother had just uttered to be true. Not that it mattered. The only focus just now was heroin. The only focus when he woke up was heroin. The only focus when he went to sleep was heroin. The focus was heroin.

As he watched Fe walk away disappearing into the distance, in a rare moment of reflection these days mainly as the heroin usually blocked everything out, Tam felt saddened and almost bereft. He knew Fe was both worried about him as well as hurt at what his friend and brother had become. He knew that look on Fe's face, he knew his friend felt helpless and that he had given up trying to help. Tam wondered how he even got here as he stared into the depths of emptiness. He thought about his parents and how they had successfully managed to contribute absolutely nothing to his life; Tam thought about the others – Sanny, George, Butch and Daisy, they would all have his back without question. Tam knew he let everyone down. He had let himself down and the pain and loathing he felt for himself because of this was almost physical. That's why Tam needed something to block out all the pain.

Fe walked into the paper shop, lifting the Daily Record and scanning the front page. "Thatcher wins rare third term as PM." Fe offered a derisory smile. The iron lady had little fans in the area, and Fe struggled to understand how this bitch had not been called out. The dyslexia that had tormented Fe in school was still a prominent part of his life, however Fe struggled on, ensuring the newspaper sat pride of place at his dining table each day. Fe worked mainly with the pictures, but effort is effort in his eyes.

"Did you see your Tam over at the new build Kevin?" Brenda questioned, nodding in the direction of his dear friend.

"I did that pal." Brenda was the owner of the small paper shop. She was a good woman. Curvy and blonde, with the hearty laugh Fe always found warmed him when exposed to it. Brenda had often helped the young Fe out during the period his father had left the family with nothing.

Sticking an extra loaf of bread in, or a wee wrap of chopped pork for free. She was the epitome of the term community. Look after your own, and keep that togetherness feeling alive.

"I know it cannot be easy for you to see him like that son, but your mam did everything she could for that boy, trust me son. Many a time I had her crying in here with worry over him." This was news to Fe, who did not realise just how invested in Tam his mum had become.

"A just need to leave him to it Brenda, he won't listen to me pal." Brenda smiled, knowing full well the man in front of her had no doubt tried to rid his friend of the affliction of drug abuse.

"It's they McDonald bastards, flooding this toon with that crap, someone needs to fill they bastards out." Fe nodded at Brenda's account of actions required.

Walking into the living room, Daisy smiled at him, a warm smile that once upon a time could clear Fe of all his troubles.

"I passed our Tam on the way to the shops, what a fucking nick he was in." Daisy looked at Fe, wishing she could take the turmoil from him, knowing how much it hurt him seeing his friend in such a sad state.

"What are your plans today then?" Daisy asked, attempting to change the subject. "I need to go down to Grangemouth and meet with big Tiff, he has been having some bother with one of the young teams trying to come up. He wants advice. And don't worry, I am not getting involved, just advising him on the steps he needs to take." Daisy looked at Fe with the uncertainty that had become all too common in the relationship.

"You just remember you're a dad now Kevin, the last thing we need is a war coming to this door." Fe turned around, visibly angry with Daisy's statement

"You do not think I fucking know this Daisy, but he is sitting on two kilos of my product. I canny have him getting taxed and losing the fucking lot. If I feel it is getting too much for him, then I will be taking the gear back and letting him get on with it!" Before Daisy had the chance to respond, Fe had burst out the front door and made his way down the couple of steps leading to his car.

The glorious Opel Manta Fe had spent many joyous journeys in had been replaced by the powerful BMW. Fe took immense pride in knowing he was one of the first people in Kemlin to have a CD player in his car. The money coming in from drugs clearly being spent wisely. The thought of living under the radar clearly a foreign concept for Fe. He had no job yet drove around in a car that would take a lifetime of giros to afford. The stylish Red E30 M3 was every bit the car of choice for drug dealers, and Fe knew he was top of his game. As he sat inside the beautifully cut cabin of the car, the CD player came to life as the engine purred under that beautiful iconic BMW bonnet. As the sound of Dire Straits filled the vehicle, Fe took off for his destination.

Grangemouth was only a few miles away from Camelon, but it felt alien to Fe. The heavily industrialised area was surrounded by clouds of smoke high in the sky as the various refinery's pumped gasses into the air. It was a tough area, filled with tough young gangs all coming up trying to make a name for themselves. The competition in Camelon had been almost non-existent for Fe. The McDonald's had no interest in making a move on him, with the grip they had on the heroin trade more than financially making sense for them. A war is an expensive thing. The price of soldiers and loss of business can be a high one. It was a costly product neither faction fancied. But Grangemouth was different. These young gangs had nothing to lose.

One of those gang leaders had been big Tiff. A giant of a lad Fe had come across a couple of years earlier when the young man had approached him to buy speed. Fe had set Tiff up about a year ago, and the relationship worked well. Tiff bought copious amounts on a regular basis, and Fe ensured the quality of the product remained high from his sources in Glasgow. However, Tiff had phoned him the previous day sounding unusually spooked. This was not like him. Fe knew the young lad could handle himself, and he had a good pool of young soldiers around him to manage the patch they commanded. So, for Tiff to reach out looking for help, Fe could not help but be intrigued.

Chapping the front door, Fe looked around while he waited for a response. The area was surprisingly relaxed. Well-kept gardens, all maintained by proud homeowners. It would be a tough point to sell the fact that behind this door is one of Grangemouth's biggest drug dealers. Fe could hear the various locks on the door become undone. In all, it took nearly thirty seconds to unlock all of them. As Tiff opened the door, Fe offered a smile to his friend.

"You reckon you have enough locks on that door sir, fuck me, what have you got that needs to be hidden that well." Tiff looked nervous, failing to offer the expected laughter from Fe's attempt at humour.

"Come in man, quick." As Fe entered the property, Tiff proceeded to lock up every nut and bolt on the door, clearly assuming the presence of Fe in the house was still not enough to keep them safe.

"Fuck sake big man, something has you spooked!"

Tiff sat on the edge of the couch, his long-toned legs holding up his muscular arms as they leaned against them. Fe could not help but admire Tiff's physique. He was about six foot five and built like a panzer tank. The genetics of the young man far superior to that of Fe. His long-chiselled head, with a peppered beard shaped around the curvature of his face. Slick sharp hair made Tiff a clear stand out. That alpha male mindset clearly present in the young man. He was twenty-one or twenty-two Fe told himself, unsure as to his actual age. Fe had always told himself, if shit ever turned south with Tiff, he would have to smash the big man up with a weapon, as he just couldn't see how he could defeat a man of this stature with just his hands. An outcome Fe hoped would not be needed.

"So, are you going to tell me what the fuck is going on, or should I guess?" Fe announced, clearly hinting to the young man that he was busy, and time was a precious factor in his world. Even though Tiff was a giant of a man, Fe always maintained the thought that he was on top. That he could cut the giant tree down whenever he sees fit. Any show of weakness in this world would be capitalised on by apparent friends in a heartbeat. Truth be told, there was no such thing as friends in this universe. The drug ethos was simple. Domination of competitors at all costs. As Tiff lifted himself up from the slumps of his chair, he looked Fe in the eye, the turmoil fighting in his mind screaming out for help.

"I have been getting followed Fe. I didn't think fuck all of it at first, but it started happening all the time. Everywhere I fucking go now, I see them." Fe's chest tightened in on him. He had come down to see his young protégé with the intentions of sharing tactics to warn off other young teams, hopeful of taking over Tiff's patch. Tiff had not even said it, but Fe knew exactly who had been watching him. He held off until the full story had been laid bare.

"Fucking just sit their Fe, on the motorbike. They have some crazy picture of a dog on the back of the jackets they wear, never seen anything like it." Fe looked at him, deciding to play the confused card, he wanted to see how much the young lad knew.

141

"From what I hear, they are a biker gang from the bottom of the country. One of my boys who does a bit of running, his mam works on the council planning department. Apparently, this biker gang have bought the old football pavilion behind the gas works." Fe sat listening, ensuring every point was saved in his mind. "I have spoken to a boy I knew from Barlinnie, and apparently they are looking to start a chapter in Grangemouth. I had no fucking idea what a chapter was, but he says it's just the biker gang moving in to take over another area. He reckons this mob are a big deal. The K4's they call themselves. He reckons they will work me over and take control. Fe I am no built for a war mate. I just wanted to make some money and enjoy my life. I can deal with a few wee fannies coming through tooled up, but my pal reckons these cunts are armed, and I mean proper armed. Fuck sake Fe that was never part of the plan we set up."

Fe did not respond, as he sat back in the comfortable leather sofa, analysing everything his young friend had shared with him. Tiff watched Fe with intent, waiting for some form of direction from the man who had mentored him up to this point.

"How much are you sitting on just now?" asked Fe as he looked over at his young friend.

"Just under a Kilo left Fe, and about four bars of smoke." Again, Fe went into a state of silence, working out the best course of action.

"What we are going to do is, you punt that as quick as you can, then we will make out there is a drought in the pipeline of distribution. Allow you to keep your head down and work out how these bastards want to play it. They must have eyes and ears down here, so you play it business as usual. If you just suddenly stop, they might think you are on to them, and I reckon they would run over you without thinking. You need to show a sign of strength. We all do."

Tiff bent over, running his hands through his hair as he realised the magnitude of the problem they had moving in on them. Fe made a point of not mentioning he too had been visited on several occasions by the bikers. But in his mind, he realised his full operation was under scrutiny from these bastard bikers. This was not good. The thought of going to war with a biker gang was insane, and one Fe could never win in a million years. But why hadn't they just made the move and got on with it? What was it with all the reconnaissance? That part Fe did not understand. As he rose to his feet, he advised Tiff to phone him should any other issues arise. He made his way out to the car and offered one final parting nod.

Fe set off to return home, knowing there was only one person who could potentially answer the various questions he had running round his mind. The very point that none of the boys had ever dared raise in the past was going to have to be exposed. Fe needed answers, and he needed them quick. The bikers could move into the new club house any day now. With this in mind, Fe made his way to the destination which might just hold some of the answers.

Chapter 21

The devil exposed

"There you are my best pals!" Fe declared as he dropped to one knee, both dogs pouncing on him with an explosion of excitement. Every time Fe was reunited with Lola and Loki the Rottweilers, it was the same thing. It would take Beast an eternity to get them to calm down, they had such a bond with Fe.

"So how can I help you Fe, we didn't have you planned in for ink today did we?" A confused Beast still trying to work out why his friend had come to visit.

"I need a word with you big man, and I am not going to lie, it's going to be uncomfortable for both of us." Beast did not respond, his eyes fixed on the man standing across the kitchen from him. Eventually he joined the party with a subtle shake of the head.

"We better go into the living room for a seat then eh?" Beast suggested.

Making their way into the living room, Fe realised he had never actually been in here before. Despite the many visits to the property in the past, business had always been conducted in the kitchen. Fe was amazed with all the sights filling his visual senses with intrigue. The room was filled with different action figures and memorabilia of different movies from over the years. The predominant theme was horror, although science fiction held a stronghold in various locations. The floor had been littered with various electrical components, all which Fe had never seen before. He was unsure as to what was going on, as it looked like Beast had been preparing a device unknown to Fe.

"Are you making a fucking bomb or something sir, what is all this stuff?" Beast began to laugh at his good friend, the ignorance displayed was no surprise to him due to the secluded life the local environment he survived in.

"These are all computers Fe, different monitors and keyboards." Fe looked on with confusion.

"What the fuck is a computer, never heard of it big man. Is it like one of those microwave things?" Again, Beast laughed at the outburst from his companion.

"These things will run the world one day Fe, you wait and see, this is the future." Fe laughed at the assumption from the giant standing in front of him.

"If you say so big man" retorted Fe who was clearly unconvinced.

"So, what can I help you with Fe?" Beast questioned, instantly changing the tone and atmosphere between them. Both men sat at opposite sides of the room, Fe sinking into the large couch that had been dented and misshaped by the colossal mass of both dogs, who had clearly spent many an hour lazing over it.

"The K4's?" Fe studied Beast for a response.

"So, what do you need to know about them?" Beast remained unperturbed by the mention of the biker gang.

"We have all had our wee suspicions over the years, and it makes fuck all difference to us if you are or not. The past is the past." Beast scanned the room, not actually looking for anything, but as an involuntary measure while his brain computed the information he had just received.

"That was a long time ago Fe, in another lifetime almost. I am not that man anymore. I want a quiet life, just me and my dogs." Fe could see his friend had been reluctant to share details of his past, unsure if he had been ashamed of it, or just not willing through loyalty. Either way, this conversation was not going to be an easy one.

"Why do you ask? I mean I have known you since you were a young laddie, why are you questioning me now?" said Beast genuinely interested as to why this would ever need to be brought to light when the history wants to stay history.

"I think they are gunning for me." No sooner had the words left Fe's mouth than did Beast come alive. Unaware, he had lifted himself a couple of inches from his chair, his head was now firmly level with his young friend, his eyes opened wider.

"What makes you think that? Fuck they don't have any business dealings anywhere near here. Nearest clubhouse is in Glasgow, and any talk of a move to smaller areas had never been raised. At least not in my time." Fe knew he had to be careful. For all the respect he had for Beast, he could not be sure he had his full loyalty. He knew only too well that biker gangs are like a family, and if Beast still had connections with them, Fe could be giving away his full game plan. Not that he had an actual game plan to run with.

Fe explained: "It started off just once in a blue moon. A biker sitting at the end of the street, then he'd speed up when going past me. They appeared outside my mam's, and outside my house. And they have been scoping one of my boys in Grangemouth. He is proper rattled, to the point I think I might lose him."

"They are sizing you up, and the fact that they have made more than one appearance tells me they like what they see. The reality is Fe, the wee visits to your house, those are just scare tactics. They will be getting all the intel from someone who knows you well. Someone you trust." Beast looked questioningly at Fe.

The room fell silent, as if the last few words that left Beast had almost been a submission of guilt, at least in Fe's paranoid fucked up mind.

The silence was broken by Beast who asserted, "I am not working against you Fe. I will not say it again as I am not a fucking parrot. I have not spoken to anyone from that world in years. Truth is I did time for the gang in prison. Promise always was, you keep your mouth shut, no snitching, and they take care of you when inside. I kept my side of the bargain. But they bastards shat all over me. My ex-wife left on the outside with fuck all. My young kid left to fight for the scraps. I gave complete fucking loyalty to those bastards. Five fucking years of my life!"

Fe sat in shock as Beast explained the events of his past. He had no idea Beast had served time, certainly not five years. And he had no idea the mass of a man, the big scary looking biker, actually had a family once upon a time.

"What happened to your wife and kid?" Fe asked with the softest of requests, hoping not to add any more hurt.

Beast lowered his tone and sounded despondent. "She left me. Five years is a long time. Fucked off with another man. No idea where they are now. I spent a time searching for them, but she changed her name a few times. Every time I got hot on the trace; I would be met with a dead end. Eventually I just had to accept that part of me was gone."

Fe sat back in the chair, shocked with the words being shared in the small living room.

"You must miss your kid." Beast looked down, as a tear rolled down his cheek, the man mountain purposely dropping his head in an effort to hide this potential sign of weakness.

"I think about him every day. It is hard. But I hope one day he comes looking for me. All I have left is hope, and that's what keeps me going." As he took in a deep breath to compose himself, he lifted his head, the previous hurt on display now shifted to anger.

"When I got out, they expected me to carry on like fuck all had happened. All in the past they would tell me, and bitterness had no place in that world. Well fuck them. Loyalty is all a man has, and if I didn't have that, there was no way I could continue."

"And they let you just leave? I mean I have heard these things are for life," Fe asked, curious about the manner of departure.

"The way they'd seen it I suppose, was that I was a broken man. Useless in their eyes. The hunger was gone. The brotherhood bond broken. They had contributed to that more than anyone. Killing me was instant but allowing me to live this existence was proper punishment for my lack of loyalty. Fucking loyalty, it makes you laugh doesn't it. Zero fucking loyalty when I am doing five years, yet absolute fucking dedication expected when I return. So, they left me. Just let me walk. Fighting the demons in my head each day. That's the fucking battle. That's the fucking war!"

The pain inside Beast was obvious, and a part of Fe kicked himself for making his friend relive these memories again. He couldn't imagine there had been too many times Beast had shared that story. One thing was for certain, any concerns of loyalty Beast might still have harboured for the biker gang, those thoughts were long gone.

"They are opening a chapter in Grangemouth." Beast looked up as the declaration hit him.

"Who told you that?" Beast enquired, still in disbelief.

"It was a source from my boy down there, he said his guy was legit. And the council have signed everything over." Again, silence filled the room.

"Do they know you are living here now?" Fe queried.

"They will know. Anyone considered a potential threat will always earn a tag. Just to make sure I stay in line and don't get any fucking ideas."

Fe ran his hand down the back of his neck, looking up to the thick artexed ceiling, with the gravity of the mess he was in starting to appear.

"So, what am I dealing with here then Beast?" The ex-biker looked up, eyes focused with those of his counterpart, ensuring no doubt remained after he had finished what he was about to share.

"They are bad bastards Fe. Money is everything. They run a code of loyalty, and the soldiers will fight to the death for that. And they will be armed. With the connections they have around Britain, you can be sure they are ready for a fight. This is not one you can win. They will destroy you, and everything you love." The brutal assessment of the situation was laid bare for Fe.

"The president is a fucking animal called Sean Mac... Some of the boys will call him Sean, with the older one's using 'Mac'. Both the same person. He is like no man I have ever met. He fucking charms the boys into this life with promises of solidarity and freedom from the usual shit your average nine to five will have to endure. The confines of a normal life broken, instead a nomadic existence with the brothers around you... Fucking reality is that you're just a fucking number doing his dirty work for him. Any disobedience is met head on with force. Hence why no cunt ever questions him. Make no mistake Fe, he is a fucking smart man. Very smart. That brain-dead image of a biker you have in your head, get that firmly to fuck. This guy is a tactical fucking genius. He runs these boys like a military unit. They are untouchable."

"So, what the fuck do I do then, just fucking roll over and let them fuck me?" Fe now becoming filled with rage at the thought of everything he worked for being taken away.

"You keep your family safe Fe, and you do what they tell you to do. That's the only way." Beast advised, warning Fe of the seriousness of the threat.

Fe spent a minute or so considering Beast and his proposal. "Fuck that Beast, they want a war they can fucking have one!" Fe now becoming galvanised by the surge of adrenaline. He had never feared anyone since Harris. And that cunt taught him bullies are not worth shit when you expose them. When you fight back. As his friend got to his feet and began to pace the room, Beast dropped his head into his hands, knowing only too well the young maverick meant every fucking word of it.

"Will you help me?" The very words Beast had prayed would not come out since the mention of the K4 Rottweilers was announced.

"We can't win this one Fe, and I cannot go back to that world. I am sorry son, but this fight is yours. I have advised you on what you should do. The choice of using that advice sits with you. But I am too old to go to war." Fe nodded his head, knowing it had been an unfair request in the first place, and one he should have thought over properly. That compulsive behaviour Fe was famous for again coming to the forefront.

With Fe making his way down to the car, he turned to find Beast watching him from the kitchen window, a look of sorrow etched over his face. He had lost a lifetime of potential happiness to this group of bandits, and now he was in danger of losing one of his closest friends. The punishment seemed relentless. Fe nodded his head as he took off for his next destination, unsure in his mind where that was. The options were many, but the winning solutions were few.

Chapter 22

"Read all about it!"

Walking over to the counter, newspaper firmly tucked under his elbow, Fe grabbed a couple of cans for the house. The thought of socialising in the pub, with the potential threat awaiting him, held no appeal at this moment in time. As he shared the usual pleasantries with Brenda, he scanned down to see the headline from the local newspaper. "Body found in Local Park!"

Fe felt the wave of anxiety ride over him. There was no logical reason for this. The town had thousands of people populating it. People died all the time. Junkies killing each other over the price of a tenner bag. Young gangs taking things too far with the various weapons being exposed to enemies. Nobody had made any contact with him, so he had no reason to feel concerned over this. He found himself picking up pace as he walked home. The urge to read the report of the incident, but also ensuring safety from the shelter his home would offer.

"Body found in local Grangemouth Park. The popular spot for dog walkers and families alike are shocked to the core with the discovery of the body of a yet unidentified male." Fe could not help but allow his imagination to swerve to Tiff. His big friend that had shown great concern for recent events. Surely, he was just being paranoid! Fe kept telling himself this as he picked up the phone and entered Tiffs number. As each repetitive drone of the phone rang out, dread filled Fe. Then suddenly the ringing stopped, as a nervous voice offered a sharp hello at the other end.

"Is that you big man?" Fe blasted, hope now fighting against the dread in his body. "Is that you Fe?" Tiff questioned at the other end.

Fe could not hide his relief. "Thank fuck sir, I seen the body found in the park, and well..." Fe decided to hold off finishing his sentence.

"I've seen it. Couple of junkies I am told. Fighting over some fucking bird. One of the smackheads hit a Killshot with a blade. Caught the artery. The boy bled out in minutes. Fucking sad stuff, but you know what fucking junkies are like." Tiff offered the parting comment with a derisory tone, despite the fact he was a drug dealer, potentially creating future heroin addicts.

"How are you keeping?" Fe asked, as contact had been kept to a minimum over the few days since the last visit.

"Aye all good Fe. I have that money sitting here if you want to come and get it." The invitation would be a welcome change to the solitude of the four walls in the house.

"I will pop down later today. I need to sit with the wain for a few hours." Both men agreed a time and Fe put the phone down, relief overwhelming him.

Despite everything going on, that time spent with his son was special to Fe. Everything in his life, the drama and the violence, all of it flooded away when his little man looked up at him. He was a little character now, emulating his father even from an early age. That superhero status Fe had held for his father, no doubt coming round to take effect for him. Fe was now the hero in the eyes of his child.

With Daisy arriving home from the doctors, Fe stood and placed his leather jacket on.

"Where are you going?" Daisy questioned. "I need to go and see a man about a dog" Fe hit back, knowing Daisy was about to give him the usual shit. "You have barely been here since the baby came home from the hospital. What happened to all those promises of being a better man? You are fucking more distant than you have ever been. I feel like I am living here on my own. I feel like I am losing you Kevin. You care more about these fucking drugs than you do about us!"

Fe did not respond, slamming the door as he walked away from the very place he had promised sanctuary to his better half. Fe was angry Daisy did not have faith in him. He had failed to update her on recent events, fearing more than anything else the pressure the news would add to her. "Does she not fucking realise I am looking out for her?" he asked himself. The apparent selfishness in his mind from her grating at him.

As he pulled up outside Tiff's house, fear and alarm began to fill his body. The ultra-cautious Tiff, who had more locks on his front door than Fort Knox, had left it sitting partially open. Maybe he had expected Fe's arrival, both men having agreed the time he would pop down. Surely that was it. Doubt still filling Fe, he slid the hammer into his leather jacket, allowing it to be local enough should he have to use it. As he made his way down the short path, he called out to his friend.

"Tiff, you their pal? It's Fe. I am not just wanting to walk in pal so if you could come to the door, that would be great." A few seconds passed with no response as Fe's dread increased, now concerned as to the potential scene awaiting him behind this door. The thought of turning round and walking away fought over in his mind, however he needed answers. If his friend were in trouble, Fe would help!

Stepping over the threshold, the feeling that he was not alone filled his body. As he made his way along the hallway, he decided that adopting a silent approach would be the better option. Worst case scenario he walks in on Tiff, the big man shitting himself. "No doubt the big idiot would be sitting with his trousers down in a compromising position while watching some adult minded video." A smile crossed Fe's face, hopeful that this version of events would hold the truth. As he pushed open the door to the living room, he felt resistance. Fearing the nature of the restriction on the other side, he gently pulled the hammer from his jacket. As he used his brute force to clear the door, he found there had been a chair partially lodged against it, still wide enough for someone to pass though, which hit Fe as being very strange. The recent paranoia Tiff had displayed probably led to this action. "You cannot be too safe" Fe told himself. As he scanned the room, he heard a noise coming from directly above him.

"Surely the big arsehole has not been in his bed all this time?" Fe knew Tiff had mentioned taking Valium to help him sleep. He had got the mother's little helpers from his neighbour, and his testimony had been that they made all the difference. The Valium had no doubt knocked him out, and Fe's rustling around his home probably woken him up. As he made his way upstairs, he called out to his friend, again there was no response. He decided to keep the hammer in his hand, unsure if the noise had simply been a floorboard creaking due to the age of the property, or indeed his friend just waking, and potentially blurred from the effects of the Valium.

Nudging the bedroom door, Fe could see the reflection in the large wardrobe mirror showing the clear outline of an adult in the bed.

"Fuck sake sir" Fe roared, now dropping the hammer down at his side as he walked freely into the room. "What a fucking fright you gave me sir, you are needing to lay off them blues, fucking sparked out drug dealers are not the most productive of things." Fe adapting a comical tone as the adrenaline in his body subsided. The figure in the bed offered no reaction.

Walking around to the side of the bed, that adrenaline he had allowed to fade away suddenly gripped him like the hands of a giant. At the base of the bed, just next to the wooden side unit, was a pool of blood. Fe's eyes slowly lifted to the figure under the covers, only the sight of hair being visible at that moment. As he slowly lifted the quilt, his heart sank to the depths of his body as he tried gallantly to fight it off. Tiff was here. He had been here the whole time. But the response Fe had prayed for was never going to come.

The blade had cut Tiff from ear to ear, the gaping wound on his throat testifying this young victim had a bloody ending to his short life. The guilt washed over Fe like a sandstorm of remorse. This was his fault. He had got the young man into this world, promising wealth the young man had only dreamed of until that point. He had also promised protection should the time ever come. He had let Tiff down. The boy was scared, and Fe had instructed business as usual was the best way to deal with it.

Fe stood back, computing everything that must have taken place before his arrival. With brutal force, the bat smashed into the back of his head, instantly knocking him out and sending him crushing on top of the lifeless body settled out on the bed...

Chapter 23

"Let me introduce myself"

The weight of his lids battled with his broken blue eyes, the light hurting as the protection of darkness was snatched from him. Every part of his body was screaming out in pain. Various figures came in and out of sight, as the muffled chants of conversation swirled around him. "Good evening Mr McAfee. It is good to have you back with us, that was quite a sleep you had there." As Fe attempted to locate the direction of the voice, the turning of his neck sent waves of pain shooting to his brain. The last thing he could remember was looking down at the lifeless body of his young friend, and now waking up to this.

"You will no doubt be wondering why we have gone to so much effort to have you join us tonight. The fact is Mr McAfee, you are an incredibly special person in our new world."

Fe's eyes slowly adjusted to their newfound surroundings, with the realisation that he was a long way from the comforts of home. This looked like an old barn, and the smell of shit did nothing to detract from that theory. The floor littered with hay trails, scattered in no great pattern, telling Fe the care and attention this place had once been accustomed to was long gone. He could see remnants of old farming machinery, long since utilised, scattered around, parts torn from it for salvage before resting in the rustic open grave they stand in today. The same grave it looked like Fe might just inherit. The barn door smashed down the centre, no doubt attributed to a forced entry. This fact highlighted the chances of someone coming to Fe's rescue were on the same par as Tiff suddenly rising from the dead. "Fuck fuck fuck!" Fe knew this was a disaster. Even with his unique outlook on life, he couldn't see past this one.

Walking in his line of sight for the first time, Fe could feel the rage build inside him. His veins pumping the adrenaline around his body. He fought with the restraints holding him to the old metal chair. Every struggle only feeling like him being locked further into place.

"Do we look like fucking amateurs Fe. C'mon now, behave yourself. You can struggle all you want; you're only moving when we say you move. That's how this works." The man in front was everything Fe had ever visualised a biker to be. His frame resembling the base of an oak tree. His head cast well over six feet high, with trunk like arms holding vigil each side of his body. His arms held a mixture of tattoos and battle wounds. Fe could see endless scars littered across the landscape of this man, each telling a story of a battle once fought. The patch on his vest was different from the others he had seen. Blazoned on the front was the word "President." His thick leather trousers coated his monstrous, no doubt steroid sculpted legs. His face filled with every bit of hatred one-man could harbour. His jawline scattered with patches of hair from a bold attempt at a beard. Clearly the follicles were not working in his favour, but nobody had been bold enough to point this out. His hair was slicked back, Fe unsure if it had been from hair product or simply good old grease holding it in place. He could only imagine what this guy would smell like. Fe guessed he was around late thirties, maybe early forties.

"Fuck me your even uglier than I imagined. I mean don't get me wrong, you're all a shower of fuck ugly bastards, but I half expected you to be a little less painful on the eyes." As the words left Fe's mouth, the two soldiers standing behind Sean squirmed, no doubt the first time being exposed to anyone ever daring to speak to their leader in that manner.

Sean began laughing at this, looking round at his soldiers, all of whom were unsure how they should be reacting. Nervously both began to chuckle.

"He told me you would be a bit of a character, but I didn't expect this level of fucking comedy genius." Fe looked around, scanning to look for any familiar faces. Beast had said someone had to be feeding them information. Was that parasite here just now, about to take in the demise of the man they obviously despised.

"Who fucking told you?" Fe hit back. Sean started to walk closer.

"Now now Fe, you think a man like me gets to be in positions like these by just handing out my sources on request. Behave yourself. I thought you were better than that. I was actually looking forward to the war you had no doubt promised me. They did say there was no chance you would just roll over and let me take your empire. But the fact it was this easy? I must admit I was a bit disappointed."

Fe looked up, rage shooting out him like the bullets from an old spitfire. Every muscle tensed at the binds that confined him.

"How about you let me go and I fucking show you a proper war. C'mon big man, show your fucking boys how tough you are man to man."

Sean continued to laugh at the very notion. "You see Fe, I learned long ago that men like you, they are just not smart enough to know when they are beat. That old caveman mindset rolls out and the balls between your legs start doing all the talking. Well you just tuck those wee balls back inside your wee trousers and listen to me."

The jovial nature that Sean had displayed was now turning serious.

"I fucking own you now. Putting a bullet between your fucking eyes right now would be the easy thing to do. Too fucking easy though Kevin, and a waste of a good bullet if you ask me. It is Kevin isn't it? I reckon we should stick to Fe though, for dramatic purposes. Then I have my boys, oh god they would love to have some fun with you. Pair of evil little bastards that they are. Trust me Fe, you would be begging for that fucking bullet by the end of it. Oh no Fe, I have bigger plans for you. You see Fe, you now work for me!"

Fe looked at him dead on, refusing to allow the urge to blink take effect, ensuring he was hearing this fucking maniac properly.

"Are you off your fucking rocker? You think I am going to work for you? You must be mad. You just load that gun and do your best, as the only thing you will be getting out of me will be a final breath. And even that will be fucking cursed, I promise you that." Fe dropped his head down to the floor, looking at the bloodied mess covering him from the earlier attack. He knew they had obviously kicked the shit out of him after the initial bash to the head. He had been in enough battles to know what a good kicking feels like.

Sean turned to his men, again laughter filling the air at the efforts of the young captive in front of them. He nodded at one of the men, who slowly made his way over to Fe. Sensing the oncoming threat, Fe took in a deep breath, readying himself for his final moments. The bullet he expected did not come. His vision of emulating the demise of Tiff at the hands of the same blade, did not come. Instead, the scrawny skin headed thug carrying out Sean's orders placed a thick brown envelope on his lap. Fe, unsure what was going on, lifted his head slightly, just enough to notice the thug going behind him and starting to cut at the binds that held him. Within seconds the strain that had been cutting into Fe's wrists was free. The ropes around him fell to the ground. He was a free man.

"Before you get any fucking heroic ideas of a great escape, I suggest you open the envelope," said Sean continuing in a serious, menacing tone. As Fe slowly got to his feet, the pain was too much to bear. He could identify broken ribs, and no doubt various other broken bones. They had definitely done a number on him. Ensuring he did not give off any sign of weakness, he held himself straight. He held himself tall. He held himself strong. Is that the best you have got? The reality though was much different. Defeat was already declared. The fight over. As Fe opened the envelope, his eyes remained locked on Sean. As the envelope fell to the floor, Fe slowly lowered his gaze. What he would see next changed everything.

"As you now see, you fucking belong to me! You are now property of this brotherhood until we decide otherwise, do I make myself clear?" Sean now unable to hide his arrogance as the realisation sank into the depths of Fe's mind. As he looked through the photos, dropping each one after inspection, he was met with a series of different family events. His son at the park, his wife out having lunch with friends. The thing that startled Fe the most, was that in each photo, you could see the figure standing taking in the sight of his family. That figure clothed in the gang colours. Fe realising his family had been completely unaware of the onlookers. The pictures then led to those of his mum, and then his dad. They had even captured photos of his friends. Fuck me, if this were happier times; Fe might think he was looking at a family photo album.

"There is not a thing I don't know about you. Where you live, where you hang out? Who you love, who you fuck, hell, I even know who you hate... You see Fe, information will always be the most effective weapon in any battle. Fuck, I have walked past you in the street a couple of times without my patch on and you had no idea. That my friend, is fucking power!" As Fe got to the last photo, all others scattered around his feet like parts of him broken off, his mind suddenly engulfed with rage. The anger consumed him when the final picture showed just who had fucked him over. Just who had been feeding the bikers all this information about him. He had initial concerns Beast had set him up, those concerns subsiding after his frank chat with the big man. He immediately recognised the familiar face in the photo looking up at him, and the tattooed arms wrapped around Sean's shoulder. Old enemies seldom allow the past to be the past, and clearly this was one Fe should have buried properly.

"Ah, that's a familiar face is it not Fe. Yeah, I do love the angle on that one. I feel it really flatters my waistline, what do you think?" Before Fe had the chance to offer a response, the doors to the barn opened. The man that had haunted Fe only moments before from the picture, stood in front of him, confirming this was no sick joke!"

"I bet you didn't expect to see me did you Fe, blast from the past is it not?" As Fe dropped the final picture, he held gaze with the newest member of this dysfunctional party. Those Doc Martens that had been tucked into the tight denim jeans now replaced with leather biker trousers. The chequered shirt infamous with the scene swapped for the colours of the biker gang.

"Good to see you Conner."

It had been noted years before that upon his release from prison, Conner had left the area not long after, although no one paid much attention. He was no longer a threat to Fe's world, so why would he care? That lack of judgement looked to have cost Fe his future, as that long beaten enemy he had tucked away in the history books was now more prominent than ever.

"So, what is this then, you didn't have the fucking bottle to hit back all those years ago, you had to run and get yourself a fucking biker gang to come at us? Fuck me Conner that's quite a fucking stretch of the imagination, even for you pal." The anger in Conner's face was impossible to hide, his teeth gritting together as the venom poured from the gaps.

"You fucking turned my boys inside out ya cunt. Fucking wiped them out. And a fucking ambush no less. What happened to the idea of a fucking fair fight?" Conner raged, as his body actioned to get the fight on right now, with Sean having to remind him of his rank in the situation, and who made the calls.

"Your fucking men ripped the jaw off Tam, smashed his house up, battered fuck out his girl. Don't fucking talk to me about fair game you patronising wee prick." Fe now firmly invested in a scrap should Conner want it.

"Ladies, ladies, can we please remember our manners, my god we cannot have anarchy take over this adult civilised conversation. Your right Fe, Conner did leave town that day. And he made his way to our front door. He earned his patch, been a good fucking lad for us. And then a few years ago, he told me about this young hard man. This bold warrior who had taken advantage of his absence. Well, we decided to pay you a visit, but what do we find? Well you have only gone and managed to create a small fucking empire. And as businessmen, you can see why that would show interest to us. So, let me tell you what is going to happen, and trust me Fe, it will fucking happen, or I will wipe out every fucking member of your family while you watch. Then you will live the final days of your miserable life with that guilt placed firmly around your neck."

Sean moved in closer, with Fe holding his ground, knowing the easier option would be to potentially fight it to the death right now, and hope they just fuck off and leave him. But he could not risk potential follow up on his family, especially with him out the picture.

"So, here is what happens. You go back to your wee life, the big gangster drug dealer. You continue to make us money, and we allow you to live. You do anything to jeopardise that, and we drop the fucking bowels of hell on your world. I was thinking eighty/twenty split of all profit to us sounds fair, considering you could be floating down a fucking river just now, I reckon that's a pretty good deal. What do you think Conner?" As he turned to look at his recruit, the grin on Conner's face burned the inside of Fe's very being.

"So, what do we say Fe, do we have a deal? Oh, and I might call on you every now and then to do a little extra curricular for me, free of charge, naturally." Sean making it clear Fe's subservient role in the pecking order.

"What kind of stuff?" Fe responded, looking confused at this last part.

"You don't ask fucking questions; do you understand me!" No sooner had the outburst hit Fe, was it followed up by a sharp right hook to the broken rib's Fe had been subtly nursing. As Fe dropped to the ground, the punch was followed by a volley to his head by Conner, no doubt the anger festering in him coming to the boil.

"Now now Conner, that's enough" Sean joked, as Fe struggled to remain conscious.

"Before we part ways, tell me, how is my big friend Beast getting on? Great boy he was. Could have been vice president in our whole organisation had he not started all that shit when he got out. Fucking shame. His slag of a bird fucked off and left him, and somehow it was my fault. C'mon now." Fe looked up, as the fresh blood mixed with the hardened extracts from earlier.

"He is more of a man than you will ever be!" Fe declared, proud to know the man Beast was.

"Of course he is son" Sean sniggered, before driving his boot into Fe's head, knocking him out cold.

Chapter 24

The monster under the bed

"Is that Fe?" exclaimed a startled Sanny as he focused on the lifeless body which lay under the lamp post outside...

He had been standing at his living room window while George and Butch sat on the couch rolling joints and discussing the new releases filling the charts. The bikers had thrown Fe out a moving van, naked, with nothing but his heartbeat, which at this point was fighting to remain in this world. As Sanny and Butch rushed out of the house, George ran to the cupboard to grab some blankets. As they lifted a bloodied Fe inside, they wrapped him up and sat him on the couch.

"Fuck me sir, who the fuck would do this?" George cried, pain filling his voice at the torment his friend was in. "We need to phone a fucking ambulance, and the fucking polis by the looks of it as well" George continued.

Once Fe caught the mention of police, he stirred from his unconscious state. He attempted to say something, but the gang did not pick it up. Sensing his friend was attempting to speak, Butch moved in and asked him to repeat himself.

"No fucking polis!" Butch looked up at the gang and informed them Fe did not want police.

"The first thing the ambulance will do when they see him is inform the polis, so we are fucked on that matter." Sanny declared.

"No ambulance" Fe responded, now able to just about communicate with the group.

"Fuck sake Fe look at the state of you man, your nearly fucking deed sir. We need to get you some help, as a' don't think a fucking plaster and a Bovril is going to fix this." The boys knew Sanny was talking sense, but if Fe insisted on keeping this in house, that's what they would do.

They began to clean him up, clearing away the dried blood scattered over his body. The looks around the room were that of disbelief. They had never seen their friend like this. Fuck, they had never seen anyone like this.

"I cannot have Daisy staying in the house on her own, you need to get me round the road." Fe looked at his boys with a sense of desperation and a look of helplessness that none of them had ever seen. The cocksure leader of the pack had always been impressive to others. You admired him. He had that something that most men only dream of. But this shell of a man was not Fe. This vessel was an imitation of the friend they knew. This man in front of them was scared. Terrified even.

Sanny handed Butch four Valium and told him to give Fe a hot cup of tea, and down the hatch with the blues. Hopefully that would take the edge off the pain. While Butch made his way back to the living room, Sanny had pulled away to phone ahead for Daisy. The shock of the men standing at the door with a broken Fe was too much of a shock for any person, as the boys could attest to. At least if Daisy was ready for the event about to unfold, she could prepare herself. As Fe dropped the four tablets down his neck, he sat back in the chair, head looking to the sky wondering just how the fuck he had ended up in this position.

"Whoever it was Fe, we will fucking get them back. You understand me pal. No cunt does this to one of our boys." Butch delivering words that prompted Fe to reach out and grasp him by the hand.

"You are a good man Butch, a fucking good man. And I love you brother." A tear began to roll down Fe's battered face, his emotions no longer contained within the vessel that was his heart. As Sanny walked back into the room, he placed his hand on the old metal fire grill, lifting the poker up to push another log on. "We need to keep him warm and comfortable."

The house had been shared by the three men after a series of events had them all agreed that the fairer sex had in fact not really been the fairer sex at all. Each man holding a story of how the bitch had broken their heart. So, the collective decision was the three of them get a wee house together and live the playboy lifestyle. It made sense, and Fe had often been jealous of the freedom the young men had. He loved his family, but he loved the pleasures in life as well.

The flat had a series of posters and pictures depicting rock stars, movie stars and villains of the past. The imagination of Butch would allow you to find dragons in battle with sword wielding, scantily dressed warriors. It was everything you expected from a property with no female contribution. The kitchen looking like world record attempts for stacking as many dirty plates as possible. The living room table scattered with ashtrays, all filled with the roach of a joint smoked to the burn. You would also find the old remnants of speed deal wraps Fe had given the gang; the only thing left being the magazine envelope it had been packaged in. The flat screamed for some TLC, but the boys gave less of a fuck about that than they did about the paint drying on the wall.

Sanny took his seat on the old wicker chair. He looked over to Fe. He was now feeling the effects of the Valium kicking in, and the pain being a bit more manageable.

"You going to tell us what happened then Fe. We know you don't want us being part of that world, but you need to have a bit of fucking respect and realise you cannot sit in front of us in that state and expect us just to keep our fucking mouth shut. It's time to talk Fe." As Fe looked around the room, the collective nods of the head in agreement with Sanny told him the game was up. They were big boys, and in all honesty, he could do with every bit of help he could get right now.

Explaining from the beginning about the bikers scoping him from his mum's house, to the point of bringing baby Kevin home and them being outside. The body he found in Grangemouth, and the trip to the abandoned barn. He described the conversation with Beast, having to share all details as he knew they would look at him as a threat if he didn't. And then ultimately the return of Conner, and the new agreements in place for Fe's best working practices.

"That fucking dirty skinhead bastard!" George roared, clearly enraged by the fact that Conner had brought this world of hell to Fe's doorstep. "I fucking knew we should have finished that bastard off when he got out the jail. I fucking knew it." Fe looked at George, wishing he could turn back time and agree with his friend all those years ago and finish Conner off with a fucking axe to the head. That would have saved all this bullshit now firmly placed at Fe's feet. Fe could feel the Valium kicking in good now, as he felt the urge to fall asleep. The boys refused to allow this, concerned about potential concussion, and wanting Fe to stay awake and alert if possible.

"So, what does this mean now Fe? You're just expected to put yourself in danger on a daily basis and these bastards take all the profits? And whenever they decide they have some dirty work for you, it's a click of the fucking fingers and Fe comes running. What kind of fucking set up is that going to be? That's no life for any cunt." Fe looked up, visibly angry with the statement Sanny had just made, he put the haze of the Valium hit to one side and blasted back.

"And what is it you expect me to fucking do then Sanny, just allow these bastards to destroy my fucking family. To destroy my friends, to destroy every fucking thing I care about. I cannot let that happen. I do not have a fucking choice. I do what I am told and hope to god they get fucking bored with me."

Before Sanny could offer a response, Fe staggered up and walked over to him.

"I am sorry brother; it's just this whole fucking situation is about as fucked up as it could get. And I don't see any way out." Sanny got up and hugged his best friend, with Fe making the noise you expect when in pain.

"Fucking hell big man, gently does it." The full gang began to laugh.

Once they got to the car, it took a couple of them to lift Fe into the front passenger seat. He refused the offer of a seat belt, thinking what fucking additional damage could be inflicted upon him on top of what he currently had. As they made their way round to Fe's house, silence filled the vehicle. Each man was trying to find their own interpretation of what had happened, and no doubt attempting to offer some kind of fix for this. The main thing was that Fe knew he was no longer alone in this fight. He has his boys, the boys who had cheered as Harris fell to his arse, and who had gorged on the mar's bars Tam had provided. The soldiers who had smashed up the McDonalds in the playground, and the warriors who had dished out vengeance to the skinheads. They had been through everything together, so one more battle was fucking gladly accepted by them.

Pulling up at the bottom of the three steps leading up to the house, they could see the front door open, with Daisy standing waiting on their arrival. The panic on her face was plain for all to see. As the men aided Fe into the house, George shut the front door and joined them at the dining room table. Tears streamed down Daisy's face as she struggled to control her emotions. She held Fe by the hand, unable to drop her gaze from him. Sanny could see Fe was out of it with the Valium, so he carefully explained everything his friend had shared with him to Daisy. Her facial expressions changing as each part of the story laid out. Sanny knew there was no point buttering the story up, Daisy needed to understand how serious this was.

164

"Then why can we not just run away. Just start again somewhere new. Fuck all the drug money, we don't need it. As long as we have each other." Daisy pleaded with Fe as if the only possibility for the family's wellbeing had been her suggestion. Fe looked up, clearly taking in everything that had just been said.

"It's not as easy as that doll, they know everyone. Even my fucking dad. If we run away, they just go to the next person closest to me. They will wipe the full fucking family off the face of the earth. And where would we go? They have connections all over Britain, we would always be looking over our shoulders. It would never end." As the desperation filled Daisy, she broke down again, her head dropping to her hands, which sat perched on each thigh. She knew they couldn't just abandon those they loved, leaving them to deal with Fe's mess.

"The way we see it Daisy, this is our fight too. It was not just Fe who smashed the skinheads that day, we all did. And Conner is looking for that revenge. The only reason the bikers are entertaining it on this level is because they got a sniff of the money Fe was making." As noble as Sanny's gesture had been, Fe knew the looking glass was on him, and he had to work with this alone.

"I need to try and get some rest boys. I really appreciate everything you have done, but you boys get yourself round the road and get to bed," said Fe offering the gang a way out of the night's drama.

"I don't fucking think so Fe! Me and George will take a couch each and Butch will do the first round of guard duty. We will swap every three hours. You and Daisy away upstairs and get some rest!" The offer from Sanny was not up for discussion. Fe smiled at his group of friends.

"Well I guess I am fucking stuck with you shower of ugly bastards then eh." The gang all began to laugh at this comment. As they helped Fe upstairs, he rested on top of the bed covers. Each of them planted a small kiss on his forehead, declaring their love for him in the process.

Daisy joined him in bed. She turned to him. "What are we going to do Kevin?" Fe looked up to the sky. The man that always had an answer for everything replied, "I don't know Daisy, I really don't know."

Chapter 25

New rules

The weeks following the attack had been surreal for Fe. Tiff's body had been found, along with a quantity of drugs and cash. The police put it down to a dispute between rival dealers. Fe knew that this meant they unofficially didn't give a shit about it. They would never find his killer, as they would never look properly. Fe was pretty much bed bound for almost three weeks. His body needed time to heal, and his mind needed time to process all that had gone on. The guys had taken turns to stay over each night. One of them would sleep on the couch, firmly assuring any follow up attack would be met with resistance.

After the second week, Fe advised them to go home, realising they could not live like this forever. He had to install some form of normality in the lives of those around him. He lay in bed for hours at a time, drifting in and out of sleep, battling with the logic of what was a dream and what was reality. The problem was that the nightmares began all over again every time he woke. At least in his dreams he would be paraded with happier times. Dreams of the gang as kids, dreams of faraway happiness with Daisy and baby Kevin. Waking up scared him. Waking up meant dealing with reality.

"How are you feeling son?" Jackie asked as she squeezed tightly on his hand. She had been visiting most days, and firmly taking on the belief that this was her fight also. As any strong mother would, even as an adult, Kevin was still her son. Still her baby boy. Any troubles he was going through, she now inherited.

"I am fine mam; I just need to get back on my feet now. I need to get everything back to normal," Fe explained as he fixated on the pattern running across the bedroom ceiling. He had spent the best part of three weeks scanning every aspect of his self-imposed prison cell. He hated this bedroom now, and every recent memory it harboured.

"Well if you feel strong enough, then I think it would be the best thing for you." It was clear Jackie did not know how to deal with a situation like this. For a parent that had an answer to every trouble her son had ever faced, this one was beyond her.

Fe made his way downstairs; he was met with Daisy playing on the floor with baby Kevin. She looked up and smiled, relief sweeping over her as the potential for some normality creeping back into the family home might just be a distinct possibility.

"How are you feeling?" she questioned, observing that Fe was fully dressed with shoes on.

"A lot better. I need to go and make some pickups. The guys have been sitting on the money for weeks now, so I need to clear things and reset." The disbelief from this announcement was clear on Daisy's face.

"Kevin you almost died, and less than a month later you are talking about collecting dirty drug money. Is this a fucking joke?" Any civilised relationship which had manifested while Fe was incapacitated was now being put to the test once again.

"I don't have a choice Daisy. They are expecting money. I cannot just fucking sit in my bed and pretend this isn't happening." Daisy knew deep down Fe was right, however she had become falsely reassured by the cocoon created over the last few weeks in the house. The sanctuary and safety of the four walls housing them had been a refreshing change from the chaos that had become normal life.

When Fe made his way out the front door, the direct sunlight hurt his eyes. The exposure burned for a split second, and he stood still while his body adjusted. As he scanned up and down the street, it was clear the world around him kept turning as normal. The neighbours completely oblivious to the trauma recently inflicted on the family living in the property only a few feet away from them. Behind closed doors, many surprises lay await.

He had called ahead to a few of his smaller dealers, and the assurance that the money was ready for collection was made by each of them. As he made his way down the Camelon main street, he would scan all the faces looking at him. Was it a coincidence? Had these onlookers been spies for Sean and his group of outlaws? The sacred blanket of familiarity, which this area had offered him complete with security and safety now felt a million miles away. Camelon was now just as dangerous as any other part of the world. Even more so now, as they knew where he would be ninety per cent of the time.

Cutting down the side of the rugby parks, Fe caught sight of a motorbike pulling out of the car park. Normally the threat of anyone following him had been nothing more than some throw away paranoia. Fe found his issue to be the car he was driving, it was the only model like this in Falkirk, so he stood out like a sore thumb. He convinced himself it was just a coincidence the biker had been in the car park and spotted him. However, the threat now was very real. Fe decided to go back on himself, not willing to expose the location of his dealers. As he turned at the roundabout and made his way back towards Camelon, the biker followed. As Fe made a couple of sharp turns at the last minute, all mirrored by the biker, he realised this tail was for him. Realising this could go on all day, he pulled into a stop just behind his old high school. The biker stopped about twenty feet behind him, and Fe could clearly see the biker had turned his engine off. He was waiting for the biker to get off and approach him, but nothing. Several minutes passed as the standoff turned into a stalemate. Realising this game of cat and mouse could go on all day, he stepped out of the car and slowly made his way towards the two wheeled nemesis.

"You want to tell me why the fuck you are following me? I have fucking agreed to his demands, but you need to let me make a fucking income." The biker looked at him stone faced. "Are you fucking deaf?" Fe roared, his anger now moving towards boiling point.

"Get on!" The biker demanded catching Fe by surprise.

"What do you mean get on? Why the fuck would I get on your bike?" The biker looked at him, focus unwavering.

"I will only say it one more time, Get on!" Fe realised he was in no position to argue. He walked up to his car and made sure everything was locked and secure before returning to the Harley and swinging his leg over.

"No helmet for me?" Fe said sarcastically. The biker did not offer a response.

Making their way to the new clubhouse in Grangemouth, the realisation of just how close the enemy now were from him really hit home. They would always be only minutes away from controlling their new puppet whichever way they saw fit. Turning a sharp corner, they faced mesh wire gates, a guard on either side opening for them. Crossing the red ash car park, they pulled up outside the new pavilion. He could see the bikers had already made their mark. The décor of the exterior marked in several areas with the logos and motifs of the gang. As Fe stepped off the bike, the escort who had brought him down grunted and nodded towards the doors to the clubhouse.

Once Fe made his way up the steps, he turned again to take sight of the audience watching his every move. He counted at least seven guys, and three times as many bikes parked up. The dogs which had played a massive part in this culture walked freely around the yard. A large beast had offered the occasional growl as he passed, but none of the dogs ever looked like they would attack. Clearly the training for each animal was on par with the training each soldier in the gang had received. Everyone must have discipline to make an organisation work, including the pets.

He pushed open the double doors, which reminded him of the entrance to an old saloon bar from a John Wayne movie. He was immediately met with the sound and smell from the proprietors of this unique establishment. That stale scent of sweat, when personal hygiene is no longer a concern, mixed with the alcohol exhaled into the air. It was everything Fe had expected. The noise attacking his ears was thrashing rock music, the speed of which Fe could not understand how anyone would find any pleasure in it. The area resembled the worst pub Fe had ever entered years ago in Glasgow, the duration of his stay that time cut short due to firearms officers raiding the place. He wondered just what the authorities would find should they ever make a move on this hell hole. The bar was propped with various hairy bikers, all thick with tattoos. The clouds of cigarette smoke made the effort of breathing more of a task than it had to be. Life expectancy in places like this certainly wouldn't meet the national average. The floor was sticky, and each step felt like a challenge on the thighs. The walls smeared with Nazi memorabilia and other far right ideology. The propaganda machine for this lot clearly didn't have much work to do.

The chance of an unwelcome stranger walking into these parts looking to quench his thirst were close to none. Inside the property were more dogs, and Fe realised he had lost count of how many he had seen. Did they outnumber people? Possibly so. He also had no doubt the dogs smelled better than the owners who looked after them. Fe was almost certain of that.

Fe could see several doors leading off in to separate rooms. As he scanned the faces, all of which had taken an interest in his presence, he wondered when Conner or Sean would make their grand entrance, no doubt the fucking pinnacle of this shit show, Fe told himself. A large balding man with a spider web tattooed on the side of his face began to make his way over to Fe. As he got closer, he nodded with the intent of Fe following him. Fe knew he had no choice and offered chase to the leader. As they marched along a series of corridors, Fe quickly realised any form of escape from this place would be futile. He was already lost. Every area looked the same. Every door offering nothing unique about it. As they came to a second set of double doors, he saw a plaque hanging from it saying, "meeting room." He assumed this was where the big boys camped out, no doubt plotting what kind of misery they would unleash to the public. Many a death was no doubt authorised behind these doors. Fe just had to make sure it was nobody he cared about was at risk of becoming the subject of discussion.

The giant with the spider web looked down at him, instructing Fe to wait where he was. As he trudged off, occasionally bumping into walls as the various chemicals in his body fought it out, Fe realised making him wait out here like a naughty schoolboy was just another one of their power trips. He had to realise they were in charge. That's how these things work. Break the man. Then make the man. Only the new man is a shadow of himself serving his masters.

He could hear muffled voices coming from behind the doors. As he stood taking in the scenery, his heart suddenly jumped out from his chest. The sound of three gunshots rang out, one after the other. He instantly checked himself for any holes, assuming he would be the natural recipient of any gunfire. Realising the shots had been fired from behind the door, the urge to turn and run, taking his chances against thirty odd bikers, ran through his mind. Before he could come to any agreement between his brain and his legs, the door suddenly creaked open. Out walked two bikers, one on each side holding a dead weight. As they dragged the lifeless body along the corridor, neither men acknowledged Fe at any point. It was like this sort of thing was completely normal. Nothing to see here.

"In you come Kevin" the thug instructed from inside the room. Fe instantly recognised the voice to be that of Sean, the realisation confirmed as he stepped into the large meeting room. He was shocked to see the décor in this place. It was not in tone with the sights he had seen up to this point. Expensive woods, each carved to create splendid pieces of furniture filled the room, with books of fiction lined along one of the walls in a large bookcase. The centre of the room had a hand carved table, emblazoned with the sign of the biker gang. That big Rottweiler beautifully crafted to honour the centre piece it had become. This was some serious work Fe told himself, and clearly the wealth which the gang had accumulated had been filtered to the top end of the gang. He could see Sean enjoyed the finer things in life. Expensive bottles of whiskey, cigar boxes containing large Cuban smokes. It resembled everything Fe had seen in the gangster movies from Hollywood. Maybe that was the point? Fe seeing that these guys were the real deal. Was that the point of the gun show while he had waited outside? Did those guys get out of sight and the dead weight suddenly stand up and order a Jack Daniels while he sparked a cigarette up? This world was alien to him, and at this point, anything was possible. He had to remember that.

"Ah Kevin, apologies for the wait. You know how it is. Sometimes people just forget their place in the machine." At either side of Sean sat massive male specimens of the breed he had seen littered throughout the property. These two were enormous, clearly size mattering even when it came to choosing your pet. Both dogs seemed to be ultra-obedient, but he had no doubt they would shred him to pieces with the click of a finger. Sean could see Fe sizing up the dogs.

"A real thing of beauty are they not. I heard you were a bit of a dog person. Hell, we could set you up with a puppy, for the right price." Fe looked Sean dead in the eye, clearly unimpressed by the offer.

"What do you want with me? I thought we had an agreement?" The two other members of the room, both sitting at either side of the table, did not seem impressed by Fe's blunt response.

"Now now Kevin, no need for that tone, after all, we are all good friends now. And I see you healed up pretty well. You see that Kevin, good genetics. I knew you were a strong man." Sean said laughing at his own comment, with his two cronies suddenly offering a chuckle. Fe stood silent, unimpressed by the remark.

"It appears you have not made any payments for three weeks. We agreed weekly payments did we not? This is not the start I expected from our new working relationship. Fuck Kevin, I thought you were a businessman." Fe could see the question was not a joke.

"Are you fucking serious? I have been in bed the last three weeks hanging on to my fucking life with every ounce of fight in me. The ability or even fucking thought of me collecting and dropping to you were way down my fucking list of things to do."

Fe went to continue, but Sean exploded out from his seat, launching himself over the table and tackling Fe to the ground. As he pinned himself over Fe, saliva oozed from his mouth and landed on his victim's face.

"When I tell you do to something, you fucking do it! I don't care if you have a fucking machete hanging out your arse with one of my dogs hanging off your fucking balls, you do what I fucking say when I fucking say. The only reason I haven't torched your miserable fucking existence yet is I want to see you make me rich first. Do we understand?"

Fe slowly nodded his head, as Sean continued to hold his only inches from Fe. The smell of Cuban cigars sickened Fe, but an update of his oral hygiene was surely warrant enough for a bullet in the head. As Sean got back to his feet, he dusted himself down and sat back in his chair.

"Now, where were we? Please don't make me do that again Kevin. You will find I am a very fair man. Just do as you're told and this wee enterprise of ours will go like clockwork. Now, Conner will collect the money from you Friday evening each week. And Kevin, you don't mind me calling you Kevin, do you? I know we agreed on Fe, but the ring Kevin has to it just really fucking does something for me. That's the name of your boy isn't it? Yes, I see what you did there. Keep the old family heritage as strong and traditional as you can. Good man Kevin. I never had kids of my own. Plenty of women. Oh, let me tell you there have been women. The thought of raising some little bastard however never held much appeal to me. How is your bastard Fe?"

Fe could feel the rage exploding inside him, but he held strong, knowing he was no good to his young son dead. He needed to get out of here, get home and keep his family safe. The drop with Conner was two days away. That gave him enough time to get the funds together, and stave off the war for another week.

"Well I think that concludes business for this week, but I will be in touch soon with a little job for you, so you keep yourself fit and healthy. When I hand out jobs, I expect them to be done properly."

Fe made his way back to the front of the clubhouse, with the realisation that this was now official hitting him. This was his life now. He found himself wishing for the simpler times when he and Davie would make their way to the foundry for a day's work. Even the threat of having to listen to Patrick's shit would be a welcome change to what he was now dealing with. As he stepped out on to the red ash, he realised the chaperone who had brought him here was long gone. He would have to make the return journey home on foot. His recently healed body was in for a treat.

Chapter 26

Keep calm and carry on

"You must be fucking pleased with yourself!" The words fired at Conner as he held his hand out to take hold of the bag. "What the fuck happened to you? You were a Kemlin boy Conner. You used to play fucking football with us down the Easter Park. Sleepovers at Sanny's house. And now you bring these fucking maniacs into our world. How do you think this is going to end? You think they are going to finish once they are done with me? This is never going to end. They are going to rip the arse right out this town and you my friend are the fucking catalyst behind it all. Fuck, if you had come and asked me for a fucking straightener, I would gladly have given you it. We were only fucking fifteen-year-old boys. Just wains Conner. Your fucking grown men gang of arseholes destroyed Tam while you were in jail. You knew we had to hit you back."

Conner looked Fe in the eye, that smug grin lighting up his face from ear to ear.

"You silly cunt, you think this is just about Tam, fuck Fe you are even more stupid than I thought. We are taking over here. We take over everywhere. We will consume this shite hole of a town, and when we are done, we will move on to the next. This isn't personal, you're just a casualty of war. If it wasn't so fucking easy to tax you, you would be dead already. You do realise that, don't you? You're never going to see thirty years old, I can promise that, but if you want to make sure your son does, you just keep these drops regular, and no fucking funny business. I know you are a crafty little cunt, but you will need to get up early to get passed me. I won this Fe. I won the battle... I won the war... You lost."

Fe wrestled with the thought of the hammer in the back of his jeans. He could end this right now. He could open Conner up in the middle of the street, dash home and collect his family, then get the fuck out of dodge. But the battle only becomes a fight for those he loves. His mum. He couldn't do that, it was unthinkable.

"We done?" Fe questioned, seeing no reason to continue this interaction now Conner had the money.

"We are indeed, unless you want to go for a pint and talk about old times?" Conner suggested sarcastically.

Fe made his way back to the car, turning to see Conner starting up the Harley. How did this happen? Of all the scenarios he could play over in his head, this was the last one. He needed advice, he needed help. He needed a friend.

Making his way into the kitchen, Beast got the gun ready and loaded it. "This is going to hurt" Beast advised, looking at Fe with a hint of sympathy.

"Nothing I am not used to" Fe replied, laying down on the table with his back facing the sky. As Beast ran the tattoo gun into his skin, the red-hot sensation filled Fe. It was a familiar feeling, and one which took Fe back to the good times. Thirteen years old and stopping during a tattoo session so Beast could give him a draw of a joint. The two of them laughing as they discussed the world and all the fucked-up things that made it wonderful. Beast sharing stories of memories involving acid and mushroom trips, the young Fe captivated by the life his friend had lived.

Today was different. Beast tattooed in silence, both men considering how they could get Fe out of this mess without losing any of the dear friends they shared. The usual cries Fe made when it would get too sore, followed by Beast telling him to man up, or woman up as he often added. Today Fe could not register the pain. The part of his brain offering the fight or flight logic was preoccupied with the troubles that had found him. Beast finished off the design, a half-naked woman flying on what looked like a ram with wings. It was certainly unique, and Beast was surprised that Fe had sat through the full three-hour session without taking a break.

Fe placed his shirt back on, and Beast invited him into the living room for a smoke. As they opened the doors to the room, the dogs who had been locked away pounced at Fe, delighted to see their dear friend. Fe found himself jumping nervously at this, clearly the trauma of the environment Sean had exposed him to still having an impact. Beast noticed this flinch, and reassured Fe all was ok, and he was safe here.

"I know man, I know. It's just..." Before Fe could finish, Beast walked towards him and clasped his arms around, pulling his friend in for an embrace. Through everything that had happened, Fe had tried to keep the warrior act up as much as he could. But this sign of affection from

175

Beast caused Fe to crumble in a ball of emotion. He thanked his dear friend and promised him he would not let this shit beat him!

"I know you won't Fe. This is not over yet. You are still breathing. We just need to work out how the fuck we get you out of it." Both men spent the rest of the afternoon, moving well into the evening discussing the situation. Fe taking in all Beast knew about Sean. The better he knew the enemy, the more chance he would have of defeating him. The cannabis soon turned into alcohol, and before Fe knew what time it was, he was having his car keys taken off him as Beast advised he could get them back in the morning.

"I better get going big man, she will start nipping my head when I get home." As Fe made his way along the street, merry from the alcohol levels in his body, his troubles suddenly vanished, his mind taken by thoughts of fishing and friends.

Walking into the living room of his house, his merry demeanour was about to be replaced by something a lot darker.

"Where the fuck have you been? You told me you were going to drop the money with Conner, and that was fucking eight hours ago. I thought you were dead. Have you any idea how worried I have been. I phoned everyone and nobody knew where you were. And you stagger in drunk like nothing has happened. Like the last month has all been a fucking bad dream. You selfish fucking bastard." As Fe stood taking the verbal assault from Daisy, he realised he hadn't mentioned the fact that he was going to see Beast. The military planning, conscious of every aspect when he had been high on the speed had shifted to this reckless individual bumping from pillar to post.

"What's the big fucking deal? I am home now. I don't fucking need you nipping my head every time I take a piss. I have enough fucking shit to deal with just now. You are sitting here like fuck all is going on. It's me that needs to deal with it all." Fe raged back at Daisy, who stood dumfounded by the outburst.

"Is that so Kevin, you think I am sitting in here watching TV while you deal with all this on your own. Have you any fucking idea what I have been going through. Worrying that you might never come home. Scared in case someone knocks on the door and wipes our full family out. This is no life. You promised me everything when we got together, and now you can't even look after your fucking son. How are we going to manage with another one on the way?" Daisy now in tears as she allowed herself to drop to the couch, sinking down with a wave of fear riding over her.

"What did you just say?" Fe said looking at Daisy, wondering if the drink had caused him to pick her up wrong.

"I am pregnant Kevin, you're going to be a dad, again. And the track record with our first son is hardly glittering. How are we going to manage this with two kids?" Fe, despite all that was going on, found a smile plant itself across his face. With all the bad news lately, this was good news. This was the news he needed. Another reason to fight this war!
"Are you sure?" Fe questioned again, worrying this might be some messed up tactic during an argument.

"Of course I am sure! Two months now Kevin. You are going to be a dad again. I never said anything with everything going on, but the chance of me hiding it will soon be out the window when I become the size of a beached whale!"

Fe dropped himself down beside Daisy, throwing an arm around her as he promised everything would be ok. The words simply fell on deaf ears, Daisy already resigned to the fact that life will never be the same again.

"I am going to bed Kevin, you come up when you are ready." As Fe moved in to give Daisy a kiss on the cheek, she got up and walked away before he could land it. As he picked up the sound of each footstep, his mind and body were not yet ready for bed. As he walked into the kitchen, he knocked back the kickboard at the bottom of the cupboard, exposing the blue carrier bag. As he pulled it out, placing it on the dining room table, he proceeded to pull out a large bag of speed. Since all this started over a month ago, Fe had managed to stay clean the whole time. But enough was enough. He needed stimulation. He needed to feel alive again, for as long as he could still call himself alive. As the bitter taste passed his lips, he sat back and wondered what Sean was doing right now. How does a man like that spend his evenings?

Fe allowed his mind to wonder, before suddenly hearing a knock at the door. He quickly grabbed the serrated knife from the kitchen drawer and slowly walked towards the front of the house. His heart, now beating at an unhealthy rate due to the combination of amphetamine and worry of who was on the other side of the door. He shouted out, using the most aggressive, masculine tone he could "who is it?"

The relief washed over him as the voice on the other side replied "Its Davie ya fanny, open the door. I am fucking Baltic out here!" As Fe unlocked the latch and swung the door open, his brother came towards him and landed a hug.

"Why didn't you just walk in, you know you don't need to chap my door, you're my wee brother for fuck sake!" Fe almost forgetting that times had changed. "The door was locked Fe, I tried to walk in."

Both men sat sharing a bottle of whiskey. Fe would intermittently hit the speed, with Davie indulging also. The conversation moved fast. The earlier effects from the alcohol he had shared with Beast had now worn off as the speed took over. He was alert. He was capable. He was powerful. In his mind, the proper Fe was back! Davie and he discussed the best plan of action. The reality was, despite all the help offered from Sanny and the boys, the first option Fe would run with if planning an attack would be using Davie. He could not bear the thought of having to explain to other parents how he got their son injured or worse in a war he had started. At least his mum understood the need for Davie to get involved.

"She's pregnant." Fe dropped the news out of the blue, Davie sat unsure if it was just the speed talking nonsense, or why his brother hadn't mentioned it earlier.

"Different class Fe. Even more reason to finish these bastards off then." Davie had morphed into a mini Fe. That fearless mentality would shine bright in the young man, now fully grown and every bit the man Fe was. The respect Davie had earned on the streets now matched that of a younger Fe. The brothers were a formidable pair, and not one to be taken lightly. The bold Davie having no concerns with taking on a full biker gang! Just him, Fe and a couple of grams of speed. If only it were that easy!

Chapter 27

Times, they are changing

Twenty-six years old. The age a man begins to settle down, put the party lifestyle to one side and consider starting a family. It was the next chapter of life for your average young man. However, twenty-six for Fe was one of chaos. The battle with the biker gang had not been the only thing keeping him up at night. Fe was now firmly in the grips of a speed addiction. He was drinking most days when not high on amphetamine, helping the comedown as he would tell people. He had two beautiful kids. Young Kevin, and the newest member to the fold, Darryn, should have been the catalyst to get his act together. But the dreams of summer holidays and reading bedtime stories were just a fantasy, Fe now consumed by the very thing that was supposed to fix his life. Speed had promised to be the gateway to getting out of the game quicker. Bigger profits meant a faster route to the top.

Young Kevin was now four years old and starting to realise the erratic behaviour his dad would display was not normal. The constant excuses Daisy would make for him, with young Kevin finding disappointment to be one of his biggest emotions. His father always promising the world and simply not delivering. With young Darryn looking to celebrate his third birthday in only a matter of weeks, he would no doubt soon inherit the same feelings his older brother had.

It was 1990, the start of a new decade. If ever the chance or reason to want to start again were clear, then this could be it. He could say a big Fuck you to the 80's and all the madness that came with it! Sadly, things only looked to be getting worse in the world of Kevin McAfee senior.

The payments to the biker gang were still regular, however Fe was finding himself with less and less, Sean expecting an almost set figure each week, but Fe was unable to keep up supply due to his own failings. His customers had become disillusioned by his antics. Failing to turn up. Supplying the wrong weight of product paid for. Younger competition had also entered the picture. Years ago, Fe would have blown this competitor out the water with an iron fist! But now he sat back and allowed these parasites to cut into his business.

The rise of the party drug ecstasy also hit his profits hard. The kids no longer wanted the buzz of speed, instead they pursued the euphoric ability to dance all night while telling each and everyone around how much they loved them. The infinite flow of money going through the household had long dried up, and any profit Fe was accumulating was quickly swallowed down his throat, that bitter taste reminding him each time of who he could have been.

Fe was a mess. He would vanish for days at a time without informing anyone. Arriving back in a catatonic state, fishing rods in hand, speaking gibberish as Daisy attempted to make sense of it all. He would go off to the Lochs and rivers around Scotland, filling himself with amphetamine and not sleeping for days at a time, his mind completely mashed with the effects of the drug. Daisy tried in vain to bring the old Kevin back, desperately hoping they could make the best of the situation they were in. But the autopilot life she found herself living, matched the solitude of spending days at a time on her own with the kids. Jackie attempted to help the best she could. Offering Daisy as much aid with the two kids as possible, but even she could not get through to Fe. The last three years had been hell on earth for Daisy, and she was not sure how much more she could take.

Even Conner and Sean had become disillusioned and bored with Fe. The kick they would get from tormenting this strong young man had gone. The former was replaced by an empty shell that would turn up to drop offs. When the various jibes were fired at Fe, he would simply look on in a trance. It got to the point that they just started sending a prospect to collect the money. The war with Fe was over. He was defeated. The epic battle that could have been was no more. And the moment Fe stopped paying, it would be a bullet in the head, body in a shallow grave and continue like nothing happened.

The world for those around him had also changed. Both Sanny and Butch had now become fathers, and naturally that eagerness to fight had diminished, which is natural for a father who cares for his child. They all had something to lose now, that carefree teenage spirit now truly gone. Life for Tam also looked very different. After being busted selling heroin to an undercover cop, Tam was sentenced to six years in prison. It had only been a couple of months since the sentencing, but Fe had managed to get a visit lined up to see his good friend. It was not something Fe particularly looked forward to. The relationship with Tam had been a strained one. The friend he had grown up with turned into a very different person after years on the heroin. That happy go lucky young guy who could hit the balls off the back of a bull from a hundred yards with a stone had now turned into a recluse. Painfully thin from years of self-destruction.

Just before he got the jail sentence, he and Sandra had split up. Despite being away with it ninety per cent of the time, Tam realised she was bad news. Sandra couldn't be blamed for Tam's habit; he chose to take the drugs. But she was hardly a good mentor for a fourteen-year-old boy. Tam feared that after the two had split, it had actually been her that contacted police to have him set up. The bitterness of no longer having Tam to feed her habit caused the move to rat on him. Whatever the source of the grass, none of it mattered now. He had six years to think things over and hopefully return a better character.

Fe made his way through the car park towards the entrance of the prison. Fearing the morning's intake of speed might not be enough to hold him through a full hour visit, he sprinted back to the car, reaching into the glove box and forcing another half gram down his neck. The boost was instant. He knew his tolerance for the drug was now dangerously high, and that initial high all those years ago in Risky's house was only something he could dream of. That feeling was short-lived, and the bits and pieces which held a pale similarity to that initial high were all he could hope for now.

Walking into the entrance area, Fe was met with the sight of two burly prison officers. A third officer sat behind a small metal cast desk. The floor was a hard concrete one, the prison itself very dated. Barlinnie was known as one of the most dangerous prisons in Britain. The officers did not look too dissimilar to your run of the mill police officer on the street. Official uniform with various pieces of equipment all fixed to either side of the brown belt should things get out of hand. Fe signed himself in, showing his driving licence as identification. He was then asked to step to one side as one of the officers approached him.

The anxiety within him instantly shot up, panic rising as he wondered why the officers had taken an interest in him. Fe had never been in a prison before, not as a visitor and certainly not as an inmate.

"Sir if I could ask you to empty all your pockets and place the contents into this plastic tray." The officer demanded, growling at Fe as if he had just broken the law in front of everyone.

"The fuck you want me to empty my pockets for?" Fe replied, panicking in case they had seen him hitting the speed in the car park, and the fact that he might have forgotten to remove it from his pocket. The paranoia

181

was spewing out of him, sweat running down his cheek, catching the collar of his denim shirt. He could feel the patches of perspiration form under his arm pits, faintly aware that the Brut deodorant he had used earlier was not holding up its end of the bargain.

"This is all procedure sir. Each visitor must be vetted before entry to the facility is permitted. If you are refusing to comply, then we must ask you to leave." Fe looked around the room, his brain screaming at him that everyone was looking his way. All the eyes. Every eye. Had other visitors seen him? Were they now looking at the spectacle that was Fe? He realised it had been days since he last slept. He couldn't even remember booking the visit for Tam, only the fact Daisy had stressed that morning that he had to be at the jail by two o'clock.

Once he emptied the contents of his pockets, panic set in! Where was his bus ticket? He knew he had one. He came through on a bus. It was only when he retrieved the car keys from the back pocket, followed by a glance out to the car park to see the once envied BMW sitting dirty and battered in a parking spot, did he realise he had driven himself through here. No part of his brain could recollect any moment from the journey. The car now scuffed and dented in several areas with the drink and drug driving it was accustomed to.

Fe was breathing hard, prompting the prison officer to ask him if he was ok?

"Of course I am ok. Why wouldn't I be ok? Do I not look ok? What the fuck are you trying to say like?" The prison officer looked taken aback by this outburst from Fe and asked for some assistance from a colleague.

"Is everything ok here sir?" Fe realised he was fucking things up, and he needed to calm it down. He was only here to visit. There was no need to be on edge. After all, he wasn't a criminal.

"I am fine, just nervous. Never been to a prison before, the place gives me the fear. Sorry if I made a nuisance of myself." The two guards looked at each other. "Ok sir if you just take a seat over there, we will call you when it's time to go in."

Taking a seat on the row of plastic chairs, Fe could feel his foot tap at a ferocious pace. He made it his new mission to calm the fuck down. As he took a deep breath, he forced himself to sink back into the chair. About forty minutes passed when the officer made his way over to the crowd of people, Fe included, who had now congregated in the waiting area.

"Ok if you would all like to follow me please, we will move to the secure part of the prison." The visitors were hoarded into a smaller waiting room, and each instructed again of the expectations regarding behaviour from them once inside. "No kissing, no touching. No passing of any goods across the table. Visiting will last for one hour."

They began to walk up a flight of stairs. Once at the top, they then entered a long room, tables dotted around each area. He could see a couple of vending machines, and a small area which had a collection of kid's toys. He stopped for a second as he realised some inmates here could be doing years at a time, with the only interaction from the kids they have taking place in this small area, with all the other criminals looking on.

Fe sat down on the plastic chair; his mind wondered to his own boys. It was as if history had been repeating itself. His father had two sons, and now he had two sons. His dad had been a bit of a fuck up all things considered. Fe then wondered what his kids would think of him. He knew the last few years had not been easy on the family. He blamed himself for parts of it, but how could he have foretold the return of Conner, or Sean deciding to move in on him. It was not fair in his mind. He had tried his best, and they had ruined things. This was their fault. They fucked everything. He was just a victim like everyone else in this war.

The reality was that this was all his fault. Every action has a reaction, and his reaction to every episode over the last five years had been nothing short of shocking. Why did he have to get into the speed? Things had been great back in the day. They were not millionaires, but rich in family and friends. He realised the last time he had been truly happy was the night of his twenty first birthday party. If he could just reset everything to that point and start these last five years again. That would be great. He promised himself it was time to change. When he got home, he was going to sit down with Daisy and fix everything. She deserved better than this life he was giving her. His boys deserved better. He was going to be the father they deserved. The father he knew he could be!

He fidgeted in his chair, looking around and wondering when he would get to see Tam. A door at the bottom of the room opened. Several prison officers walked out first, joining the other officers currently scattered around the room. The presence of security was strong, and Fe knew it would be an effort to try and smuggle anything in. Not that he had any intentions of doing that. As the prisoners began to filter into the room, families joined to gather as they embraced the loved ones incarcerated. Each prisoner holding their own story of why they found themselves locked behind bars. Fe finally caught sight of Tam, and he was shocked at what he saw.

"Hello Fe bro it's fucking great to see you." Tam gushed as he fired his arms around Fe's shoulders.

"Fucking hell Tam, you are looking great sir!" Fe could not believe the difference in his friend. The last time he had seen Tam, his friend was painfully thin, drug sick from withdrawing after his last hit, hunched over an old stolen bicycle. The new Tam was a different person. Standing strong, and clearly much heavier than the last time Fe had seen him.

"I have been clean for the last two months now Fe. Three fucking good meals a day, and I am training every chance I get. Enough press ups to give me that old strength back I had when I was a boy. You remember Fe."

Once the words left Tam's mouth, Fe began to cry. He had been accustomed to seeing Tam in a mess, which verified that the world had fucked up along the way, and it was ok for all of them to continue the manic lives they lived. But no, Tam was different now. He was better. Which only hit home to Fe that he too could get better. Fuck, if Tam could do it, anyone could do it he told himself. The truth was it had been the hardest two months of Tam's life. The reset of any life after years of drug abuse takes time. Even after the physical pain that comes from getting clean has passed, you then have the years of mental battles, trying to balance out the chemicals in your brain and allow yourself to be happy again. Tam was at the very start of this fight. He had a long way to go. But Tam was game for the fight. He wanted his life back. He had spent his full life around fuck ups. And he was determined not to be one of them.

"And how are you getting on Fe? I am not going to lie bro, your looking like fucking death warmed up." Tam was not wrong. Fe was a mess.

"You know how it is Tam, all the fucking shit with Conner and..." Before Fe could continue his rant on Sean and Conner, Tam intervened.

"Careful Fe, these tables are all bugged to fuck. These bastards are listening to fucking everything we say. Keep it light Fe, keep it light." Fe forgot his environment and had been close to messing things up again. They spent the remainder of the visit talking about old times. Fe found himself finding it incredibly difficult to hold his emotions in as Tam reminded him of things he had long forgotten, reminding Fe of the man he used to be. The man the full gang had loved and looked up to. That man he wished he could still call himself.

The officers called time on the visit. Tam and Fe got to their feet and went in for a final embrace.

"You look after yourself Fe, and don't be a stranger. I don't get a lot of visitors Fe, and it fucking makes my week when I see any of you, so it does." Fe promised to see his friend again soon, a promise he sincerely hoped he could keep.

As Fe made his way out to the car park, he turned to look at the massive prison behind him. The thought that hit him was he was on the good side. He could say goodbye to this place. Go home and makes things right. And that was the plan. Time to fix things with Daisy. Get home and be the husband and father they deserved. The drive home however required fuel, and that was in the form of another half gram of amphetamine down the throat, again the bitter taste hopefully being one of the last he experiences. It was time to get better.

Chapter 28

Tell me why

Fe pulled up outside the house. He was filled with hope. It had been a long time since he felt like this. He had purchased a bunch of roses from the garage on the way home. It was not even going to come close to making up for all the shit he had put Daisy through, but it was a start. As he made his way to the front door, he clenched his fist and gently knocked with his broken knuckles. Due to all the troubles the family had faced over the last few years, Fe always made sure Daisy locked the front door, keeping the keys inside it. He would chap the door and she could have a chance to see who it was before opening it. Again, not the way they wanted to live. The memories of his mum's front door always being open. With friends and family all walking in, seemed like a lifetime ago.

He wrapped his knuckles across the glass panel again, still not seeing any movement from the frosted window. As he tried the handle, the door pushed open. Strange, he thought. Fe started to recall events from that very morning. Had Daisy mentioned going anywhere today? Truth was he was so out of it this morning; he couldn't even remember dressing himself.

"Daisy, Daisy, its Kevin. I am back sweetheart. Our Tam is looking fucking great, you want to have seen him doll. And it has me thinking. Daisy… Are you in doll?" Fe walked into the kitchen, everything tidy and clean.

Fe thought to himself she must have popped round to see his mum. He then looked for a note. She always left a note if she was going somewhere. As he made his way upstairs, the thought of Tam filled his mind again. He was proud of his brother. Maybe prouder than he had ever been of him. Tam was trying, and that's all that could be expected of him.

Walking past the boy's room, he caught sight of the chest of drawers with the side drawer open. This surprised him as Daisy was always super cautious of keeping the drawers closed since young Darryn had hit his head on it only a few weeks earlier. He can remember her screaming that they would have to go to casualty, Fe reminding her that young Darryn had a head like his father, and he would be just fine. As Fe walked to the drawer, his heart sank. It was empty. It had previously been filled with all the boy's underwear. Had Daisy maybe moved things around? He pulled the second drawer open. Empty. Panic set in as a shiver ran down his spine. Every hair on his body stood to attention. He burst out the room and swung open the master bedroom. The bedroom he and Daisy had shared for years. He placed his hands on each nob of the wardrobe, praying to find all of Daisy's clothes inside. All the times she would come down and take his breath away with how good she looked. He prayed the clothes still hung there on those old wooden hangers. Fuck, he would buy her a new wardrobe full of clothes if she wanted. He was going to make everything better now. He promised!

The events since this morning began to play over in his head. He guessed he had been up for about three days now, but he couldn't be sure. Daisy had woken earlier than she normally does. She had been adamant about him going to see Tam today. The scenarios played over and over in his head. He had phoned everyone he could think of, and nobody had seen Daisy. She had not spoken to anyone. Just vanished. Fe fought with himself over that point. How does someone just vanish? The possibility of them being in trouble was not a concern. He knew if anyone had made a move on them, the decision to take all their clothes would not have been made. Fe knew this was coming. He could see how broken Daisy had been over these last couple of years. The problem was, he found his own pity and grief over the outcome of his life to be a more predominant focus, consequently yet not purposefully, neglecting the needs of Daisy and his family. It would appear that the selfish decision to focus on himself instead of those closest to him, potentially just cost him both his family and his future.

Within the hour Sanny and George had made their way round to the house, with Butch instructing he would be on his way shortly. As they walked into the living room, they found Davie and Fe nursing a bottle of whiskey.

"Fe I am so fucking sorry pal; I cannot believe she has done this to you!" George declared as he gave Fe a strong hug.

"I knew it was coming George. I have been a proper bastard to her and the kids. Fuck man, I had promised myself it was all going to change. If she had just given me another fucking chance to prove myself."

Sanny took a seat next to Davie, offering a handshake to the younger McAfee. He looked over to his broken best friend. "Have you any idea where she might have gone. Did she leave a note or anything like that?"

Fe looked outside to the swings in the back garden. "Fuck all Sanny, and I have phoned everyone I can think of. I had a few hundred pound in a shoe box under the bed. That's vanished. So, she is obviously intending to start again somewhere."

The reality was, none of the men at that table could blame Daisy for packing up and moving on with the kids. Fe had been totally out of control for the best part of three years now, and it was no life for a young family. It was a point none of the men seen any reason to mention to Fe. He was broken enough without them driving the boot in.

The men drank the night away, with the once thriving party atmosphere that was Fe's house now resembling a wake after the loss of a loved one. Gradually the men said their goodbyes, until finally Fe sat alone at the table. The empty beer cans littered the landscape around him. The notion that he sneaks off to bed and allow Daisy to clean it up in the morning flashed through his head. Then the realisation of his predicament kicked in. As he dug into his pocket, he pulled out another bag of speed. The chances of getting to sleep with all that was going on were slim. So, fuck it. Why not just keep going on to oblivion?

The door rattled around eight am. At this point Fe had emptied every cupboard in the kitchen, all the drawers in the living room and the unit in the hallway. Anything that might hold a clue to Daisy's whereabouts. Surely, she couldn't have orchestrated all this without leaving a clue. The psychosis setting in from sleep deprivation now firmly had Fe in its grip. He was talking to himself, analysing his life and the actions he had taken. The thinking in his mind now being discussed aloud.

Fe was distraught – how was he going to break the news to his mum? How was he going to tell her that her precious grandsons were gone? Jackie idolised those boys, her only grandchildren, and she had tried her hardest to give them as much love and stability as possible. Not only had he let his Daisy and the boys down, he had also let the other most important person in his life down. How could he look his mum in the face now? She would probably hate him for this and there would be no coming back from it. Fe was drowning is his own self-pity and while remorseful, was still trying to justify in his head why Daisy could at least have talked to him first and offered him another chance.

As Jackie walked into the living room, Fe failed to acknowledge her. His ramblings intensified, the frustration with the lack of results causing him to get worked up.

"Kevin!" Jackie roared after watching her son for several minutes.

Fe did not respond, instead lowering the tone in which he talked to himself. The focus now intensifying with the ongoing search.

 "Kevin!" Again, Jackie trying to grab the attention of her son. Still nothing.

The search now moving to the kitchen. As Jackie followed, she had taken enough of this. She grabbed Fe by both hands and pulled him tightly. Fe broke down as his mother held him.

"What am I going to do mam? She has taken my boys. I am left with fuck all." Jackie didn't have the answers, struggling herself to come to terms with the loss of her grandsons. She too was broken, but she had to be strong for Kevin.

They sat and discussed possible scenarios and how they planned on fixing this, with Fe reaching for another can of beer.

"Is that really wise just now Kevin? You need a clear head to deal with this son. Getting out of it is not going to help anyone. It's the reason you are in this mess in the first place. C'mon now Kevin, I need you to be strong, for both of us son." Jackie pleaded.

The pleas fell on deaf ears. Fe cracked open the can. He then excused himself to the toilet where he topped up on the amphetamine in his body. He told himself he needed to be sharp and his twisted logic told him the speed would help him do that.

Once Jackie left, Fe realised he was on his own. Sure, his family and friends would offer support when he reached out for it. But his partner, his best friend, she was gone. And she had taken the two things more important than anything else in this world. His boys. Fe just wanted to be a better dad than Billy had been to him. He now realised the opportunity for that to ever happen might just have passed. If anything, he was now worse than Billy. At least Billy managed to keep the family together until the boys were in their teenage years. Fe didn't even make primary school for his two. His father always told him how difficult it was for a man to keep a family. Fe always dismissed this as his father just not caring enough. The reality was now laid bare for all to see. Fe was simply not up to the task. Fe was a good dad. He was a great dad. He

189

just struggled to be a reliable person. And that constant chaos that followed him was something Daisy could no longer expose her kids to in the world they shared at home. Intentions and actions from Fe simply no longer matching up.

Part 3

Chapter 29
The speed of breakdown

The days turned to weeks, which then became months. Each anniversary would remind Fe of what he lost. He wondered what his kids were doing at that moment in time. Would they be thinking about him? Would they miss him? Fe had tried to make some sort of sense of it all. A reasoning as to why Daisy would do this. He would tell himself the boys were better off without him. That the new life they had would turn them into good men. Proper men. One day they might come back and see their old dad. He had been told stories of various sightings, and he would scramble to that area, high on drugs, frantically questioning the locals with pictures of his family. Once the realisation kicked in that it was another dead end, the process of self-destruction would kick in once again. That vicious cycle had become unbearable. He had pleaded with Daisy's family for an address, even just a phone number. Each time, blank. He had tried being polite, then going in all guns blazing. Every time, blank.

The people around him had also become darker. His lifelong friends had been pushed away by Fe, the sight of them reminding him of what he had lost. Instead Fe replaced them with 'fake' friends, only using Fe for the free drugs and misplaced ideas that somehow, they were now gangsters with the great Kevin McAfee. The truth could not have been any further away. The house that Fe had once shared with his family bringing too many bad memories, Fe decided to swap for a small one-bedroom flat. It was a grotty place, devoid of all the luxuries Fe had surrounding him in his old home. The thinking for Fe was easy. Anything that reminded him of what he had lost had to go. The pain too severe for him to deal with. Instead life became an existence. Pushing his body as far as he could in the hopes that he might not wake up tomorrow. The thought of killing himself scared Fe. He was a coward in that sense. But if the drugs would just stop him waking up. Stop him hurting. That was the target. That was the plan.

As Fe sat with the can of cider, chemicals racing around his body as the world faded away, he heard a crash at the back of the flat. Instinct told him to go and check what had made the noise. As he leaned over the sink in the kitchen, he could see the two figures attempting to remove the chain from his scrambler. Rage filled his body. Did these cunts not understand what he had been through? Did they think he would allow this shit to stand? Did he look zipped up the fucking back? The questions Fe posed to himself as he pulled the hickory shaft from the hall cupboard. Any plans of stealth and surprise on the enemy sat a million miles away from Fe. These bastards needed to pay, and the noise made no difference to him. He burst out the front door, dashing round the side of the building to ensure the intruders would have to run into him! As he neared the corner of the flat, a stockily built young guy with a balaclava over his head made moves towards Fe, crowbar in hand. The topless and barefoot Fe, only saving his blushes with a pair of old Levis jeans on, sprung at the enemy, missing his initial swing of the shaft by a fair bit. Clearly the days on end drinking had messed with his coordination.

The intruder swung the crowbar and cracked Fe in the corner of the head, Fe crashing to the ground. The second accomplice joined in looking over Fe, who looked out of it. Both men began to laugh. "Aye the big bad bastard Fe is not much of a hard man now, is he?" As the words landed on Fe, visions of his boys dashed around his mind. Laughter at bath time. Stories of the good-looking Mob at bedtime. The dyslexic stories he would create for his sons, littered with mistakes, but bursting with love. These memories causing a surge of fight to return to the fallen Fe. He crashed the shaft into the kneecap of the balaclava wearing thug. As the man dropped to the ground, Fe swung the bat again, smashing his victims jaw out of position....

" Aaaarrgghhh" Fe roared, raw rage filling him like the hulk. As the second intruder ran at Fe, who was still kneeling on the ground at this point, he launched himself at the attacker's right leg, sinking his teeth into him. The unorthodox attack offering great effect, as the shrieks of pain filled the air. As Fe fell back into the wall, sitting on the wet ground as it soaked into his bruised arse, the second attacker, now requiring a tetanus jab, decided to run off, leaving his comrade sprawled out on the ground, his jaw still swinging aimlessly.

As Fe slowly lifted himself to his feet, he looked down at his attacker. Any urge to offer help void, Fe instead spitting on the young man who aimed to cause him harm with that faithful crowbar. As Fe began to walk back to his flat, the noise of the sirens filled the empty streets. As the blue lights stopped outside Fe's front garden, the officers burst out the car screaming at Fe to get on the fucking ground! Fe stood in shock, struggling to understand how being potentially turned over by two robbers equated to him being the bad guy, clearly lending no thought to the broken man sprawled out, lifeless and beaten behind him. As the officer got within two feet of Fe, he swung a punch, landing it directly on Fe's temple. Fe dropped to the ground once again, the cuffs locked on to his wrists, the burning from the cold metal registering with Fe ever so slightly, yet still not enough for him to worry, instead offering a deranged laugh.

As he slumped over the back seat of the cop car, he drifted in and out of consciousness, the adrenaline that had spurned him on to fight now subsiding, his injuries taking control of his body. Arriving at the local police cells, Fe was escorted into the holding area, with the charge Sergeant looking over his desk at the topless crusader smiling at him. "How are you doing big man, busy night for you?" Fe questioning the Sergeant as if they had been friend for years. The Sergeant refused to acknowledge Fe, instead looking down at the paperwork which had held him up the best part of this shift so far. The nightshift was always a battle for officers. All the arseholes of the village making an appearance as the pubs spilled out its contents to the world.

"Name?" The Sergeant requested, glaring down at the busted inmate.

"Fe"

"Your full name ya daft cunt"

"Daft cunt? Daft cunt is it. That's not very nice now, is it?" The Sergeant looked unimpressed with Fe's questioning.

"Listen son, this can go one of two ways. You can be a good wee laddie and play the game, let me fill this form in, then fuck off to your cell before court on Monday morning. Or, we can do it the other way...and trust me son, you dinny want it the other way."

As Fe began to laugh uncontrollably, the charge Sergeant nodded to the officer behind Fe, who promptly smashed the baton into the back of the new prisoner.

As Fe lay beaten in the cell, he began to laugh at himself. This was different. This was a bit of a change, he told himself. As the lights flickered, he drifted off to sleep.

As Fe was filtered into the holding cell under the court, he was greeted by a familiar face. "How are you doing Fe, fuck me sir you have looked better. What the fuck happened to you pal?"

"How are you doing Higgy son?" Fe winking at his old friend. The memory of the battle in the Key club against the Bog boys flooding back to Fe, and the desire to be back once again like the man he was. He missed that Fe, the confident young guy, transformed into this stranger. He knew he probably should have been embarrassed by his appearance, but the reality was he could not give two fucks. If wee Higgy had an issue, he would no doubt keep it to himself, most of Kemlin now aware of how unhinged Fe had become.

"What you in for Fe? A got fucking busted for a couple of ounce. Scunnered with it sir. I was only fucking holding for a friend" said Higgy smiling at this last point as he winked at Fe. "Some fucking boy Higgy, so you are sir!"

As Fe stood in the dock, he swayed side to side, the combination of a lack of sleep mixed with the various substances that would cling on to him like a bad habit.

As the judges and lawyers discussed Fe, he stood idle. Contradictory to the stuff you see in the movies, real life crime is a mundane thing. Paperwork and whispers holding court. Fe simply an unused extra in this circus. After a few minutes, Fe's lawyer approached him. "Remanded until your intermediate diet. Sorry Kevin, I tried my best" The lawyer solemnly updated Fe of his fate. Fake empathy struggling to hold up, Fe knowing he was simply a number in this wee bastard's book. "Jumped up wee prick that he was", Fe telling himself he needed no cunt. Send me down! Let me be punished! Without warning Fe roared out at the top of his voice "We are the mob!"

Chapter 30

Throw away the key

As the beaten old wagon pulled up outside Barlinnie, Fe looked up to the sky. The weather was miserable. Intermittent rain had battered the van during the journey to Glasgow, and to the place Fe would now call home. As the fresh air stung against the cuts on Fe's broken face, drops of rain caused Fe to drift away.

"Some fucking weather for catching monster pike" Fe declared, the confused guard handcuffed to him looking on in surprise.

"Is that right captain, if you say so" The guard said hitting back, clearly disengaged with current events, and unwilling to involve himself with any form of human social interaction. As they entered the main building, the clerk signed Fe in.

"One hundred and forty day lie down?" the small ageing officer questioned, as if the answer was not in his possession before Fe even pulled into the car park.

"Apparently so big man, unless you fancy taking these bastard cuffs off and allowing me to go on my way. I might even get hame in time for a bit of Take the high road."

"I see we have a smart cunt joining us. Let's see how long that lasts. Handsome young laddies like you in there will be passed around like a fucking dirty magazine." The grin from the desk officer being shared with the handcuffed guard.

"Is that so? Well a' better make sure I don't disappoint any cunt then eh" said Fe hitting back, leaving the guard unsure of how to take the comment.

As Fe was stripped and searched, the hands that scanned him would hit damaged parts, pain shooting to Fe's brain. The drink and drugs now almost completely worn off. This was now the sober reality. However, Fe stood strong, like a battle-hardened Viking unwilling to share secrets of tactical planning with the enemy. As he was led down the corridor to the main remand hall, the thick nicotine stained walls offered a harsh faded yellow ocean of brick. The map of yellow broken up by the evenly spread battered blue steel doors, each with a hatch at the top and steel plates holding the lock. As he looked up, he could see another two flights of cells, with the top row offering a harsh row of red doors. Fe wondered why they would use different doors? Had this been the real prisoners on the top row? Would he be a small fish? A nobody? The only person he knew in the prison at this moment was Tam, and the chance of bumping into him had been slim and none. This was remand, and Tam was in a different wing with convicted prisoners. As it stood, Fe was still technically an innocent man until trial. Not that the walk to his cell would offer any indication towards this fact...

As Fe walked into his cell, he was met by a small Glasgow native glaring up at him from the bottom bunk of the metal framed bunkbed. The only other furniture holding up the room being a small table that had been carved with a thousand names. Across from the table stood a solitary chair under the steel bars leading on to the free world. Fe looked around, assessing his new environment. "Where the fuck is the toilet?" Fe observing something was missing.

"Ah we have a first timer here do we not? Behave yourself son, the only fucking toilet in this hell hole is the warden's throne. We slop out and clear a few times a day. It's nothing fucking pretty son, but you will get used to it." The old timer said, updating Fe on proceedings.

"That's you up there," said the roommate nodding to the top bunk as Fe weighed up his new co-pilot. Fe did not respond, instead lifting himself to the top bunk and lying back on the coarse sheets. This was up there with the most uncomfortable place Fe had slept, but within minutes he was asleep.

Fe would wake every so often with the noise coming from outside the cell. He had never heard anything like it. The screams, the empty threats of attack amongst prisoners. He was in the jungle. And it was every man for himself in this world. Fe could feel his stomach beginning to twist and turn. He had spent the last few months abusing opiate painkillers, and the withdrawals had begun to introduce themselves. Fe would twist and turn throughout the night, the involuntary spasms of his arms and legs causing him to kick and punch out into fresh air, the sudden movements shooting alarm to the prisoner directly under Fe.

The next day Fe was fully in the grips of an opiate withdrawal. His temperature playing games with him. Body on fire, clothes being torn from the body to offer some sort of respite, then suddenly all blankets being held tight as a cold rush swept over him, the thermometer within his body simply unable to take control. Fe refused the chance of breakfast and lunch, informing the officer he was unwell. At dinner time his co-pilot had convinced the guard to allow him to take a sandwich back to the cell for Fe.

"You need to eat son and get that fucking shite out your system. That fucking smack has a lot to answer for," said his new friend offering advice to the younger Fe.

"Am nae fucking smack head, and you will do well to remember that auld yin. And you can take that sandwich and ram it clean up your arse."

"My apologies son, although I have had a fair few bad rattle myself in the past going it cold turkey, and I can tell you, if your no a smack heed, your making some fucking impression of one!"

Fe did not have the energy to argue back. Instead turning to the wall and praying the bugs in his head would fuck off and leave him be.

For the next four days, Fe battled with the signals in his brain screaming out for more pills. The battle to regain control of his bowels, now freed from that opiate back up, paired with the need to slop out made this the worst four days of Fe's life. If someone was to offer a bolt gun to the head, Fe would smile and agree. Anything had to be better than this.

By the Friday, Fe stirred from his sleep. It had been five days of no sleep and constant pain, but he realised he must have had a few hours' sleep, as he instantly felt a million times better. As he scanned the room, he realised this was the first time in five days he had accepted he was in prison. The blur up until this point was wished away by the delirium. But this was real. As he swung his legs and dropped down to the floor to take a piss, his co-pilot called out to him.

"The names John McAvoy, but you can call me Jock. Suppose it's about time we got to know each other then eh?" As Fe turned to the small, heavily tattooed man sitting on the bed, he guessed the old boy must be pushing his late fifties, maybe even early sixties with a decent paper round. The receding grey hair exposing a couple of faded head scars. Thick glasses Jock wore, Sellotape affixed to one of the arms, reminding Fe of his own dad. Fe guessed Jock was probably a someone once upon a time. But he knew a man that age would probably struggle with this new generation of criminal, the sort who are lacking the respect and values of the previous era of gangster.

"Listen, I have been a bit fucked up the last few days. If I came across as a bit of a fanny, just ignore me. It's been a tough week" Fe said regretfully, remembering his mum didn't raise an ignorant man.

"Ah don't be fucking daft son, this place has a different effect on all of us. It's the place where fuck ups need to wake up. Fuck, half the boys in here canny even remember why they had been arrested in the first place. Full of the drink and Valium. You finally straighten up and you have five year up your arse to think about what you did. But hey, this is remand, and we are all innocent on this wing, at least until the lawyers hang us out to dry."

Fe began to laugh, realising this whole fucking circus was brought to him. He was minding his own business when they two wee bastards attempted to turn him over. What the fuck was he meant to do?

"Just do me a favour son, keep yourself to yourself until your court date. The main jail has structure and society, but these bastards in remand are feral. Nowhere more dangerous in this prison than this fucking shitehole. Trust me son."

As both men exchanged small talk, they could hear the locks opening from cell doors as the prisoners filtered out to make way for breakfast. As Fe walked out to the landing, he realised his initial blurred perception of the place upon walking in had changed. He suddenly spotted the light tiles on the floor, with the scattered blue blocks making up misplaced patterns. The other prisoners now also looked real, instead of the wall of madness that hit him when walking in, just shouting and cheering from the gaps in the steel doors. They now represented real people, with real troubles.

As Fe made his way along the landing to collect his food, he took a seat at a small round set of tables. They had been permitted to one hour per day socialising. And a couple of substandard meals a day. Scanning the room, he could see a hive of activity breaking out in each corner. Relationships between strangers being formed, along with reunions of those who regularly enjoyed a vacation at her Majesty's prison. Jock sat beside him, and immediately played out the law of the land, highlighting the known outlaws like a who's who? The cardboard warriors who would maybe chance it against Fe if they felt brave, and the real deals who would straight up rip the jaw from Fe and smile.

As both men got stuck into the porridge, a gang of young burly men walked towards the table. The leader of the gang was around six foot, arms carved to offer maximum effect for the evil bastard look he was clearly shooting for. His shaven head covered in scars and battle damage. The clean face accentuated by piercing green eyes.

"You know who I am?" The stranger fired the question at Fe, who had returned his gaze to the leftover porridge sticking to his bowl. He hadn't eaten in five days, and he would be fucked if this arsehole was going to spoil his meal, even if he was a mean looking fucker.

"None of my business pal." Fe responded as the spoon aimed into his mouth for the target.

"My name is Spider, and this is my fucking wing. You make sure that registers with you while you rattle into that shite they dare to call scran in this fucking dump."

Fe immediately began to laugh, almost choking on the porridge. "Spider? Fucking Spider? What kind of evil bastard calls their wain Spider? Fuck sake sir, no wonder you look that angry. I feel for you pal, I really fucking do." The shock of Fe's assessment caused silence to fall over the room, even the guards refused to offer any response.

"The fuck did you just say, you have no idea what I am capable of, I will..."

Before he could finish, Fe exploded: "Listen to me you silly looking bastard, you don't have the faintest fucking idea what I have been through, so if you fancy a fucking pop, take it! Fucking take it! I fucking want you to!"

As Spider looked around the room, unsure of what the fuck was actually going on, he nervously responded "You just watch your back, I am warning you!"

Fe did not respond, instead lifting his bowl in order to lick the rest of the porridge from it.

"I am taking it from that wee outburst, the porridge was not up to the standard you expected?" The question from Jock caused both men to burst into a fit of laughter. Fe lay on the top bunk; his knees straddled up as he processed everything on his mind. One hundred and forty days until trial was potentially on the cards, then fuck knows whatever else they decide to fire at him once the trial actually comes around. It could be years. He knew he had wasted that boy outside his flat. He was glad. For a moment it made him forget what he had lost. He wasn't an animal, but sometimes that animalistic behaviour allowed him to escape reality.

Escape his loss. He missed his son's. Truth be told, he missed Daisy even more. She reminded him of a time when he had control. When he had a life. She symbolised the normality that he had truly fucking blown out the water with his behaviour.

Chapter 31

A web of trouble

The message sent to Spider that day was clear, Fe was not to be fucked with. Fe knew trouble would not come for him. He was well aware when a potential threats arse had collapsed, and if Spider was top boy in this place, Fe had fuck all to worry about. The issues in his mind lay outside the prison walls. They sat inside the walls of the court, and how they would choose to deal with him. He knew a big sentence would be the death of any drug empire, not that he gave a shit. But that would give the bikers the chance to finally finish him off. He wondered if that would really be a bad thing?

It had been almost a month since Fe joined the ranks of the Bar L loyal. Today was a day all the prisoners looked forward to. That one hour when they get to feel normal as family and friends come to spend some valuable time.

"Visiting time" The warden roared as the men filtered out of the cells. As Fe made his way into the communal visiting room, he scanned for that friendly face. He felt his heart sink as he saw Sanny and George sitting at the table. The tears began to stream down his face. He had not expected this reaction. He had seen his friends a million times, but he couldn't remember the last time with a straight head.

"Fucking hell Fe, what's with the water works ya big poof", Sanny laughed, offering a comical response as the tears began to flow from him also.

"Awe I have missed you boys, that's no lie I can tell you. Fuck sake sir, how have things been?" As the group shared tales of their lives over the last month, Fe felt a warmth fall over him.

"The thing I canny work out, the thing that really bothers me, is those two bastards knew who I was. They said my name before I snapped them with that bit hickory. What cunt would be daft enough to steal my fucking bike? Surely to fuck that canny be right." As Fe looked on into the distance trying to work out the answer to that question, George turned to look at Sanny. Both men looked nervous.

"What is it?" asked Fe, noticing the expressions on his friend's faces.

"The wee cunt you lit up with the bit of wood, that's fucking Craigy from the Bog's laddie," answered Sanny, looking on solemnly as the news sunk in.

"You're fucking joking me? Why the fuck would that wee bastard have a problem with me. Fuck, me and his auld man had a scrap years ago, but it was fair game. Fuck, the cunt tried to chib me with that big fucking daft set of dusters, do you mind of that Sanny?"

"I do Fe, but apparently this wee bastard has taken exception with you laying his auld man out. He has turned seventeen and fancied a bit of retaliation. Apparently, the whole bike theft patter was just to get you out the house," said Sanny, looking at Fe as he processed this information.

"Seventeen? He is just a fucking boy. You're telling me I opened up a wain!" declared Fe, the realisation hitting him. "Is he ok?"

"Fuck that wee cunt Fe, don't you even worry about him. We are going to have a word with him and try get the charges dropped."

Fe interrupted quickly, "You don't fucking touch him, do you understand. This is my problem, and I fucking deal with it!"

As the guards began to instruct prisoners to return to the holding area, Fe stepped up and hugged it out with his old friends.

"I mean it, no cunt touches the boy"

Fe returned to his cell, and the image of the young boy laying broken and smashed on the floor hit him. It haunted him. His actions in the past now had to be answered for. A few days passed and Fe had decided to write the young man a letter. It was an open letter to him and his father, Craigy. In it he explained his life growing up, the happiness he once had and the misery that followed. It detailed how he considered himself a monster, and that he deserved everything that came his way. At the end it begged the young man that one day he might forgive Fe for the pain he caused.

As the locks of the door opened, Fe lifted his head to see what was going on. It had been over three months since his first night in Barlinnie, and the place had started to grow on him. The structure it offered had been something Fe had missed. The fresh, clear head he would wake with each day. Fe could understand why many men would become institutionalised in places like this. Once society writes you off in the outside world with criminal convictions hanging round your neck, then sometimes prison life actually offers proper society to these broken men, as fucked up as that might seem.

"You have a visitor McAfee, let's have you" ordered the guard instructing Fe to follow him, the door closing on Jock. As Fe was escorted into a small room, he was surprised to see his lawyer sitting waiting.

"The fuck are you doing here?" Fe questioned, knowing this useless bastard was his only chance of staying out of prison for the next five years!

"Kevin, I am here to tell you the charges against you have been dropped. We have some paperwork to go over, but we should have you out of here by the end of the week."

Fe looked on in shock. He had been facing a serious assault charge that the Procurator Fiscal had been pushing to change to attempted murder. How the fuck does all that just vanish? "You on the fucking noise up? Cause I am warning you, if this is some kind of sick joke, I will open you up like a burst couch."

The lawyer laughed nervously at this "No joke Mr McAfee. It would appear the main victim has written a declaration stating he intimidated you, he instigated the initial assault and he had the intentions of causing serious harm to your person. You simply defended the threat against your life, as any man would."

Fe sunk into his chair. It had been months since he had written the letter to the young boy, and at no point had he even been close to suggesting the young man change his statement. As Fe returned to his cell, the shock was still evident on his face. As he explained the update to Jock, the old man smiled. He had grown fond of Fe, and the relationship between the two blossomed.

Jock had a son once upon a time, a young lad a lot like Fe. That alpha male mindset inherited from Jock. However, the mind of his young son locked horns with Jock, and the relationship died. It had been years since he had seen his own son, but Fe reminded him of what he had lost.

"You remember Kevin, the world is going to be just as ugly as when you came in here. You need to be strong son, or me and you will no doubt have to cross paths again."

"Cheers Jock, I appreciate that pal. You look after yourself when I am gone. You promise me that!"

"Many a man has tried and failed to take auld Jock down, so don't you worry your wee cotton socks. I will be just rare."

Chapter 32

This is the end

As Fe sat on the stained couch, his eyes scanned the walls surrounding him. This was home, but it felt more dangerous than any jail cell. He had been released a few weeks earlier, and sincerely tried to make amends for all he had done. However, the solitude of nights alone, with just him and his thoughts, meant that it did not take long before the drink and drugs moved back into pole position. For all the promises a prisoner can make behind bars, the cold hard reality of the outside world, now an enemy to anyone with convictions, can sometimes be too much to defeat. Falling back into old habits is often the only route.

The supply chain of drugs coming to Fe had vanished, the months spent in prison clearly unacceptable to the dealers from Glasgow. In the eyes of these Gangsters, business was business, and the show must go on. The truth was, that even before the prison experience Fe had the pleasure of, the dealers from Glasgow had become disillusioned with Fe's erratic behaviour. In the summer of ninety-three, almost three years since Daisy left, the plug was pulled on the supply from Glasgow. This now opened a new wave of issues. The biker gang had long left him to his own devices. As long as the money continued to come, they had no reason to enter into contact with Fe. The prospects collected the profits each week. Fe had put up a futile resistance to the cut from Glasgow, but the reality was he no longer cared. The days of dealing drugs had come to an end. Now the purpose of his life would be to take them. The fact that the bikers might put a hit out on him posed no concern. Part of him wished for it. Just turn the lights off and let him go to sleep. Let him rest. He was tired. So tired.

"What do you mean there is no fucking money this week?" the biker raged at him, knowing the prospect of returning to the clubhouse without the profits would see him in bother.

"What fucking part of it did you not understand? I have lost my source. If I don't have a source, I don't have drugs. If I don't have drugs, I can't make any fucking money now can I." Fe responded, a grin etched on his face at the thought of the bikers finally experiencing a bit of stress from him. After all, these bastards had taken everything from him.

"You realise you are a fucking dead man once I go back to Conner and Sean with this. Your days are marked." The full-on threat launched at Fe, who smiled in response.

"Son, my days have been marked since the day I was born. You tell your fucking president to come at me with everything he has. I will be waiting." As Fe walked away back to his car, he wondered how they would finish him. Bullet? Maybe that gang beating he had been promised that would turn him into a pulp? It didn't matter. Nothing they could do would come close to the hurt he had experienced over the last three years.

Pulling up in the beaten-up old escort, Fe looked up to the kitchen window. The window he had spent many a happy time in. It had been a long time since Beast had spoken to Fe. The initial reach out when Daisy left to try and help his young friend had been spurned by Fe. As he rattled on the front door, he wondered what kind of reception Beast would offer. It did not take long to find out. As Beast opened the door, the shock on his face at the state of his young friend was impossible to hide. Beast was visibly shaken, and caught Fe off-guard as he lunged towards him, throwing his arms around and pulling the young man in for an embrace. Fe could not remember the last time anyone had hugged him. It had been a long time. The decision to reject everyone, to close himself behind that door of his and hit the self-destruct button, had caused him to forget the emotions that still shone a small light inside him. The light flickering to stay alive, it was still there.

"I have fucked up big man, I am so sorry." Fe realising the level of friendship he had offered over the last two years was hardly acceptable.

"Come in ya daft cunt, don't be silly. You are here now. C'mon in and we will get you cleaned up. When was the last time you had a wash Fe? You smell worse than the dogs." Beast joked, knowing the statement was not far from the truth.

"I have cut it with the K4's Beast, I didn't pay them this week. They will be coming for me. I should not have come here Beast. This is not your fight." Fe looked at his friend despairingly.

Beast stood for a moment as the details of Fe's outburst sank in, and no doubt the outcome that would arise from this.

Fe continued, "I fucking lost my source. They cunts in Glasgow said I was a mess. They cut me out Beast." Beast walked into the living room, turning down the music that had been filling the house before Fe arrived.

"Don't worry about any of that just now. Here, I've run you a bath, get yourself in it and I will see if I can find some clean clothes that'll fit you. You're staying here tonight Fe. And I am not taking no for an answer. You will need to fight me to try and get back out this house."

Fe began to laugh at the ultimatum. "Well I am not going to argue with that then am I. Look at the fucking size of you. I reckon you would ride me before you burst me."

As Fe soaked in the warm bath; a strange feeling ran over him. A feeling he had not felt for years. A feeling that the chaos of his world would not allow him to experience. He was calm. He was relaxed. He was happy. He smiled as he submerged his head under the water. As he wrapped the towel around him, Beast handed a set of clippers into the bathroom.

"Get that fucking birds' nest off your head. You look like a fucking bishop for fuck sake. And that beard as well. Captain caveman came to visit they will be saying." The short-shaved head everyone had been accustomed to seeing Fe with, the clean sharp look it offered, had been replaced by a carefree bundle of mess that perched on his head. The thick moustache which made him resemble his father had been swapped for a thick matted beard. Once Fe had cleaned up in the bathroom, he made his way into the living room again.

"Who the fuck is this stranger in my house? I have seen this guy before, long time ago mind you" Beast joked as he handed Fe a joint. "That's the only drug allowed in this house now Fe, you understand that?" Fe nodded his head, the thought of hitting the speed was the last thing on his mind.

The men spent a few hours chatting away as the dogs curled round the feet of their old friend. It had taken a few minutes for both dogs to remember Fe, the recent look he had inherited clearly catching the friendly beasts out for a moment.

Before long, Beast announced he was ready for bed. "I have set you up on the couch Fe. Plenty covers, but if you get cold during the night you come and give your big pal Beast a cuddle!" Both men roared with laughter at this comment "Good to have you back Fe." Beast did not wait for a response from this comment, leaving Fe in the living room on his own.

Fe sunk into the couch, scanning the ceiling of the property. He had the realisation that he couldn't remember the last time he had actually lay down to sleep. Recently it had been a case of hitting the speed as much as he could until his body collapsed, then waking up two days later to start again. But his body was clean tonight. Within minutes he was sleeping, and seven hours passed without any interruption. As the birds began to sing in the morning, Fe woke up and looked out the window. He wondered if he had any visitors at his flat last night. He knew he was safe in this house. They would never suspect him coming round the corner from his own property when a hit was out on his life. Nobody is that stupid!

Beast began to stir upstairs, and Fe could hear the footsteps through the ceiling. He was a big man, and any chance of anything about him being subtle was out the window. It was like a giant readying himself to come down the bean stock. As the men sat down to a morning coffee and some toast, Beast asked him what his plans were.

Fe said "I honestly don't know. Yesterday I was more than happy to let these bastards wipe me off the face of the earth. But I don't know, maybe things are worth fighting for." Beast looked at him dead in the eye with a glance Fe had never seen before. There was a serious, almost desperate look from his friend.

"Fe, they ruined my life, and it took me a long time to get back to normal. If your serious about going at these bastards, and I mean serious. None of this getting crazy with the speed. I mean straight headed. Taking our life back. I am with you."

Fe could not believe Beast was willing to go to war with the bikers with him. He had been warned in the past that this was a fight they could not win.

"Why the sudden change of heart Beast? Don't get me wrong, I am fucking made up at the fact your willing to help. But why now?" Fe had to ask the question before moving forward.

"Truth is Fe, they ruined my life, and I accepted it. But they have now ruined your life. Where does this fucking end? They are poison. Like a virus. And I have had enough." Fe nodded his head. The desperation that filled him the previous day had now lifted and was replaced by a flicker of hope. In fact, more than a flicker, with Beast at his side they might just be able to get Sean and Connor to fuck once and for all. The old Fe was back!

"You need to get stronger though Fe. That speed is going to be ripping out your system shortly. We need a few weeks to work things out and get ourselves a plan. I think if we..." Before Beast had the chance to finish his sentence, the door went.

"You expecting anyone?" Fe questioned, panic filling him that this could be it. His life suddenly meaning something to him again.

"Not expecting anyone" Beast replied as he slid the kitchen knife from the cutting block. "You wait here, if it kicks off you come and help." As Fe sat waiting in the kitchen, he could hear the front door open, the faint murmur of talking picked up from the gap in the kitchen door. No shouting. That was a good thing. Wasn't it?

Beast walked into the kitchen, the look of dread filling his face. "You have a visitor" Beast instructed. As the kitchen door slowly opened, the adrenaline was pumping round Fe's body.

"How are we doing Kevin?" Relief washed over Fe as he sprung to his feet to greet his dear friend.

"Tam! What the fuck are you doing here? When did you get out? Fucking hell you are looking great sir!" Beast began to laugh behind Fe. "And you ya big bastard, you had me fucking shitting myself there."

Beast continued to laugh. "Sorry Fe I couldn't help myself; you're fucking face though sir." The room filled with laughter as Tam explained he had been released the day before.

"I got out early for good behaviour. Apparently, I am a reformed character. Who fucking knew eh? I went to your house, but these fucking Randoms answered. Said you had moved out. Gave me your new address. Then when I couldn't find you there, I went to your mums. She told me you were in a bad way, and that you barely spoke to her anymore. I phoned a few of the boys, then worked out you might be here. Fuck sake Fe I am so sorry about Daisy and the boys. I should have been here to help you." Tam moved in as he once again hugged it out with his best friend.

"I am sorry I stopped visiting Tam, you know how it is mate. I was not in a good place." Fe dropping his head at the shame of letting his friend down.

"Don't be fucking daft Fe, we are together again now, that's all that matters." Tam reassured his friend and brother.

Fe began to explain the recent events, and Beast's agreement to help deal with the K4's while Tam sat listening intently.

"Whatever you decide to do Fe, I have your back." Tam declared wholeheartedly.

Fe looked at his friend with confusion. "You are just out the jail Tam, you canny risk going back for me!" Fe said adamantly making it clear it was his intention to do this without Tam.

"Fe, if it were not for you and your family, I probably wouldn't even fucking be here. You are my brother, and if you think you are facing these cunts without me, you are even more fucking stupid than I remember," Tam stated categorically.

"You will stay here Tam," Beast instructed. "The less traffic we have coming in and out of here the better. They'll not know who we are, who's involved or what we have planned." Tam nodded in agreement with this. "You need to phone them Fe, make contact and tell them you're going on holiday with your mam, trying to get yourself clean so you can start making them money again. Make sure they think you are sorry for what has happened, and you want to make things better. Tell them when you get back, you'll have a face to face with them. That gives us time to get you fit and healthy again." Fe nodded at this plan, realising it was the best they had.

"What about the rest of the boys?" Tam asked, wondering if they would ask the rest of the gang for help on this matter.

"I'd rather not Tam. They are all good men, but they have their own lives now. I have fucked up one family already, I don't want to be responsible for fucking up another. Our Davie will be on side. The four of us just need to work out the best way to hit these bastards. And hit them fucking hard!" Fe could feel the life he once had filling him again. The dead shell he had been for the last three years was slowly coming to life! Fe was coming back!

"You should use the phone box on Wall Street. We don't want to phone them from a landline in case they trace it" Tam suggested, knowing the dangers that awaited them had been very real. "You want me to come up with you?"

Fe smiled at the offer from his old friend. "It's fine Tam, I will be fine. I am only nipping out to straighten things up then I will be right back!" The assurance from Fe was delivered to both men, but the worry filling the room could be tasted and was clear to see.

Chapter 33

The job

Fe stepped into the small phone box. He could smell the stale piss from where someone had no doubt showered the place on an earlier visit. "Dirty bastards" he told himself as he wiped the phone along his denim jeans, not realising the irony of his thoughts and actions in that Beast had just forced him to have a bath for being a dirty bastard and committing a similar offence. The smashed windows on either side of the phone box reduced the privacy available for the call. Not that it mattered. He didn't plan to be on the phone long. He had a direct line to Sean. He realised while typing the numbers in that he had not actually spoken to Sean for several years now. A couple of rings played out before the line went live at the other end.

"Hello, is that you Sean? It's Fe here." The silence felt like a lifetime before the user at the other end began to talk.

"Afraid not Fe, this is Conner. Sean is out visiting a family friend just now. In fact, you might know her. She lives in Kemlin. Goes by the name of Jackie." As the words rang through his head, the phone dropped, now left swinging at his knees. The graffiti covering the walls of the phone box now blurring over as Fe swayed from side to side.

The door of the phone box burst open as he launched into a sprint, bolting down the street as the destination of his mother's house now became the most important journey he would ever make. All those times he had been running home at night when the streetlights came on, his mum always telling him the lamppost was his alarm clock. As he pulled up outside the small archway leading into the front garden, he noticed the two Harley Davidsons sitting in the cul-de-sac across the road, previously obscured by houses as he entered the street. As he made his way along the path, the sight waiting for him on the other side of that front door filled him with dread.

Pulling on the handle of the front door, he slowly walked into the property. He could see almost instantly that the big pair of leather boots had been poking into sight from the kitchen. He slowly walked into the room to find his mum sitting at the table, Sean sitting on her left with a burly prospect sitting on her right. Jackie looked terrified, the cups of coffee sitting in front of each individual offering a false sense of normality.

"Have they hurt you mam?" Fe blurted out in desperation wanting to take his mother as far away from this fucked up scenario as possible.

"C'mon Kevin, are you not going to say hello to your old friend. It has been a while." Sean was grinning arrogantly, smug with the control he had over the situation. Fe refused to drop the gaze he had on his mum.

"Have they hurt you mam?" Fe repeated his earlier question.

"She is fine Kevin, for fuck sake. What do you take me for? We are not animals. Your mum just made us a coffee. We were about to get the baby photos of you out, but hey you're here to join us now!" Sean continued "Now mummy here, you don't mind me calling you mummy, do you? Mummy here was blissfully unaware of the little arrangement we had in place Kevin. The arrangement you have suddenly decided to stop honouring. Not good Kevin, not good."

"They have cut me off. I don't have any way of getting it in, so I have fuck all to sell. What do you want me to do? I explained all this to your boy when we met." Fe pleading to Sean in an attempt to calm the situation down.

"Yes, he did tell me you found the whole situation quite funny. I must admit, not the reaction I would expect from you. But it would appear we are both different people from the men who shook all those years ago. You have been a nice little earner for me Kevin, tell me, how am I meant to keep going without that?"

"I will do whatever you need me to do, just don't hurt my mum!" Fe said, pleading for the safety of his mother. "You can do whatever the fuck you want to me, but she is a good woman. Please." The desperation in his voice now impossible to measure. Tears started rolling down his cheek at the prospect of these bastards causing harm to the first woman he ever loved!

"Well Kevin there is no reason for anyone to get hurt, certainly not as long as you do what I ask of you. And remember Kevin, my patience with you is running thin. I have been a very fair man to you over the years, but you just keep letting me down. What will it take for you to learn your lesson?" As the final word left Sean's mouth, he slammed a punch into Jackie's jaw.

"NO!" Fe roared as he leapt towards the enemy. His advances brought to an abrupt end as the prospect pushed the handgun into his gut, making clear that the next move will be the end of him. As Jackie lay unconscious on the floor, Sean sat back in his chair, taking a drink from the cup.

"I will tell you what Kevin, your mummy makes some cup of coffee, don't you mummy, a grand cup so it is!"

Fe looked him with deathly eyes. "What do you want from me?" The look on Sean's face turned as the discussion now moved to serious business.

"Kevin, I am hoping I have made my point here today, I wouldn't like to ever have to come back and pay Mummy here a visit. I honestly don't think it would end well for anyone. So, here is my plan. Here is what I want from you. The McDonalds."

The name ran through his head. Fe knew Sean did not have to say anything else. He knew exactly where this was going. "I hear you have a bit of history with the dear McDonalds. Well, I have had my eye on their little heroin empire for a while now. They have made quite the name for themselves. But the thought of me losing good men over it. No, I am afraid that doesn't sit well with me. So, here is what's going to happen. You are going to take them out. You are going to take over the business they kindly hand over. And Kevin, you will not fuck this up. Your chances have run out. I want that heroin run. I want that business. You really want to deliver Kevin. I cannot stress that enough. If I wipe your family out of the picture. I make you live every day with that on your conscience, and trust me Kevin, that will kill you before any bullet does."

Once Sean got to his feet, the prospect dropped the gun from Fe and placed it back in his waistband. "You have one-week Kevin. And remember, I have eyes fucking everywhere."

As the front door closed, Fe dashed to his mum, lifting her in his arms as he sat on his knees cradling her. He could see she was beginning to come round. "I am so sorry mam, I never meant any of this to happen." The surprise from Fe from her response confirmed in Fe's mind the next step.

"It's good to have you home Kevin, it's been a long time since I saw those eyes. My boy is back."

Both mother and son began to cry, holding each other tightly as they remained on the kitchen floor. Fe called Beast, who made his way round to Jackie's house with Tam.

"Well that didn't exactly go to plan" Beast declared as he placed the milk into the coffee for Jackie. As he turned to hand the cups out, he could see Jackie at the table, Fe and Tam on either side of her.

"This is a great day. I have my boys back. It has been too long boys. It's time to screw the nut. Enough of this shite you are both involved with." Jackie glared at both of her sons.

Fe looked puzzled as he turned to his mum. "You did just see the big bad bikers in here a couple of minutes ago, I didn't imagine that did I?"

Jackie smiled. "I saw them Kevin, but I also see you. My boy is back. You have been lost for years. But your back. You will fix this. You always fix the problems in this family. I trust you son." Fe gave out a breath as his eyes widened. The expectations from his mum simple enough. If only….

"What are you thinking then Fe? The McDonalds are not fucking mugs anymore." Tam pointed out with a frank expression on his face.

"You best go and fill your pockets with stones Tam, we are going to fucking need them!"

Chapter 34

Old enemy

The exterior of the property was the victim of years of neglect. Two old cars, both stripped and mutilated for parts, obstructed the view to the rear of the building, with a busted old shed perched on the hill in the back garden. Behind the back garden ran the Forth and Clyde canal. The lack of objects or cover made a rear entry attack almost impossible. Unless they planned on lifting the shed and carefully placing it down every time someone looked that way, mirroring something from an old Tom and Jerry sketch, the only option would be head on at the front door. The windows had been blackened out, and any trade usually ran from a side door of the building, via the way of a hatch. The door was fully loaded for protection. If the authorities had any designs on raiding the place, they would need a tank to get through. The steady stream of junkies filing into the garden and leaving with the freshly scored poison secured in the pockets of a tattered outfit, leaving the McDonalds a tenner richer than before.

They sat in the badly beaten old escort, the car giving the impression this was just another junkie waiting to score. Fe realised the McDonalds must have been raking it in. The brazen fact they were dealing right from the comfort of their home told Fe they probably had an agreement with a few senior police officers. No doubt a back hander each week to keep any official police interest away from them. Or a pair of police informers, grassing on other dealers to allow them to monopolise the market and stay in business themselves. Fe knew the depths these two would stoop to. The old legacy of a gangster code was alien to these two thugs.

"Fuck me Fe, I remember the days you used to drive around in a big BMW. Fucking changed days my brother. This thing smells like a gang of junkies had a fucking gang bang in the back of it!" Tam said laughing at his own comparison.

"Thanks for that Tam" Fe replied, grinning at his friend. It was good to have the old Tam back. It was good to have a friend again. Fe could feel the pull of speed which had given solace to his mind and body for such a long time screaming out for a top up. He had taken a Valium when he woke up earlier, helping to take the edge off things. He had promised

Beast and his Mum that he was finished with the speed, and he intended to stick to that.

"Right Tam, you are up!" Fe directed, advising Tam it was time for him to do his thing.

As he stepped out of the car, his fresh clothes and sharp look offered no clue of a man looking to score some heroin. As Beast sat back in the passenger seat, eyes fixed on Tam, he sparked up a fag. The thought of smoking a joint before battle was not one that held much appeal. So, it was cigarettes only for the foreseeable future, the length of which could be determined by the end of the day if the McDonalds had their way! As Tam walked past the old cars, he turned back to glance at the battered escort. With a nod of the head, he disappeared out of sight.

The bang on the steal door rang out as Tam stood, anxious at the thought of buying heroin for the first time in years. He had been selling his own stuff before the prison, but the product always came from the McDonalds. The battles and sides of childhood mattered not to a junkie. The McDonalds took immense pleasure in Tam's misery. As several moments passed, the small hatch on the door eventually opened.

"How much you after?" the growling tone from the other side of the door asked.

"I need bulk, looking to start punting again with the twin's permission. I need a meet. And it needs to be today." Tam made the request as calmly and confidently as possible despite feeling understandably apprehensive. The dealer on the other side of the door fired back at Tam with a response Tam was not hoping for.

"The twins only see people on appointment. What's your name?" Clearly the monkey at the other side of the door was a new guy and recruited during the three-year holiday Tam had been enjoying on behalf of her majesty.

"Tell them it's Tam." A few minutes passed before Tam could hear the series of bolts unlocking on the other side. Tam adjusted the blade tucked tightly into the back of his corduroy trousers. The man behind the door was short and stout. His arms thick, with a once youthful face looking tired. Tam guessed he was around thirty years old, and probably better utilised as muscle than being a glorified receptionist. Wearing an old Scotland top, his look told Tam he was disillusioned with life on the door. It was a thankless task, and hardly the glamour the world of a gangster would expect. Dealing with junkies through a hatch each day, smelling the putrid breath from a rotten mouth full of teeth.

"I need to search you first!" the monkey declared. As Tam raised his arms, he realised turning up armed to one the biggest dealers in the town was not the best way to kick things off.

As the doorman ran his hands down the inside of Tam's leg, Tam began "Fucking sin what they did to the last boy they had on this door." The doorman stopped in his tracks, as his head tilted to look Tam in the eye, the distraction working.

"Fucking four years the cunt was on here. Then they get busted, and he takes the hit for it all. Fucking ten years up his arse. Poor cunt only wanted to provide for his family. But hey, at least they will be looking after you properly. Surely they don't want anything like that happening again."

The dealer got to his feet, stopping the full body search prematurely. "You coming the cunt, or is that the truth?"

Tam grimaced his face "Fuck sir, do I look like the kind of cunt that wants to lie about the two biggest gangsters in Falkirk. Not me. I'm just here to get a start. I meant nothing with what I said. Just forget it." The doorstep dealer nodded as he gestured for Tam to follow him. The full body search had stopped just shy of the blade.

Making their way through the hallway, the smell of Cannabis was overwhelming. Tam noticed a door left open which led to a room that housed a small forest of plants growing, as well as the various paraphernalia used to create a crop all doing the job. Further ahead was the door leading to the living room. He had been here years ago and remembered the layout of the property. The door was bashed and beaten, holes covering most of it. No doubt from fits of rage from the two fucking McDonald lunatics.

Walking into the living room, he could see not much had changed over the years. The beaten-up chairs and couch remained in place, with the walls covered in different liquids splattered over recent times. An alcohol stained carpet sat battered under his feet. It was clear whatever the McDonald's were spending their money on, it wasn't the fucking house!

"They really were a pair of black bastards" Tam told himself. Tam was surprised by the number of bodies in the room. He could see the twins sitting at a table next to the window, with two strangers joining them. The rest of the room filled with empty beer cans. Tam imagined an operation this big would warrant vast numbers of soldiers. The head count of five in the property surprised him. Unless they had a room of men hidden somewhere, ready to attack. He wouldn't put it past the McDonalds. You don't get to the top of your game by being soft, that's for sure!

"Ah Tam, they told me you were getting out shortly." Clearly the many contacts the brothers had in the prison system were feeding them intel from behind bars. "You are looking well. I wonder how long that will last once you start pumping that fucking shite back in your body. Once a junkie always a junkie, eh Tam." The level of respect they had for Tam was well below the expected mark. The twins had not aged well. Years of abusing their body with alcohol and junk food had left them bloated and pale. Both men had enough designer gear on to look the part. The jewellery hanging off both like trophies of the victory over other dealers who dare step up to them.

"I am not here for a score" Tam replied, with both brothers lifting up in the seats housing their mass of weight.

"Is that so Tam, and what are you here for then?" Barry McDonald questioned.

"Fe is looking for a meet with you both, today. He promises your safety in return for a meet." The twins looking at each other before bursting into collective laughter.

"That junkie bastard is promising us safety. Fuck me I have heard it all now. What is it? He thinks we have Daisy locked up in the cupboard?" Stevie McDonald's outburst causing the room to fill with hysterics, Tam remaining straight faced. "Oh fuck, you are actually being serious. And what does he want with us then Tam?"

Tam looked at both brothers, conviction in his eyes as he tried to sell the prospect of a meet. "He didn't say. The only thing I know is both firms are in grave danger if we don't react."

The laughter in the room vanished, as the twins looked at each other, without exchanging words. As if a deep bond shared by the twins gave them an advantage over anyone looking into their world.

"When and where would this proposed meet take place then Tam?" asked Barry.

Tam suggested the meet take place in two hours at the sluice area on the canal, both brothers again turned to each other.

219

"No cars. We would need to walk a fair bit to get there. Only an old dirt footpath. Out of sight except your occasional dog walker. If you planned on hitting us, that would be a fucking mighty fine place to do it. Would you not agree Tam?" Barry indicated making it clear they were not that fucking naive.

Tam looked both men in the eye, the point he was about to make hopefully making the difference with any decision made.

"If I wanted to hit you, I could have wiped one of you out when I walked through that door." Tam responded, gesturing to the beaten-up door as he pulled the large blade from the back of his trousers. "Not bad for a dirty wee junkie eh? We don't want to attack. We want to talk." Both brothers threw a snarling glance at the doorman who had failed miserably to do his job by disarming any potential threats. No doubt he would be dealt with later.

"You have your meet Tam, but we fucking warn you, any fucking funny business and you cunts will be blown away. Now get the fuck out this house before we change our mind."

As Tam made his way to the door to leave the property, the defeated doorman nodded his head at him. "Well played ya cunt."

Tam smiled and nodded his head as he made his way to the world waiting for him. As he jumped into the car, Fe started the engine and took off. "We are on" Tam declared; a smile etched over his face having achieved the first victory in this forthcoming complex battle.

Chapter 35

The meet

Fe stood anxiously, dust kicking up in the air as he skimmed his sambas across the ground. "What time is it now Tam?" Fe asked for the tenth time in a matter of minutes.

The McDonalds were supposed to be there forty minutes ago, and Fe feared they had changed their mind on the meet in this secluded area. The truth was, if anyone had asked him for such a crazy meet, he would have laughed in their face.

"Look," Beast declared, as the sight of a group of men appeared in the distance. It was too far to make out if it was who they were expecting, but the chances of a separate group of seven burly men turning up at the same chosen venue at this point in time was unlikely.

Fe had chosen this spot for a reason. Once in place the chance of a quick retreat was impossible. You couldn't get cars up here. And any unwelcome guests would be spotted a mile off. As the McDonalds got closer, Beast confirmed the head count as seven.

"I thought you said they only had five Tam?" Fe said looking at Tam with a puzzled expression.

"They did only have five, but I am sure a mob like this can muster up another couple of boys no bother. Fuck sake Fe, you do know who we are dealing with here. You do realise how hard this is going to be!" Tam looked on at Fe, catching a smile light up his face. It reminded Tam of the deranged prisoners he had seen during the prison riot. The smile had Tam on edge. It had been a long time since he had seen Fe, and he wasn't quite sure what his friend was now capable of, but he was now about to find out!

As the McDonalds got to within about thirty feet, Fe readied the blade in the back of his denim jeans. The battle that had been building since they were eleven years old was potentially only moments away.

"Well Fe I must admit, your looking better since the last time I saw you. Fuck, that day we passed you in the car I was half expecting you to try and stop us and ask for spare change. It looks like our old foe might just be back to his best." The laughter lingered between the seven men as the task of belittling Fe started immediately.

"And I see you are still a pair of fat ugly bastards. I suppose some things don't get better with age. Pity that eh." The reply from Fe causing both brothers to turn red, the group of men behind them fighting to hold in their laughter.

"Still a fucking cheeky bastard I see. So, you want to tell us why we are in the middle of fucking nowhere talking to two junkies and a fat fucking tattooist. Hardly the fucking squad you are used to Fe is it? Sorry we have not been formally introduced before. Its Beast isn't it? See Fe, we did our research, and we knew the only cunt still willing to entertain your pish was these two fucking bums." As the less than flattering remark landed at Beast, the big man stepped forward, eyes locked on Barry.

"You fancy coming ahead for a straightener then, just me and you. We'll see who the fucking bum is?" All eyes moved to Barry, who appeared uncomfortable and awkward in his demeanour, clearly a call out from Beast wasn't something he relished. Fe could not control the smirk that appeared on his face, clearly impressed that his old friend had not lost any of his fight and bravado.

"Tell me why we shouldn't open every single one of you cunts up right now?" Barry hit back, as the machete tucked away in his jacket suddenly made an appearance. The other men behind him now using this as their call to expose the weapons they had. Various knives and bats showing they were more than ready for a battle.

"I was sent here to turn you cunts over by the K4 Rottweilers. You heard of them?" The brothers looked at each other, with Stevie then returning his attention to Fe.

"We knew you had been working with them, a few years back one of our boys got us up to speed. What the fuck do they want with us?" Stevie asked in genuine surprise.

"They are looking to take over everything you have, control the heroin coming in and out of Falkirk. These guys are the real deal. I had been paying them each week to keep the peace. But I lost my supply of speed coming in, so now I am not worth the shit on their shoes. They guessed I could prove my worth by doing their dirty work and turning you cunts over. Save any blood being lost by their own men."

Both twins looking concerned at this news. "And you fucking reckon you and the two musketeers beside you are fucking capable of that. Fuck sake Fe you must be off your fucking head. You cunts are going to get buried where you stand, how does that sound?" Steve grinned sardonically.

"If we wanted a fight do you think I would be standing here sharing fucking small talk with you two ugly fuckers? Look, I know you fucking hate us. That's a given. The amount of shit we have fired at each other over the years. It goes without saying I would love to drill a fucking axe right through each of your fat heads right at this minute. But what will that achieve? If I smash you boys up today, and hand them the keys to your empire, I am still a fucking dead man. They will have no need for me after that. And if you boys smash us up and walk away from here, I promise you by the end of the week you will be joining us in the dark corners of hell. You cannot win against these people. At least not without someone who understands their structure. Understands the layout of business model they have." The McDonalds looked at each other, that non-verbal communication again coming into effect, while Fe and his men waited, carefully scanning the opposition for any moves.

"So, what is it you have in mind then Fe? Surely you are not expecting us to join sides with you. The McDonalds and Fe's fucking merry men, now that would be a headline." The cronies around Barry all began to laugh, but the expression on Fe's face was deadly serious.

"That's exactly what I am suggesting. They gave me a week from yesterday to turn you cunts over. That gives us a week to work a plan to hit these bastards, end this once and for all and take our town back. I am done with the drugs, so you are welcome to the speed and cannabis world when this is over. That lets you expand into a bigger market, with fucking zero resistance. What do you think?" The proposition from Fe now becoming very real. Silence fell over the group of men, as the gears in the collective McDonald minds went to work.

"I want your assurance that this isn't a fucking set up. You are a man of your word Fe, so you fucking give me that, and we have a deal." As Barry looked at his brother, who nodded the head in agreement, Fe began to walk over.

"You have my word boys. All I have said is true. I just want my family back. I just want my life back." As both groups shook on it, Beast stepped forward, the mass of the man causing the McDonalds to step back a couple of feet, just in case he was ready to attack.

"I have one thing to add. Their leader, Sean. He belongs to me. Nobody touches him. We wipe these bastards out, but he's mine." Beast made his intentions very clear to everyone to ensure there was no interference when he finally gave Sean what he deserved.

Barry and Stevie both began to laugh at the request. "Whatever you want big guy, you just make sure you keep your attack on the right team." Fe nodded at this request, knowing Beast had more reason than anyone here to want Sean. That was the spoils of war for Beast. Fe knew how Beast felt and had the same sentiments towards Conner. He wanted to be the one who drove that blade deep in his back. That piece of shit who had brought all this trouble to them, he was a fucking dead man!

"We will be in touch over the next couple of days. You get as many good men as you can. They have about thirty strong behind them, so this won't be easy. We will meet up to go over layout of the compound, access points and what we do once inside. This needs to stay between the men standing in front of us just now. If they get wind of any sort of fucking ambush, they will wipe us all out before we have time to shake it. Sean is a smart bastard, and this is not his first war. He will be half expecting something like this." As the group of men took in Fe's comments, the collective nods sent a message of confirmation.

The McDonalds turned and walked away, with Fe and his men sitting down next to the water. Once the McDonalds were out of sight, Tam looked at Fe with concern filling his face.

"You reckon we can trust them Fe?" Beast was also now looking at Fe for guidance.

"I don't think we have a choice Tam." Fe stated with all honesty.

Once they returned to the flat Beast called home, Fe relaxed into the sofa as Lola and Loki swarmed him. Both dogs jumping all over him, the smile planted firmly on his face. Tam settled down with a cup of tea, as Beast rolled a joint for the men to share. As they smoked their way through the best part of a quarter, the three men shared memories from the past. Tam explaining to the guys what his time in prison had been like, with Beast offering a comparison with his. Both men had spent time in Barlinnie, and the long serving prisoners they had both met inside turned out to be mutual friends. Their world was a small world. By ten o'clock they had all settled, the various containers of food that had been attacked after the munchies kicked in, now empty as they lay strewn around the room. The men all forgetting the impending war coming up as they laughed the night away at the adventures of Cheech and Chong.

Fe knew he could relax as his mum was safely resting at her sister's house. Fe had instructed her and Davie to move out until all this was over. That night Fe slept almost ten hours, the regeneration of his body well under way.

Chapter 36

War

"It's on!" The words passing down the line as Sean smiled at the other end.

"Well done Kevin, I must admit, I had my doubts about you son. But it looks like you have a bit more of that good stuff left in you than I first thought. We might just have use for you after all of this." Fe gripped the phone inside the piss stained phone box. The scent that had previously made him grimace had now faded to a gentle reminder of the good people in this community.

"I am going to need help. They have at least twelve men, and I only have four. You need to send me at least seven good men. There is no point me going on a fucking suicide mission. Trust me, these guys are making a fucking fortune. I scoped out their house. The traffic going through that place is frightening. This will be a game changer for us." Fe now firmly giving the impression he was one of the gang.

"You remember any point during our conversation where I offered you manpower? I must have forgot that part Fe, as I was pretty fucking sure I told you to get this done within the week." Sean commanded, clearly not happy with the suggestion that his men would have to get involved.

"The reality is, I go in with four men, and we're all fucking dead. Then you are going to have to send your men in anyway, and by this point they will be waiting for you. No doubt increasing their numbers, making the task that much fucking harder than it had to be. You know what I am saying makes sense!" Fe knew even Sean wasn't stupid or stubborn enough not to recognise the truth in his argument.

The line at the other end sat silent for a few moments. "Five men! And I mean it Fe; I want that fucking set up for myself. You better deliver it, or I will hunt your wife and children down and execute them where they stand." Sean snarled, the comment causing Fe to grip on to the phone as if he were attempting to crush it in his bare hands.

"I understand" Fe replied through gritted teeth.

"So, when are you hitting them?" Sean queried.

"We thought Saturday night would be the best time. They'll all be out of it. They don't do drugs, but they are big drinkers, and Rangers are playing that day, so no doubt they will be full of it after the game. It makes the job of turning them over that bit fucking easier. What do you think?" asked Fe as he outlined his proposal.

"You are starting to think like a proper leader now Kevin. It's a shame you didn't have a bit more self-control, you could have been a powerful man, instead of the fuck up that is already taking up too much of my time. My boys will be with you Saturday at eight pm, how does that sound?" Sean said, sounding as if he was now becoming bored with the interaction.

"Eight pm is perfect. Tell them to get me outside my flat. My boys will be waiting, and I think..." but before Fe could finish, the line went dead. "Fucking prick of a man" Fe said aloud as he placed the phone down and turned to leave the phone box. Outside Beast, Tam and Davie all sat in the car, watching the episode from the comfort of the vehicle.

"We're on! Eight pm this Saturday. He's agreed five boys for the fight, which means we have five less men to run through when we hit them." Fe said, happy with his idea of splitting up Sean's gang. Divide and conquer he told himself. The rest of the guys smiled, finally a bit of good news in a world which seemed destined to only share bad. Everything was going according to plan.

Saturday night arrived as the men stood in the car park behind the local junior football ground. They had fourteen men in total. The McDonalds had turned up with ten, along with Fe, Beast, Tam and Davie taking the total to fourteen.

"And how many men you reckon they will have Fe?" Barry shouted out, with all heads turning to Fe.

"I reckon about thirty in total. Minus the five who will be standing outside my flat like spare pricks until the penny drops. So, we just need to make sure we get the job done before they return. Sounds simple enough, eh." Fe quipped light heartedly.

Barry looked at Stevie and laughed "And you had to decide to pick on this crazy bastard all those years ago, I fucking told you he was worth the wide swerve." Fe began to laugh at this. After years of a very public civil war, the locals had put their differences to one side to take on the outside enemy looking to destroy the place they loved.

227

The men filled the air with small talk, when suddenly a car pulled into the car park.

"You expecting anyone Fe?" Barry shouted over.

"Not me Barry" The reply from Fe posing more questions than answers. As the car parked up, Fe felt his heart kick that little bit harder as he gulped down his shock.

"What the fuck are you doing here?" Fe declared in astonishment, looking at the three men joining the party.

"You didn't think we would let you cunts go to the dance without us, did you?" Sanny began to laugh, as Butch and George stepped out of the car.

"How did you even know?" Fe replied, still shocked to see his best friends.

"You know your Davie cannot keep his fucking mouth shut" All heads now turning to Davie, who offered an embarrassed grin.

"Sorry Fe, but they would never forgive me if anything happened to you and they hadn't had the chance to help." Fe smiled at Davie's frank admission.

"Boys, these bastards are not going to go down without a fight, and you all have families at home waiting for you." Fe pleaded hoping he could convince the men to think twice and return home. The thought of losing more loved ones than necessary was simply too much for Fe to process.

George stepped forward. "Fe, you promised us a proper fucking war when we were sixteen. That big return battle with the skinheads. Well that never happened. Then the talk when we had been drunk was always about smashing fuck out the McDonalds one last time. Well it looks like there is more chance of us getting our hole from the McDonalds now than getting a fight. We are all fucking best pals after all. So, the way I see it Fe, you fucking owe us a good scrap." Both camps began to laugh at this point, with Stevie McDonald walking up and shaking George's hand.

"Well how the fuck can I argue with that" Fe replied, the smile cemented on his face. "Right boys, that's almost half seven. Time to get our game face on."

As the gangs split into separate vehicles, Fe joined Beast, Davie and Tam inside the Ford Sierra they had borrowed off his aunty earlier that day. Every vehicle was clean, they did not want any possibility of the bikers catching wind of their plan and offering early resistance. As they made their way over the bridge at Lock sixteen, Fe looked back at the place he had grown up in. He prayed that he would once again return to these streets. He would be thirty years old next week and saw that as the perfect age to start again. He just needed that chance to be the man he once was. The man he should have been. Just one more chance.

They passed the college on the left-hand side of them, with Fe catching sight of the five bikers heading in the opposite direction. Any concern he had previously harboured of Sean disbelieving them was now out the window. The plan was falling into place. As the men all pulled up round the corner from the pavilion, they parked the cars and huddled by the bus shelter on the right-hand side of the road. If anyone were to look, it would just appear as a large group of friends waiting to catch the bus. Maybe for a stag do or some other group event. They could see the clubhouse ahead, and the two guards stood at the front gate. The saving grace for them had been the fact that most of the other bikers must be inside. The heavy rain pouring down upon them made the prospect of standing outside an unwelcoming one.

"Right Tam and Davie, you know the plan. On you go." Fe said ordering his two men to kick off proceedings. As both men began to stagger up the road, the attention of the two guards became fixed on them. Both men bouncing off the walls and hedgerows as balance became the biggest fight. A pretentious argument broke out between the two, and when only feet away from the two guards, Tam turned and smashed his fist into Davie's head. Davie dropped to the ground but staggered back to his feet and proceeded to kick Tam up the arse, the half-hearted attempt by these two drunken bums offering more of a comedy show than any threat.

The two guards began to laugh, but realised they had to get these drunken idiots away from the front of the clubhouse. Any unwanted attention could cause problems for the gang and the illegal activities taking place behind closed doors.

"Right you two jakey bastards, away with you. Take your fucking shite to the next street along before we flatten the both off you." The clear threat from the biker falling on deaf ears as Tam and Davie continued to grapple. As the two guards got closer, Tam and Davie suddenly pounced at them, each holding the selected biker in a headlock, squeezing until the life drained out of them.

The bikers, who were taken off guard by the attack offered little resistance, the strength of grip making it almost impossible to fend off. Clearly the work outs Tam had punished himself with during his time incarcerated had paid off! Once the conscious state of each man had been left behind, they picked them up and discarded them in the row of small bushes working in front of the larger ones.

"Right let's go!" Tam gestured quietly. The small army of men chased along the street, holding form as close to the side as possible to avoid detection, they finally stood in front of the mesh gate. Fe gripped the bolted lock and pulled until the gate sprung free from its restraint. The McDonalds pushed it open as the group of men filtered into the wet ash car park. It was a miserable night, and Fe was glad the last fight he might ever have was at least inside! As the men stood outside the double doors leading into the clubhouse, they could here that repetitive thrashing of heavy metal spew from the seams of the door.

"Fucking hell, they deserve to die just for their fucking taste in music" Sanny joked, the calm head the big man always displayed forever present.

Fe knew the dogs would all be in the kennels at this time of the night. The kennels had been situated at the back of the building. That was one less thing to worry about. Fe would have had more concern hurting a dog than he would a human.

Fe looked around, realising his life had come full circle. Tam, Sanny, Butch, George and Davie all standing side by side ready to do battle. The promises of young boys as they played cowboys and Indians, vowing to always stand by each other whatever happens in life was now being put to the test. All the mistakes Fe had made over the last few years, none of that mattered now. And the enemy for so long was now the brother who would win this war with them, the thought of it keeping the spirit alive. As Fe looked at Barry and Stevie, the smiles bounced from each set of men. The McDonalds. The bane of his fucking life was now ready to die beside him. Before anything else, before religion and before class, they were Kemlin boys!!! And nobody fucks with Kemlin boys!

"This is it then boys. Every one of you go in there and fight for the people waiting at home for you. Fight for your family. Fight for your kids. Fight for your freedom." Fe said as he offered encouragement to all his men.

Barry shouted over, "Fuck me you can get the boys riled up ya wee Fenian bastard. No wonder you were so fucking hard to beat when we were boys." The men all smiled as Fe stepped up to the second step, hands now on the door. Fe nodded his head, eyes locked on the team. The second nod of the head... Anticipation now exploding from each individual. Adrenaline causing uncontrollable shaking, shaking that would not settle down until the punches started to land. With the third nod of the head the group burst through the doors, charging towards every corner of the room as violence went off like a bomb dropped on a small village.

The bikers fought back in response. The initial shock causing them to lose several men. The weapons thickened with blood and pain. The cries rang out as men forced body parts back into place to allow the fight to continue. This show must go on! Fe drilled his head into the biker who had escorted him to the clubhouse on that first visit. The cocky little bastard that told him to "get on." He now wished they were still taking in the cool breeze of the Scottish wind hitting them from under the open top helmet. Fe was like a man possessed. The fight for survival so raw, it added a strength he never knew he had. He gouged the eyes out of the biker until the screams and writhing of body parts were left to fight for any part of life still available.

The McDonalds had not been built for street fighting, certainly not at this age. Instead the tunnel vision of each man solely focused on anyone wearing the patch of the K4's. The blades entered men with ease, sharpened to offer as little resistance as possible. They cut down the enemy like a lumberjack looking to get home after a long day's graft. As Butch smashed the knuckle dusters into a large biker's chin, he looked back with a distorted grin. Almost as if he enjoyed the impact of the brass dusters. The biker grabbed Butch by the throat, launching him into the wall, following up with the exposure of the razor blade which ripped down his arm, slicing the rose tattoo in half. As he lifted the blade again, that cocksure look on his face died as Tam drilled a glass shard into his neck. Blood sprayed out like a beautiful red waterfall rolling down a human hill.

The biker fell to his knees as Tam offered Butch a crazed smile, Butch reciprocating with his hearty laugh. The chaos of death and gore around them somehow found amusing by Butch. As Sanny lay on the floor, with two men kicking him, George challenged at one with the pool cue, taking him to one knee before smashing his skull against the bloodied bar next to him. As the other charged at George, Davie swiftly intervened with a flurry of hands. The dazed biker was attempting to retaliate, but Davie was too quick. As the biker got down to pray, Davie sank his teeth into his ear, pulling off the best part of the lobe, spitting it across the bar and planning to have it for a trophy after the battle.

Sanny got to his feet and then rushed the biker holding Beast against the wall, attempting to open him up with the butcher's blade, a blade thick with blood from an earlier casualty. As the war ensued, Fe broke away, navigating through the door he knew would eventually lead to the meeting room.

"Fe!" A voice called out, catching Fe and stopping him in his tracks. As Fe turned, a bloodied Beast caught up with him.

"You ok big man, you don't look too hot?" Fe said clearly concerned for the wellbeing of his friend.

"Let's finish this!" Beast hit back, clearly unfazed by the various wounds littered over his body.

Once they got to the meeting room, Fe stopped and signalled to Beast that they had arrived at the destination. Fe smashed through the door with his size eight samba, the force bending the tight leather footwear back, pain shooting up Fe's right leg. He didn't think that one through. The pain instantly subsided as he stood only a few feet away from Sean, with Conner on the opposite side of the room. The expression on Sean's face was one Fe had never seen before. The arrogance now replaced by the genuine look of concern, even fear.

"Have you any fucking idea what you have done. You stupid fucking cunt. We are the K4's! This thing is bigger than me. When the other chapters find out about this, you are fucking dead men. Your full family will be erased from the fucking history books," exclaimed Sean, praying that the threat would cause the young attacker to turn and walk away.

"You ruined my fucking life. You destroyed everything. And the man standing behind me, his story is exactly the fucking same. You're a monster. And it's time to put that monster to sleep. The fucking game is up Sean." Fe declared, clearly unimpressed by Sean's threat.

"Tell him Beast, you know what is going to happen once the news of this gets out." Sean said, now pleading with the ex-biker to neutralise the situation.

"Your correct Sean, I do know what would happen if we made a move on your chapter. That's why I phoned the president of the K4's in Glasgow. The president of the K4's in Hawick. The president of the K4's in Edinburgh. It's fair to say some of the old boys were glad to hear from me again. A lot of them not happy about that bullshit you pulled all those years ago. You see Sean, it turns out everyone is pretty fucking fed up with your leadership. The killing of your own. The power has got to you Sean, so when we offered the chance of getting rid of you, allowing them to avoid a civil war within the group, I am sure you can imagine they bit my hand off for this." The smile etched firmly over Beast's face as he brought Sean up to date.

"You're lying. There is no way they agreed to that. I have been a good leader. They know that. This is my fucking gang; these are my fucking soldiers. They answer to me!" Sean continued "And tell me why I shouldn't just put a fucking bullet into the head of both you as you stand?"

Beast began to laugh at this threat. "If you had a gun, you would have used it before now. Oh no, the weapons you boys had stored got shipped to Glasgow for the post office job weeks ago. Funny that eh." Sean stood shaking, the realisation that his other chapters had indeed shared information with Beast, knowing the guns had been shared with another chapter. Sean in his arrogance assumed nobody would ever make a move on him and the need for the use and protection of guns had been low.

No sooner had he finished his speech than Beast had rushed at Sean, slamming him against the wall. His massive hands wrapping around Sean's throat as he squeezed the life out of him. Sean was a big guy, but the years of hatred had built up in Beast, the life lost at the hands of this animal, had galvanised him into action, to becoming an unstoppable force.

Beast lowered him to the ground, saliva slithering down from each corner of Sean's mouth as he fought for air. Beast's face lit up at the sight of victory. Redemption after years of hurt. On the other side of the room, Conner sprung at Fe, landing several punches into his ribs. The wind was knocked out of Fe as he struggled to regain himself. The headbutt reigned in on him, knocking him across the table. As Conner pulled out a blade, he charged Fe, with Fe just managing to jump out the way, leaving the blade to lodge into the table. As Conner fought to pull it loose, Fe drilled his right hand into his jaw. As the ex-skinhead fell to the floor, Fe sunk his knee into his nose, causing an explosion of blood and snot as the bone snapped. The centre position the nose had previously enjoyed was now several millimetres out as it pointed west.

Fe walked over to the table, content that victory was now his, when suddenly the fight in Conner allowed one final charge. With blood clouding his vision, Conner freed the blade from the table, lunging at Fe with murderous intent. Before the blade could connect, Fe swung the hammer that had been concealed in his tight Levi jeans. The hammer connected with the corner of Conner's temple, sending his lifeless body to the ground. Blood trailed from Connor's ear. As Fe walked over to Beast, the big man stood up, content his revenge had been served.

The men returned to the bar area of the clubhouse. The McDonalds were aiding the henchman hired for help to the door. Tam and the boys were checking wounds to ensure none had been life threating. They had done it! They had defeated the bikers! The game was up for the enemy who believed they were too big for anyone to ever threaten. As the men filtered out into the car park, the five bikers who had been sent on a goose chase returned to the scene. As their engines died, the bikers looked over at the bloodied enemy, tooled up and waiting for round two.

"It's over. You can join them in there, or you can start your engines and join another chapter. Forget that bastard in there and the shit he put you all through. The choice is yours," Fe said offering them a peaceful way out.

The bikers looked at each other for a few moments. Then with an explosion of life, the engines roared once again as they offered a nod of the head to Fe, almost signalling the fact he had finally set them free.

As the men walked up the street to return to the vehicles which had brought them down, they could hear the distant sound of sirens. Someone had obviously informed the police of the disturbance. Not that it mattered, Fe and his men would be long gone by the time they arrived.

Once they pulled into the car park behind the football stadium again, the victors of the battle just fought dispersed and greeted each other. Earlier enemies now shaking hands and comparing battle wounds.

"I guess that means we have to be nice to each other from now on?" Fe joked at the twins as they offered a smile in return.

Stevie laughed "Fuck, I wouldn't go that far. You did well though Fe, fair play man. We are all too old for this shit now. You sure you don't want your patch back with the hash and speed?"

Fe smiled at the offer, with Beast and Sanny looking on intently, awaiting his response.

"I am fine boys. The game is up for me. Its time I started building things again. I have been a mess for too long, and that shit is only taking me back to that world." The twins nodded in acceptance as they instructed their men to break away and lay low.

The McDonalds drove off. Fe held court with the friends who had come through for him once again. "I cannot thank you guys enough. I honestly didn't think we would get through that, but you fought with the heart of lions. Let us just hope that's the last fight we ever need to experience."

As the friends moved in to hug each other, Sanny looked over at his old friend "You going to be ok then? None of that crazy shit we have been seeing over the years. Time to screw the fucking nut now Fe." The collective smiles from the others at Sanny's comment showing the gang all felt the same way.

"I promise boys. I am going to try my best to turn things around." As the gang said their goodbyes, they all went off in separate directions. Fe choosing to walk back to his flat. He could not call it his home. He had lost his home the day Daisy left with his boys. The thought of now going back to that place sober scared him. But he had to make things better. There were still people in this world that needed him.

Chapter 37

I'm coming home

Looking in the mirror, the man looking back was a stranger, an imposter, a wrong turn in the path of how things should have been. The shadow of a man now bloated from years of self-abuse and destruction only served to remind him of how too many mistakes made it hard to turn back. This was the present. This was the future. This was how it was going to be. But where did it go wrong?

It had long been a method of self-preservation to blame those around for the downfall of a character who could have achieved so much yet at this very moment had so little. A broken man both once feared and respected in equal measure, now wondering just how much more one man can take. This new world around him was alien. Only thirty years old and now barely able to remember any events since the start of the nineties.

Filling the pasta into the pot, Fe caught sight of his mum walking down the path. As she walked into the kitchen, Fe hugged her with all the love he had in him. She had stuck by him through everything. Fe was not fixed, not even close. This was going to be a long battle. The biggest battle of his life no less. Addiction is the real Beast that many must fight. "Can I have a word with you Kevin, and you better sit down for this."

Making their way into the living room, Fe was filled with a feeling of dread regarding what Jackie might be about to say given the serious look on her face. He was only used to bad news these days. It had been almost four years since he had seen the kids. He had tried to find them, but the trail had run cold long ago. He was now reserved to the fact that the chase was over.

"Kevin, a couple of years ago, I hired a private detective to try and locate Daisy and the boys." Jackie said looking at Fe and waiting for a reaction to this news.

"What the fuck is a private detective", Fe responded, thinking this sort of thing only existed in Hollywood movies.

Jackie continued. "He has been looking at schools and doctors all over the UK, and it has been a long search costing me most of my savings. But he has found them Kevin. He has found your boys."

As the words lodged themselves into Fe's head, his heart swelled with emotion. He burst into inconsolable tears as Jackie moved in to hug him, clearly the reaction exceeding anything she had expected.

"Where are they?" Fe questioned, the urge to slap himself and make sure this was not a dream coming over him several times.

"They're living in Yorkshire." As Jackie shared the location, Fe felt the urge to kick himself. Why did he not think of that? He knew Daisy had a friend in England. He simply did not think Daisy would go to the extent of taking the boys over the border and into another country. None of that mattered now. All that mattered was the answer to the next question.

"Am I allowed to see them?" The pleading hitting Jackie as if the decision sat with her.

"Daisy has agreed to a visit down there on the condition you are not on anything. Not even a pint of beer Kevin, do you understand, you can't mess this up. You need this. I need this. I want my boys back in my life." The pleas of desperation Jackie now shared with Fe.

"I won't let you down mum." Fe reassured his mum and he meant it with all his being.

The bus pulled into the large station in Leeds. Fe stepped off. He had never been this far from home before. The big city was a strange place. People bustling past one another with ferocious pace. The simplicity of Camelon was a million miles away. As he flagged down the cab, he instructed the driver to take him to the community centre roughly fifteen miles away. He knew Daisy would not be there, clearly the pain and torment Fe had exposed her to, made it too painful for any reunion at this point. The boys would be accompanied by a social worker who had agreed to chaperone them. As he handed the taxi driver the forty pounds, he muttered the words "Robbing bastard" under his breath. The taxi driver caught this comment, and fired a snarl at Fe, to which Fe offered an even more aggressive look in response. With the door of the cab still open, the driver quickly apologised. Fe slammed the door shut and began to laugh at himself as he walked away. "You never lose it" he told himself. You can take the boy out of Kemlin...

Walking up the recently mono-blocked path, he wondered what the boys would look like now. He questioned if they maybe had an English accent after four years of life around English kids. He realised any relationship in the past now had to start again. He had to make his boys love him all over again. It was a battle he was more than ready for.

Passing a large window, the visit still ten minutes from commencing, his heart sank. Standing there, now much taller than he ever remembered, were his two boys. The emotion filled him as the tears streamed down his face. The freshly pressed shirt becoming the landing ground for the onslaught of emotions. As young Kevin turned to catch sight of his dad, he nudged Darryn, the younger brother turning and smiling at the face staring back at him.

Fe had messed up. He had lost his family. Lost his wealth, lost his home. He had lost everything. But redemption is a wonderful thing. Everyone deserves a second chance. And Fe was both willing and desperate to hold on to his tightly with both hands.

THE END

We did it! From the wild phone call I made to Kelly declaring I was about to write my own book, to the endless editing between us all. The DIY book finally happened. The journey really was a crazy one, and I will never forget it. Special thanks go out to Sandra Ross. The evenings spent proofreading my work, offering valuable feedback. You really are an amazing person.

We then had my dear auntie Winnie who had to entertain my erratic moments. Me becoming the pain in the arse writer who would fail to update my mentor/editor of all the changes I had made. The phone calls for hours at a time with me ranting about this and that, and you calming me down and reassuring me all would be ok. In the end, all was ok. This was not just about writing a book. You helped me make sense of my own life and my own worth.

My amazing big cousin Zoe, who managed to create an amazing book cover despite my ridiculously short notice appeal. You are a star! From the drawings we did together as kids, to the ability you have displayed during this, you have a remarkable talent.

To all the friends and family who had to endure my embarrassing videos yet supported and shared my journey. We smashed it!

And to my wife, who without you, none of this would have been possible. You fixed me when I was at my worst all those years ago. You made me believe I was worth something. Every time I wanted to give up, you would offer those words of support, help build me back up, and carry on. I owe you everything and will spend this day until my very last ensuring I repay you with all the love I have. I love you Kelly x

AND FINALLY

A MESSAGE TO MY SONS, JACK AND LEWIS. YOU WILL NEVER KNOW HOW MUCH DADDY LOVES YOU BOYS. HOW BOTH OF YOU SHAPED THE MAN I AM TODAY. I PROMISE TO ALWAYS PICK YOU UP AND DUST YOU OFF WHEN YOU FALL. AND THE DAY I CAN NO LONGER HONOUR THAT PROMISE, I WANT YOU TO LOOK BACK AND READ THESE STORIES. THE TALES I CREATED FOR YOU BOYS.

I WANT BOTH OF YOU TO GROW INTO GOOD MEN. WITH CONFIDENCE, RESPECT AND MOST OF ALL, LOVE. ALL I DID BOYS; IT WAS ALL FOR YOU.

MY GOOD LOOKING MOB.XXX

This novel was written in memory of Kevin Mcphee. You did things the way you wanted. The rules of society merely shrugged off by you. We all miss you. We all love you. What I would give to have you read this book. I remember the stories you would write for us. Littered with mistakes, but full of love. It fills me with pride to tell you how amazing all the kids are doing. For all the faults over the years, that love you installed in us, that was the biggest thing for creating good people.

A message from Cherie

This morning I looked out my window and found, A bluebird singing but there was no one around. At night I lay alone in my bed, with an image of you going around in my head.

You made us laugh and you made us cry. You made us who we are and taught us how to be tough. But most of all, you showed us love and what family means. A love that we will never lose for you and for each other.

Love you dad.

STM XXX

To ♡

My Dear,

Auntie Janet xxx

♡ All My

Love,

xxx Ken xxx

Printed in Great Britain
by Amazon

54029852R00144